STONE COLD DEAD

STONE COLD DEAD

STEPHEN LEWIS

ARBUTUS PRESS
TRAVERSE CITY

Stone Cold Dead
Copyright © Stephen Lewis 2007

978-1-933926-02-5 Hardcover
978-1-933926-03-2 Paperback

Library of Congress Cataloging- in-Publication Data

Lewis, Stephen, 1942-
 Stone cold dead / by Stephen Lewis.
   p. cm.
 ISBN 978-1-933926-02-5 (alk. paper) —
 ISBN 978-1-933926-03-2 (pbk. : alk. paper)
 1. Michigan - Fiction. 2. Brooklyn (New York, N.Y.) - Fiction. I. Title.
 PS3562.E9755S76 2007
 813'.54--dc22
                    2007013110

Arbutus Press
Traverse City, Michigan
info@arbutuspress.com
www.Arbutuspress.com

To my daughters, Danielle, Kerri and Tracy
And as always, for Carol

CHAPTER ONE

FIRST Street, on the flank of Prospect Park in Brooklyn's Park Slope section, was layered with the shattered casings of firecrackers. The morning air was thick with the smoky residue and the acrid smell of exploded powder from the night before. Here and there metal trash cans lay with their sides ripped open by cherry bombs, but the street was now quiet, except for an occasional heavy flutter of a pigeon's wings or the sad cooing of a mourning dove greeting the new day from window sills and branches of the tall maple trees that lined the street.

As she stood next to the red '55 Caddy convertible, its top down, boxes that hadn't fit in the trunk piled on the back seat, Kelly Abrams tried to compose herself. Next to the boxes, in the middle of the seat, lay Hooper, an English bulldog. Huddled in the corner, with her eyes staring through the window at the brownstone building where her father now lived, was Kelly's daughter Allie.

"We can change our plans," Kelly said. "I can just tell him that you're coming with us."

Shoving the inch thick layer of firecracker casings aside with the toe of her shoe, Kelly focused her eyes on the door to Michael's ground-level apartment.

"He's still my father," Allie said after several moments of heavy silence.

"Yes," Kelly admitted, but..." her voice trailed off.

Dave Abrams turned from his position behind the wheel just as Kelly leaned her head into the car to whisper something to her daughter. The hair of mother and daughter blended into a mass of red except for the streaks of silver in Kelly's. Impatient to leave Brooklyn and his failure in the Bonita Mercado case behind him, Dave rested his foot lightly on the accelerator pedal. The morning sunlight bounced off the hood ornament, and a man and his daughter rode by on their bicycles. He watched as the little girl's legs pumped hard to keep her small bike abreast of her father's. A memory of running behind his own son, Jonathan, holding the back of the seat on a bicycle just the same size as the one the girl was on, forced its way into his consciousness. But Jonathan now lived with his mother in California. Dave pushed that memory back, although it left a feeling of loss that hollowed his stomach.

Kelly, too, saw the two bicycles go by and watched them until they turned the corner. Then she yanked open the door. After a moment, Allie reached down to the floor in front of her for her nylon overnight bag. Tossing it onto the sidewalk next to her mother's feet, she leaned over to the other side of the car and hauled out her suitcase. She patted Hooper's head, leaned down to nuzzle his ear, and then reached over the dog to pick up her sketchbook from the floor of the car.

The orange, stuffed head of Pooh Bear protruded from the corner of the overnight bag. Kelly pressed the head down and tried to zipper the bag over it, but it popped back up.

"Are you really sure you want to take this with you?" she asked.

Allie nodded and took the overnight bag from her mother.

"He gave it to me," she said.

Kelly picked up the suitcase, and they walked to the door to Michael's apartment. Kelly reached her hand to push the bell, but hesitated. She brushed a stray hair from Allie's forehead, and then studied her daughter. They'd had a tense conversation about what she would wear to greet her father. Kelly pushed for a sedate, flower-print sun dress. Allie now stood before her in a top that showed six inches of pale, vulnerable skin between her small breasts and the low slung waistband of her baggy shorts. It was the kind of outfit designed to catch the eye of teenaged boys. It announced her daughter's intention to assert herself as a young woman, and it expressed a confidence belied by the unnatural brightness of her eyes and the nervous tremor of her lips. Allie, having won the battle of clothing style, now seemed ready to collapse into a defeat of uncertainty. Kelly glanced at the Pooh Bear in her daughter's overnight bag and then at the rounded curve of her buttocks in the shorts. Because she and Allie had stopped visiting Michael some time ago, he had not seen his daughter grow up. What would he think? She pressed the doorbell.

Although Michael's fair hair was now gray, he looked much as Kelly remembered him. He was wearing cut down jeans that hung loosely off his slim hips. He was shirtless, barefoot, and red-eyed. A huge silver crucifix hung on a thick chain that seemed to disappear into his gray chest hairs. A dab of shaving cream sat on the point of his chin, and he swept it off with the back of his hand while offering a bright smile. He opened his arms to embrace his daughter, and as Allie stepped into them, Kelly saw a crude tattoo of a snake wrapped around a skull on his right biceps. She remembered stories she had read of men who had been away where Michael had been. Allie seemed tentative in her father's embrace, and stepped back, eyes averted after a moment. Michael held his daughter by her shoulders, looked at her and shrugged. Kelly saw that his fingernails were manicured.

"I didn't get much sleep last night," he said, and gestured toward the street, where the sun's rays, laden with dust, seemed trapped in the thick and pungent air.

"I guess kids will be kids," Kelly replied. "Especially on the Fourth."

"I don't think I know much about that." Michael's expression darkened, but then he turned to Allie. "I'll learn," he said, "I always was a quick study. Would you like to come in for a cup of tea or coffee? Both are ready."

Kelly had anticipated this courtesy. She studied his lean body, at ease against the door frame, and then his red-rimmed eyes, and fought the urge to tell him that it was just too soon. She reached for her daughter as though to pull her back toward the car, but then, remembering how hard Allie had lobbied for this time with her father, she let her hand drop onto the girl's thin shoulder and nudged her forward.

"Dave is waiting in the car," she began.

"He's welcome, too," Michael said. His tone was more than pleasant, and Kelly wondered if it was only the noise that had disturbed his sleep. The night before, she had lain in bed envisioning this scene, imagining that she would see a disheveled young woman rushing, red faced out of the apartment when she rang the bell, or that she would find him in drug-induced incoherence, something, anything that would confirm her anxiety and permit her to justify keeping her daughter from him. The truth was that he had been out of her life too long, and she could not move beyond the bad memories of the end of their marriage to believe he might be all right now. But as he stood there, except for his red eyes and his tattoo, which she could not really fault him for, she had to admit he was doing a serviceable imitation of the father he had once been, even if that were long ago.

"I'll just stop in for a minute, to see Allie settled," Kelly said.

"I'll be happy to have a cup of coffee," Allie said.

Michael turned to her, a look of bemused curiosity replacing the smile.

"Oh, so you're old enough for a morning cup of coffee?

"You know I'm almost sixteen," Allie said with a shrug and a shy smile. "You know that."

"I do. But I've been away. I only remember how you looked a long time ago." He shaded his eyes from the sun to stare at his daughter. "You look very different now. But I see you still like to draw. I remember your pictures on the refrigerator."

With a shy smile, Allie raised the sketchbook.

"Yes," she replied.

"Come on, Allie," Kelly said. "Let's get you settled."

Kelly sat across the table from Michael, her cup of tea untouched in front of her. In the chair next to her, Allie stirred sugar into her coffee. The apartment was freshly painted a bright white, but ancient cracks in the plaster were beginning to reassert themselves. The table was new, with its gleaming white Formica top and oak frame. Four matching oak chairs circled it. The rest of the apartment was bare of furniture. The old plank floor had been sanded recently, and the smell of polyurethane hung in the air.

"My furniture is being delivered today," Michael said. He glanced at the cup of tea. "What's the matter? Earl Grey was always your favorite. That's why I had some on hand for you."

"Cut it Michael," Kelly said. "Don't even think about those days."

"Right," he smiled. "Just excise the first several chapters of the family scrapbook, right?"

Kelly stiffened in her chair, her fingers playing with the handle of the cup. She raised it to her lips and took a sip.

"Please don't make this more difficult than it is," she said.

"Where am I going to sleep?" Allie asked. "There's only one bedroom."

Michael closed his eyes, as though in deep thought. When he opened them, his face wore a curious expression, a mingling of fatherly concern and something else, something Kelly could not identify, but which caused her chest to tighten.

"I haven't quite worked that out," he said. "I thought we'd talk about it. I just tossed the junk the previous tenant left here, and I've been sleeping on the floor in the living room in a sleeping bag." He turned his eyes full onto Allie. "Remember how we used to go camping at Bear Mountain, and how you would get scared at night, and crawl into my sleeping bag with me?"

Allie began to smile, but Kelly's frown stopped her.

"That was a long time ago," Kelly said.

"Oh, you'll have to forgive me. I keep forgetting those chapters have been edited out." He shrugged. "Anyway. Once my new stuff comes, we can work it out."

"I think I'd like to know now," Kelly insisted.

"No problem," Michael replied. "I'll take the bedroom. Allie can have the futon in the living room, where the television will be."

"You seem to be setting yourself up very nicely," Kelly said.

He narrowed his eyes.

"And you're wondering where I'm getting the money for all that, on a shoe salesman's salary."

"Right."

"Just a little put away from before. I'm not insulted that you ask. It's your job as Allie's mother, after all."

Kelly reached into her purse and pulled out a piece of paper. She glanced at it, folded it, and slid it across the table to Allie. Allie opened the paper, and a frown formed on her face as she read it.

"Just in case," Kelly said. "While we're on the road."

"And what exactly do you think might happen?" Allie asked. "And if it did, what good would it do to call Uncle John who is out most of the time, doesn't believe in answering machines, doesn't even have a cell phone, or a computer. And is a thousand miles away anyway? I already have your cell phone number."

Kelly stood up.

"I don't know how good the service is going to be in Canada as we ride across. Uncle John's phone is old fashioned, connected to a wire. It'll work. And I told him to stay close to it until we get there. But like I said, just in case. If nothing else, knowing you have it will make me feel better."

"Old Uncle John," Michael said. "Give him my regards. I had some good times in the summer working for him during the season."

"He doesn't farm much anymore," Kelly replied, pulling Allie's thin body hard to her. She flashed a smile at Michael, wondering if he could detect how hollow it was, and then turned to leave. She paused at the door, with her hand on the knob. She reached back toward Michael, and lifted the heavy crucifix from his chest. He seemed to tense for a second, and then relaxed. She pulled the crucifix even higher as though to look at it more closely, and then she let it drop against his chest. He began to reach for it, but then he extended his hand. She willed herself to squeeze his flesh, and found it hard and cold.

Dave started to turn the key in the ignition as soon as Kelly settled into her seat, but she held his hand.

"I'm not sure I can go. Let's just sit here for a while, so I can think."

Dave glanced at the ground-level window facing the street where Allie stood waiting to wave good-bye. Michael stood behind her, his hand, too, held in the air. Michael extended his palm, puckered his lips, and blew them a kiss. "Start the car," she said.

"Are you sure?"

"Just start the damned car."

He pulled away from the curb, and they rode in silence to the stop sign at the end of the block. He hesitated, wondering whether to turn left and head for Flatbush Avenue and the Manhattan Bridge.

"Do it," she said. "Before I change my mind."

There was very little traffic on this holiday morning, and they were soon on the bridge.

"He's changed more than I expected," Kelly said.

"You haven't seen him in a long time, and..."

"I know. Prison can change a man. But whatever he has become, whatever process has taken place, started long before that."

"Otherwise?"

"No, I don't think so. I would have left him anyway."

"Maybe it'll work out. Allie could benefit from knowing who her father is."

"That's what we all decided, and she wanted it a lot, and I didn't think I could deny her. But at what cost?"

Dave looked out of his window at the twin arches of the Brooklyn Bridge. Between them the sun glinted off the huge cables, hanging heavy in their graceful, catenary curve, and the mist off the harbor seemed to gather in the thousands of supporting wires. Above the hum of the Caddy's engine, he could hear the raucous calls of the circling gulls.

She put her palm flat against his cheek.

"I didn't expect an answer," she said.

"That's good," he replied, "because I sure as hell don't have one."

He pushed down on the accelerator and the Caddy responded with a smooth surge that pressed their backs against the seat. Beneath them a tug towed a barge heaped high with a portion of the city's daily mountain of refuse, and ahead of them lay a thousand miles of anxious highway.

CHAPTER TWO

DAVE looked back to the motel, perched on a gently sloping rise overlooking Lake Erie, and then turned to the quiet blue waters reaching to the horizon under a cloudless sky, the colors of sky and water just beginning to darken in the failing light. He sat down on the edge of grass that gave way to a thin strand of sand. Hooper stood in the damp sand lapping the water with his ridiculous tongue. Kelly said she might join him later, but judging from the way she threw herself onto the bed, he did not think so. She would lie there, exhausted, and fight the urge to pick up the phone to check on Allie.

A breeze, edged with the night's cool, rippled the shallow water, and Hooper retreated, finding a place in the sand at Dave's feet where the sun's rays still formed a circle of warmth. Weariness from the day's drive pressed down on him.

"Come on, Hooper," he said. "Bed time."

Dave found the light on in their room, and Kelly lying on her side, her arm stretched toward the night table where the phone sat. She opened her eyes as the door clicked closed.

"No," she said. "I didn't call."

Late the next day they were again driving along a shoreline, this time the flank of Grand Traverse Bay, off Lake Michigan. The bright, light blue waters of the bay looked inviting after two days on the road, the last four hours through the rolling hills and farmland east of Traverse City. When they approached the city, they saw the bold rectangular shape of the resort hotel, towering above the tops of trees.

The Wilson place, their new summer home, was fifteen miles north of Traverse on the Leelanau Peninsula, and a mile past Kelly's Uncle John's farm. They turned onto the two-track driveway that led to the old farmhouse on the crest of a hill. The house leaned slightly forward, as though it were an old bear trying to hold up its weight on arthritic knees. The driveway cut through an orchard of old cherry trees, now laden with fruit ranging from yellow to a blush of red

"Napoleons," Kelly said. "Looks like they're almost ready."

George and Eunice Wilson were standing on the porch to greet them. A pickup truck, piled high with boxes and a few pieces of furniture, sat at the end of the drive. A row of wooden chairs, turned upside down, with their backs hanging over the side of the truck, were held in place by a heavy piece of rope. Dave pulled the Caddy to a stop behind the truck. He wanted to get out and stretch, but first he turned to Kelly.

"I thought they were just going to leave the key with John," he said.

"So did I."

"You don't suppose they changed their minds, do you?"

Kelly frowned.

"No. I believe they want to do the right thing, and that means that they should welcome us. If they didn't, they'd probably feel like they were sneaking off."

"It's just business," Dave said.

"Not to them," Kelly said, her voice edged.

"I know," he relented. "I'm just trying to convince myself we're not picking the flesh off their bones."

George Wilson was a thin, hard man. Blue veins creased his arms, and his face was leathered from the sun. Eunice Wilson was as plump as her husband was lean. As Dave and Kelly climbed the sagging steps up to the porch, Eunice set a pitcher of lemonade and glasses on a metal stack table. The table's edge was flaked with rust, and the glasses were decorated with a bunch of bright red cherries, and an inscription that celebrated a Cherry Festival some ten years before. Husband and wife stood close to each other and offered their hands to Dave and Kelly in turn.

"It was nice of you to meet us," Dave said.

George shrugged, and then pointed to the pickup truck.

"Got everything cleared out," he said. "Except that table your wife seemed to have her eyes on when you folks were out here. I couldn't get it out anyway."

"We can give you a hand," Kelly offered.

"No room on the truck," George said.

Eunice smiled, shyly.

"I don't think he wants to take it with us."

"There's a story about that table," George began.

"I told them last time," his wife said.

He scratched his chin.

"Well, I guess you did." He looked again at the truck. "We're going to haul that lot down to Henry, he's our oldest boy. Lives in Flint. Has a job in the GM plant. He always was real good with machines. Maybe he can use it."

"Of course he can," Eunice said. She turned to Kelly. "Our new trailer is a bit small, and we don't need much."

"Did I show you the shaker in the barn?" George asked.

"Yes," Kelly replied.

Dave recalled seeing the ancient shaker. It was attached to the chassis of an old pickup with the roof of the cab and the sides of the bed removed, leaving only the seat sitting atop the frame. The shaker itself, which was driven by the engine of the truck, was a steel arm, ten or fifteen feet long, on a hinge with a clamp on its end. The clamp would be wrapped around the trunk of a cherry tree and the arm would vibrate causing the fruit to fall into a tarp spread beneath the tree.

"I guess it'll just gather dust now," George said, but his eyes looked hopeful.

"I don't know about that," Kelly replied. "I drove a pretty good shaker for Uncle John."

Eunice fairly beamed.

"Yes, I do remember John telling us that. Don't you, George?"

"Can't say I do," he replied. "But those cherries should be shaken off. Otherwise there won't be a crop next year worth talking about." He shrugged. "Guess that's your concern now."

"We've talked to John about maybe hiring a crew," Kelly said.

"It don't matter," George said. "With the casino the Indians have put up, and the subdivisions going up all over, our time is over."

Eunice turned and her body heaved. When she faced them again, her eyes glistened.

"I've left you some lemonade. George has the key for you. I think we'd better be on our way and let you settle in." She stepped to Kelly and embraced her. "This has been a good house for us. We pray it will be for you." She released Kelly. "George. Give the man the key."

George reached into his pocket and held out a key ring. On it were two keys, one worn and one new.

"Had a spare made up for you." He glanced at his wife. "We never needed but one." He shrugged. "Thought you might want the extra."

George took his wife's arm and guided her down the steps. They waved once before entering the pickup truck, and then they were gone.

"Sad," Dave said.

"More than you think," Kelly replied. "That son they were talking about. John told me they haven't seen him in years. His father wanted him to take over the farm, and Henry didn't want any part of it. They haven't spoken since."

They walked into the empty house, their steps echoing off the worn wooden floor.

"I still feel their presence," Kelly said.

"It'll take time," Dave replied. "For them, and for us."

The phone rang awakening them early the next morning, and they both sat up in bed.

"Are you going to answer it?" Kelly asked.

"Sure," Dave replied. "Where is it?" He stared at the night table, which held only a lamp. The ringing seemed to be coming from that direction.

"I put it on the floor, next to the bed, last night," Kelly said.

Dave leaned over the side of the bed and found the phone.

"Hope I didn't call too early," John said.

"No, not at all," Dave said.

"Good. Got to go into town this morning. I wanted to call you before I went out to remind you about the pow wow. Today's the last day. And I told Livonia Walkingstick you'd be stopping by."

"Right," Dave said. Kelly reached for the phone. "Here, your uncle wants to say hello."

Dave rolled out of bed and stood looking around the room. Kelly cupped her hand over the mouthpiece.

"It's over there," she said, pointing to the left. "Remember. It's downstairs, through the kitchen."

He found the bathroom. The shower was in the old bathtub. Dave clambered over the high side and turned on the water. The porcelain bottom of the tub had been worn rough and porous, trapping dirt in a large stain beneath the shower head. He thought he could make out George Wilson's footprints beneath the swirling water. When he returned to the bedroom, a towel wrapped around him, Kelly was just hanging up the phone.

"He said he can't make it today. Something about trying to find a part for his tractor. But he insists that we don't miss Livonia. She's a treat, he says."

They heard the beat of the drums and the chanting well before they reached the parking area adjacent to the pow wow. Dave and Kelly walked toward the music and saw a large circular area enclosed by a rope strung around its perimeter. In the middle was a pavilion where singers and drummers sat. They found an open space next to the rope and watched.

A line of male dancers moved clockwise around the circle, their feet raising dust with rhythmical shuffling steps, their bodies bobbing up and down. They turned themselves into sudden spins as the tempo quickened. They wore a variety of costumes, mostly animal skins, although some sported elaborate bone necklaces. One dancer approached them. Above his forehead was the gaping mouth of a red fox, and the rest of the animal hung down his back, jerking to the dancer's movements. Deerskin leggings reached from ankle to mid thigh. They were decorated with rows of beads and bangles that rang with his movements. His lithe body seemed almost to quiver with the intensity of energy constrained to the rhythms of the drums. His eyes shone bright, but his face was expressionless. He seemed vaguely menacing and distant at the same time. His dance steps brought him to within a few feet of them, and then his face broke into a broad smile. He waved and then danced on.

Kelly returned the wave, and then looked at Dave.

"Allie would have..." she began.

"Yes, she would," he replied. "Maybe next year."

Kelly shaded her eyes from the sun, and stared out over the circle, which was now empty. She pointed to a place directly across from them.

"I think I see Livonia. There, where the people are gathered around."

An old woman sat cross-legged in a circle of people, some Indian and some white. The whites, judging by their brightly colored clothes and the cameras dangling from their necks, were tourists. Livonia wore a large brimmed straw hat that hid her face unless she looked up, as she did now when Dave and Kelly approached. The skin of her face was like thin paper that had gotten wet and then shriveled, with her veins clearly visible in her forehead. She had a large mole on her chin. An Indian girl of about thirteen or fourteen years stood next to Livonia.

Dave and Kelly joined the circle of people waiting for Livonia to speak. The old woman moved her jaw for a moment or two, as though she were practicing forming her words, but she said nothing.

"Oko-mes-se-maw," the girl said, "tell us the story of the Trickster and the Great Turtle."

The man standing next to Dave inhaled his breath audibly, and nudged the woman next to him.

"I'm going to get something to eat," the man said in a loud whisper.

"Go ahead, Albert," the woman replied. She caught Dave's eye. "We're on vacation," she said, "and all he wants to do is leave one place and go to the next, without ever enjoying where he is, and when he does stay put, he's got to put something in his stomach every half hour."

"Please," the young girl insisted, "you know, the one about how the snails got their shells."

Livonia stared at Albert's retreating back, and then she moved her lower jaw again. This time, though, she began to speak. Her voice was strong and sonorous.

"This story begins at a time when snails had just crawled up from the bottom of the great lake, and they had no protection from the weather. One cold winter day, when the snow was falling thick, Nanabush, the Trickster, in the shape of a fox, came upon Snail."

Livonia paused and studied the faces of the people listening to her.

"Good, you are paying attention. I am an old woman, and my mind can be easily distracted by people moving about, and I might start telling a different story."

"Go ahead, continue, O-ko-mes-se-maw," the girl said. "They will listen."

Livonia nodded.

"I'll tell it straight through now, so if you have to go to the bathroom or something, you can leave. There won't be any commercials. Now, I was saying how Nanabush started talking to Snail. 'Snail,' he said. 'You look like you need a sturdy coat to protect you from the cold and the snow.'

"In his misery, Snail could hardly stir himself to look up to find the source of the voice coming through the blanket of snow. He squinted and peered until he could make out the pointed nose and bushy tail of the fox.

"'Your skin is not tough like the deer, or thick and warm like mine,' the Trickster said, 'and that is why you suffer so much. But if you will let me, I can help you.'

"'I know you,' Snail said. 'You are Nanabush, and you are not to be trusted.'

"The Trickster smiled. 'If you were a surly bear, or a proud eagle, or even a well-armed porcupine, you would be right. I would be seeking some advantage. But you are not more than an overgrown worm that all other creatures scorn, and I take pity on you. It will do my heart good to help you, and besides, I have a score to settle with Makinak, the Great Turtle, whose arrogance I have been forced to tolerate for too long.'

"The miserable Snail considered for a moment, and he concluded that he did not really have much to lose by accepting the Trickster's offer. Certainly his life could not be made much worse than it was now when it was hardly worth living.

"'What do you propose?' Snail asked.

"'To provide you with a shell at the expense of Makinak.'

"Snail still had some doubts, but he called a meeting of all his kin who lived on the shores of the great lake. They discussed the matter fully, and all but one agreed that they should take the Trickster up on his offer, no matter how terrible his reputation. They decided to tell him to work his scheme. The naysayer could continue to shiver if he chose.

"In the form of a very large, fat snail, the Trickster swam to the bottom of the lake and proposed a race to the Turtle. He told the huge reptile that all the other creatures were mocking him for his lazy ways, lying as he did for years in the same place beneath the waters.

"The Great Turtle shook in his gigantic shell, encrusted with thousands of tiny sea animals that had attached themselves to it. He swung his huge head, and the waters of the lake jumped in giant waves. He took a ponderous step, and the waters leaped onto the land.

"'I will show them they are wrong,' Makinak said. 'But I cannot leave the bottom, for if I do the waters will flood the land first as I rise, and then disappear into the earth when I step onto the shore.'

"'What will you wager to prove you are right?' the Trickster asked.

"'I will race for my pride.'

"'But your pride is nothing to me. I want something more tangible. A nice home to live in, as you have.'

"The Great Turtle reflected for a moment.

"'That is fair,' he said. `If you win, I will divide my great shell among all the snails of the world, for if that happens, in my shame, I would be forced to burrow deeper into the sands beneath the great lake.'

"'Then the prize is settled,' the Trickster said. 'All that remains is the course of the race.'

"The Great Turtle pointed his head toward a log sticking out of the bottom of the lake, about a mile away. Nanabush nodded his agreement.

"'You start first,' the Turtle said. 'You will need an advantage.'

"The Trickster inched forward on his belly, and Makinak roared in laughter, so that columns of water spewed above the lake surface.

"'I will just rest here a while,' the Turtle said to himself, and he closed his eyes. When he opened them, he could not see the snail anywhere near him. Finally, he spotted him approaching the log, for of course as soon as the Turtle had closed his eyes, Nanabush had transformed himself into a swift bass and swam toward the log. The Turtle lunged forward, and our people remember how the lake on that day rose above its borders and climbed the cliffs to threaten a nearby Ojibwe village. Once he was in motion, the Turtle's powerful legs carried him with great speed toward the log, but when he arrived there, he found Snail sitting on it.

"Without a word, the Turtle hoisted his shell off of his back. His naked skin, where it had been covered, looked as soft as a baby's, or even that of a snail.

"'You shell is much too big for me,' the Trickster said.

"The Turtle gave a mighty heave upward and the shell soared into the sky. When it came down, it shattered into thousands of pieces on the shore of the lake. The snails who had been waiting there rejoiced, and each chose a piece to cover his exposed skin. On the pieces were the tiny sea creatures that had been attached to the shell when it was whole. The one snail that did not join the wager could only shake his head and gaze at the shells lying on the beach where they can still be found today, bearing the imprint of the tiny creatures who used to cling to Makinak. The descendants of the snail who refused Nanabush's offer still have no shell. They are the most scorned creatures in the world, and come out to feed only under the cover of darkness.

"Makinak, as he said he would, burrowed into the sand on the bottom of the lake. Over the years, he grew a new shell, and as he did the level of the water rose to its present height."

Livonia's jaws continued working for a moment after she stopped speaking, and then when she closed her mouth the circle of people listening to her broke into applause. She rose slowly to her feet and extended her right arm. In her hand was an irregularly shaped stone about two inches long. She showed it to each spectator in turn, holding it in one hand, and pointing to the scalloped indentations with the index finger of the other.

"White folks call these fossil stones, but you just heard what they really are," she said. "They're all over on Peterson Beach, where Makinak's shell came to earth." She slipped the stone back into her pocket. "I have a stand, on the way to the beach, where you can buy them. If you're asking yourself why can't you just go to the beach and pick up your own, well there are a couple of reasons. One, I have the best ones, and I polish them up. Two, the story I tell gives me a kind of proprietary right."

"How do you figure that?" Albert had returned, a hot dog covered in a thick layer of mustard in one hand, and a can of soda in the other. He brushed his hand across his mouth to remove a glob of mustard.

Livonia turned her dark, hard eyes toward him. The veins on her forehead seemed to pulse.

"I could say that my stones carry my medicine, but you wouldn't understand that."

"Try me," he said, his tone combative.

"But you didn't hear the story, and the medicine is in the telling of my people's history. People have to know where they came from."

"Rego Park," Albert said. "That's in Queens, New York."

"That is where you live, but not where you are from," Livonia said.

"Let's go, Albert," his wife said, and she tugged on his arm. Albert seemed to be considering a reply, but then he took another bite of his hot dog and permitted his wife to turn him away from Livonia.

"We'll stop by your stand," the wife said to Livonia. "Albert could use a paperweight, with or without hearing the story. I don't suppose you have a copy of the story, in a book or something, do you?"

Livonia pointed to her head.

"This is the only place it is until I tell it, and that is why I tell it."

The woman ushered her husband away. Livonia kept her eyes on their backs, and then she turned to the others.

"In the story, Nanabush teaches us how we can survive, and I've got to make a living."

She smiled at the onlookers, and a man took out his wallet. Just then the drums and chanting resumed, and Livonia waved the man away.

"It's time for me to dance," she said. "Come by my stand. You'll pass it on the road to Peterson Beach."

"Or you can come to the Ojibwe Gift Shop," the girl said. "We have some of O-ko-mes-se-maw's stones there."

A shrill whistle rose above the crowd, and the girl turned toward the sound. A large Ojibwe man, carrying perhaps three-hundred pounds of flesh, much of it concentrated in his belly, waved his heavy arm, beckoning the girl. She looked at Livonia, and the old woman nodded. The girl trotted off toward the man.

As those who had been listening to Livonia turned their attention to the drums and singing, Kelly and Dave walked up to Livonia. She held out her arms to Kelly.

"John said you would be coming." She pulled Kelly to her for a moment, and then she held out her hand to Dave. Her flesh was warm, and her grasp strong.

"I used to see your wife years ago," Livonia said, "when she was a child the age of Robin, the girl who just left. I'm trying to teach the child, and she wants to learn."

"I can see you have much to teach," Dave said.

Livonia held his eyes with her own, and he felt the intensity of her gaze.

"You are troubled," she said. "Something in my story."

"Nothing in the story," he said. "A case, a woman, I couldn't protect her."

Livonia stepped closer and put her hand on his shoulder.

"You must let the circle complete itself."

"And find a shell to protect myself wherever I can," Dave offered.

"No," Livonia shook her head. "Not wherever. There is only one right place, and you must wait to find it." She dropped her hand from his shoulder and looked past him to the large circle. "Please excuse me," she said. "The next dance is for women only, and I promised myself I'd join it. I used to do fancy dancing, but now all I can manage is the two-step." She took Kelly's hand. "Maybe I will see you on Sunday, at Mass." She did not wait for an answer, but strode to the circle to take her place among the dancers.

Kelly watched her go, her face flushed.

"I used to go, when I was a kid," she said.

"I don't know which surprises me more, Dave said, "Livonia, or you going to Mass."

"I had forgotten. About her. She goes to mass at Kateri Tekawitha Church on reservation land every morning. I used to see her there, on those few occasions when I would go. Then right after, sometimes, she would tell stories like she did today, about Makinak and Nanabush. I asked her once. She said that when she was a girl, they tried to make a white woman out of her. She knew she wouldn't become one, but she liked the stories she was taught. It was all a question of understanding them the right way, the Ojibwe way."

They reached the rope behind which the dancers moved to the rhythm of the drums. They watched as Livonia moved toward them. She was separated from the other women, dancing with a powerful elegance that belied her age. As she came abreast of Dave and Kelly, she raised her head as her body uncoiled. Her eyes were half shut, and she seemed to be looking toward a place well beyond where they were standing. Then she lowered her head again and joined the other dancers.

"It's a funny thing," Kelly said. "I had also forgotten that Michael used to talk about how he should have been a priest."

CHAPTER THREE

THE   Ojibwe Gift Shop was filled with items such as plastic tomahawks, miniature birch-bark canoes, paper tepees, and postcards of strikingly attractive Native American women in traditional dress. Among this tourist fare, Kelly found a pair of genuine porcupine quill earrings.

Behind the counter, a girl sat on a stool near the cash register. Although her expression seemed mature, her body showed the angularity of early adolescence with only the hint of a curve to her chest and hips. She had deep olive skin, and a pretty face, and remarkably expressive hazel eyes. She was wearing a beige smock brightened by several lines of variously colored beads that dipped in a soft vee from the shoulders. She smiled a shy pucker of her lips as Kelly and Dave approached the counter.

"You're Robin, aren't you?" Kelly asked. "We saw you yesterday with Livonia."

The girl seemed uncomfortable with being recognized, and she looked toward a woman who stood next to her. The woman glanced sideways at Kelly. Until that moment, she had been staring to her left, out of the window, so that only half her face was visible. Now, when she turned, it became clear that she had been hiding the bruises on the left side of her face. Her jaw was swollen, and an ugly purple and ragged semi-circle rose between her high cheekbones and her puffy eyelid. Kelly started to lay the earrings for Allie on the counter, but she stopped and brought her hand to her mouth, startled by the older woman's appearance. The woman reddened and looked back toward the window. A tense quiet filled the tiny shop. The child hopped off the stool and placed herself next to the older woman.

"Yes," Robin said. "This is my mother, Frankie Asebou." She pointed to a basket of fossil stones. "And you know what these are, from Livonia's story yesterday."

Frankie lowered her head to whisper something in Robin's ear, and then she lifted her eyes, now blank with indifference. The girl picked up the earrings.

"Would you like them?" Robin asked.

"They are really very nice," Dave said. He took the earrings from Robin's hand and laid them on the counter. He ran his finger over the quills, which were three-quarters white then taupe. They were attached, top and bottom, to strands of turquoise beads, interspersed with black. "I'm sure Allie will love them," he said to Kelly, and then he turned to the girl. "We'll take them."

Frankie slowly brought her face around. Her eyes were sullen. Robin gathered the earrings into her hand and checked the price tag.

"Twenty dollars," she said. "But there's no tax."

Dave took out his wallet and handed a bill to the girl. She snipped off the price tag and slid the earrings into a small paper bag. Kelly rested her hand on the bag. Her eyes had not left Frankie's bruised face.

"Excuse me for asking," Kelly began.

"Nothing happened," the woman said.

Kelly leaned against the counter and studied her.

"But something did."

"We were in a car accident," she said. "I hope you enjoy the earrings. The price is good."

"Yes," Kelly replied. "And no tax." She faced Dave. "Do you have a card with you?"

"She said she was in an accident," he said, but his hand reached again for his wallet. She took it from him.

"I know. But just in case." Kelly opened Dave's wallet and removed one of his business cards.

"My husband's a lawyer. We just bought the old Wilson place. We'll be here all summer." She glanced down at the card. "This is the address of his New York office. I'll put our local address and number on the back." The woman did not respond. Kelly wrote the information in her quick, neat hand, and held out the card to the woman. When she did not reach for it, Kelly placed it on the counter.

"I know what 'esquire' means," Frankie said with a quick look at the card. "But I don't need him." She picked up the card, crumpled it, and tossed it into a wastepaper basket behind the counter.

"I'm sorry," Kelly said.

As they began to leave, Dave glanced back over his shoulder. Frankie was staring stonily out of the window. Robin's hand darted into the basket and retrieved the card. She shoved it into the pocket of her smock. Just then the huge man who had picked up Robin from the pow wow pushed his way into the shop through a rear door. He shifted his eyes from the woman to the child, and then back to the woman. Dave saw the man's mouth move, and the woman recoiled as though she had been struck. The child held her ground until the man stepped toward the cash register, and she backed away from him. He opened it and removed the twenty dollar bill. Apparently, that was all he found in the drawer. He slammed it shut hard enough to rock the machine, and then he retreated through the rear door.

"Do you think..." Kelly began. Her voice was tentative, but her eyes were angry. "I mean, did you see that?"

"Yes," Dave replied, "but..."

"Do we need pictures? You saw her face."

"And the man who may have beaten her."

Kelly's tone softened.

"Then you do understand," she said, "I couldn't just not say anything."

He nodded.

"You did the right thing," he said.

"You don't believe that stuff about a car accident any more than I do."

"No, I don't."

"Maybe she'll call," she said. "If not you, maybe somebody else."

"I don't think she will," he said.

Kelly took the earrings out of the bag.

"I won't feel comfortable giving Allie these. My God, that girl in there, her eyes have seen things, and her father, if that's who that man was."

"Don't" he said. "That girl is not Allie, and that man is not Michael."

Hooper lay on the back seat. His thick tongue protruded an inch and a half out of the side of his mouth, and his jowl quivered with each breath. He lifted his head when Dave opened the driver's side door, wagged his corkscrew tail once or twice, but did not attempt to get up.

Dave turned the key, and the Caddy's engine responded with a deep-throated roar. He looked back at the gift shop, at its cedar planked front, and the sun glinting off its window. Its contemporary architecture of milled lumber and glass, low slung and stark, seemed to argue with the towering trees that a century and a half ago had sheltered bark structures, home to a population that depended on the bounty of the land rather than the money of tourists for their sustenance, on the deer they hunted, the fish they caught, and the grains they grew instead of gaming in the casino and false trinkets that mocked those ancient ways. A sadness fell over him like a cold breeze from between those huge trees.

Kelly clutched the thin paper bag between her whitened fingers, passing it back and forth from one hand to another. Dave knew she was not thinking about the history of the Ojibwe. Her mind was with her own daughter from whom she was separated for the next several weeks, not so much by the miles but by something far darker and deeper. Just what that something was he did not know, nor had he been able to draw her out. She only offered platitudes when he asked her, joked about premature feelings of the empty nest syndrome. But there was more to her anxiety, and whatever it was plucked her nerves in the gift shop and now pulled her facial muscles into a hard knot and made her hands knead each other as though she could squeeze her concern into submission.

Dave maneuvered the Caddy out of the parking lot. He heard another engine start up. In the rear view mirror he saw black exhaust rise from the back of a battered, dust-covered pickup truck. When the smoke lifted, he could make out a bulky shape hunched over the steering wheel. Their eyes locked for a second, and then the man jerked his truck into gear and headed, beneath a cloud of tired dust, toward the opposite end of the parking lot where the much larger tribal administration building offered an unequal counterpoint to the gift shop. The truck disappeared behind the building.

Dave and Kelly sat in the twilight on the porch, which offered a view of the bay above the rows of cherry trees. With the failing light, the waters had darkened to a deep blue. He sipped his coffee and studied the trees.

"I hope they can earn enough for the rent," he said.

"John thinks we're due for a good season," she replied.

"Seems to me he's been saying that for some time."

"I think I remember how to drive a shaker. And I could teach Allie."

"I've never even mowed a lawn. But I'm sure Allie would love to try her hand."

Her face tightened.

"I don't know if I'll be able to get her out here next year. Or whether we should come. Maybe the whole idea was a foolish dream."

"You used to talk about this place like it was paradise."

"I was seeing it as though I were still sixteen, and even remembering how when we were teenagers and I would work for Uncle John in the summer, I invited Michael to come out for a summer job. We both needed money in those days." She sipped her tea, and fixed her eyes on the bay. "It is pretty," she conceded. "Anyway John will help us."

"Maybe you just have to get used to the idea of being here. With me. And without Allie, at least for now."

Her eyes were still fixed on the water, now almost black.

Dave waited for her to respond, and when she didn't, he opened the screen door and went into the kitchen for another cup of coffee. When he returned, she seemed to have decided to tell him what was bothering her.

"Michael hit me once," she said. "Just once. My father said I must have deserved it. My mother said her beads. I sat with an ice bag on my jaw, and wondered what the hell was happening."

"You never told me," he said.

"There isn't that much to tell."

Dave studied her face, and she looked away. He sensed that she was considering whether to tell him more.

"He did hit you," he insisted. "Was it more than once?"

Her head remained rigid for a moment, and then she nodded.

"It's not like he beat me, or anything. The one time I mentioned was the time that sticks in my mind. He was frustrated, I guess. The marriage was already over. We hadn't slept together in a year. I had almost forgotten."

"Until today."

"Yes. I saw those bruises and I felt Michael's hand on my jaw again, only this time it was much harder, and more mean spirited than I had remembered before."

The sun had slipped behind the trees to the west of their house, and the darkness, glowing faintly in the last rays, crept over the water and settled on the porch. It seemed as though the temperature had suddenly dropped ten degrees.

Dave felt an unexpected anger rise in him. He saw the hand flash through the air, and he heard the slap against Kelly's flesh. He reached the tips of his fingers to her cheek, and she recoiled.

"Don't," she said. "I can't explain it. I think of him, and I don't want you to touch me."

"I understand," Dave said. But he settled back in his chair in confusion.

~

Later that night, in bed, neither of them could sleep. They lay in an embrace, but there was still a distance between them. Kelly pulled away and sat up.

"Did you hear that?" she asked.

Dave lifted his head and listened. He heard Hooper's labored breathing, and nothing more for a few moments. Then a shutter thudded against the side of the house. He settled back on his pillow.

"Yes," he said. "I'll have to nail it down tomorrow."

"That wasn't it. Listen."

He sat up again, and this time there was a faint tapping that seemed to be coming from the front door, as though a very feeble, or indecisive, person were knocking.

Kelly stood up and reached for her robe on the chair next to the bed.

"I'm coming," he said, but she was already on the stairs. They creaked beneath her step. By the time he joined her in the narrow entrance that led from the kitchen to the door, she was talking to a slight figure framed in the moonlight.

"You'd better come in," he heard her say, and the head atop the figure shook deliberately from side to side.

"No," a thin voice said. "I couldn't."

Dave saw the expressive eyes, and then recognized Robin's voice. Kelly placed her hand on the girl's shoulders, but she stepped back.

"I only came to give you back this." She held out Dave's business card. It had been crumpled, and the girl tried to smooth it by pressing it between her hands. She glanced over her shoulder into the dark. Dave could not see anything, but he heard the rumble of an engine idling. It was missing badly and the rumble was punctuated by metallic coughs. "He's waiting outside there for me," the girl said. "In his truck. He said I had five minutes, and he's probably staring at that old pocket watch of his, and then he's going to leave."

Kelly pushed back Robin's hand folding her fingers around the card.

"Keep it," she said. "You may need it."

The girl shook her head again, violently.

"No, I can't. That was the whole point. Of him bringing me out here." She shoved the card at Dave. "Take it," she demanded. "Or there will be real trouble."

Dave took the card, and the girl stood with her hand still out, as though unsure what to do now. "I've got to get back home," she said. "I think my mom has got herself a gun." She turned on her heel and disappeared into the darkness. They lost sight of her almost immediately, but could hear her light footsteps on the gravel of the driveway. They heard the truck's door open, and for a moment the man's figure was illuminated by the dome light. He was holding up an object, pointing at it. Then he reached out his thick arm and gathered the girl into the cab of the truck, not with violence, but with a cruel determination.

The truck door slammed. The clank of gears engaging was followed by the engine's uncertain roar. After a few moments, the night was still.

Dave examined the card. Somebody had drawn thick, black pencil lines through the address and phone number Kelly had written on the back. The same hand had circled the printed address of his New York office on the front of the card. Dave got the impression that the hand was gnarled and thick, and that it labored to guide a stubby pencil in unfamiliar motions. Kelly took the card and flipped it over several times.

"Not too subtle," she said. "Yankee go home."

"She said her mother had a gun," he said.

"I heard." Kelly pressed her hand against Dave's cheek. "I know who you're thinking about—Bonita Mercado," she said. "We'll go talk to Frankie, the first thing in the morning."

For the moment, Robin's appearance, and the memory of Bonita Mercado it recalled, had drawn them together again, but Dave could sense, as they walked back upstairs, that the shadowy presence of Michael and his raised hand awaited them in their bedroom.

CHAPTER FOUR

THE sun would be up soon, but for now, the last of the night air lay like a sodden gray blanket between the bay waters and the porch where Dave sat. After Robin left, he and Kelly lay in bed together but each seemed haunted by separate demons, or perhaps one demon with several aspects. He closed his eyes, but he could not shut down his mind's imaginings, seeing Robin's terrified eyes, and hearing again and again the words "she has a gun," echoing like the shot ricocheting against a courtyard's brick walls and then transmuting to the slap of Michael's hand against Kelly's flesh, and finally coalescing in the story of Bonita Mercado.

He looked over at Kelly, grinding her teeth in a troubled sleep, her body curved into a protective curl, knees towards him. And so he stumbled out onto the porch, with his eyes dully open, staring into the darkness, listening for the first stirrings of morning. A bird chirped off to his right, and then another one a little farther off. The birds' voices sounded plaintive as though they feared what the day might bring. After a while, he discerned the rhythmical four-note pattern of the oriole, with a stress on the alternate notes, rising into the still air until they formed words, the syllables of a name and a plea he had heard many years ago, and then he knew that it was his name now carried by the bird's song, as it had been then in the voice of a woman asking for his help. The words had poured from the mouth of the woman sitting in his office on Court Street in Brooklyn, words that spoke the unspeakable, and yet she said them over and over again, pausing only to brush a tear from eyes that still flashed rage. My daughter, the words said in high pitched, clipped tones, not quite human, he thought at the time, my daughter, she said, it is not enough what he does to me, I know he has his eyes on our daughter, and she is not four years old.

Dave was doing pro bono work for Legal Aid, and his client was a woman who feared that her estranged husband—who abused her, more after their separation, who came to her apartment and beat her and even forced her onto their bed while their child slept on the couch, not ten feet away—would not be satisfied with her. The woman said that her husband had stared long and hard at the little girl, before he left the apartment, and he would be back, she knew, again and then again.

Dave secured an order of protection, knowing that it would be as useful as a curtain of reeds against the winds of her husband's need to control, the urge to humiliate, to inflict pain even on his own daughter, to use sex the way some took a can of spray paint to tombstones, as an expression of rage at his own impotence. To understand the cause was not to forgive the behavior, and Dave loathed the man, even as he filed the order he knew would not protect the woman from him.

Somewhere beyond the ancient mountain ash, its orange berries just now visible in the first light, a blue jay screeched its harsh warning, silencing the song of the orioles. Dave recoiled at the discordant note because it made him remember his almost forgotten anger and despair. He recalled, now, the end of the story, not in the words of the woman, for he spoke with her only much later, but as it was told to him by the police detective, a man in his late thirties with eyes as old as death, eyes that had seen horrors beyond utterance so often that they had lost the ability to register shock, peering instead at the world with an indifference that matched the flatness of a voice too weary to rise in indignation.

As Dave expected, and as he had warned the woman, the husband had no difficulty violating the order, and the attempt to restrain him only fueled his anger. He assaulted her one more time, and she changed her tactics, inviting him the next time into her bed, luring him away from the child who sat stonily in front of the television set. After he left, she began to throw her clothes and those of her daughter into shopping bags. She had just finished packing, tossing in a few cosmetics, when she heard his step outside the apartment door. She shoved her daughter through the window and onto the fire escape, but the stunned child crawled back through the window, her eyes fixed on the television screen, while the woman reached down to pick up the second of the two bags. By then, the man was upon them.

He did not beat her. Nor did he attack the child, as she had feared. Instead, he bound them both together and to the pipe that fed steam into the apartment. All he could find for the purpose was a cord he ripped off the one lamp in the living room. He tied it around the woman's right arm, looped it tightly around the child's left, and then secured it to the pipe. There was not much slack, and their bound arms were no more than six inches from the pipe.

It was winter. The landlord, on the order of the City Housing Authority, had just fixed the heating system. The steam hissed through the pipe, and the insulation around the lamp cord began to sweat and expand. The woman and her daughter pulled against the cord, but succeeded only in lacerating the skin beneath the knots. At last, the woman forced her arm between the pipe and her daughter's frail wrist. She held it there as her skin reddened and the tears rolled down her cheeks. She passed out, after a while, from pain or exhaustion.

When the husband returned to the apartment, he thought he smelled burning flesh. He joked about it, saying he was hungry. The woman roused herself long enough to curse. He did not get angry. He seemed never to get angry any more. He removed a clothes line from a paper bag, and with it he tied new knots, which would permit them to crawl several feet away from the scalding pipe once he cut them free of the lamp cord. While he worked, the woman clawed at him with her long nails, but the child sat in a silence from which she would not emerge for months. He smiled at the woman's attack, and brushed her hand away, gently, but with serious purpose. Then he told her to be still or he would hurt the child, who did not respond to the threat, but sat there on the floor, her eyes fixed someplace far away, rocking gently. The woman stared at her baby, and willed herself still. The man reached again into the paper bag, removed a tube, and applied a salve to the woman's burns and wrapped the wound in an old T -shirt. He heated a can of franks and beans on the stove, put them within reach of the woman and child, and then he left again.

Neither of them ate. After a while, the dark from the city streets edged over the fire escape and into the room. The child lay down. The woman would not close her eyes. She was waiting for him to come back, and she was thinking how she could kill him when he did. Then she felt something warm against her bare leg, and realized her daughter had urinated in her sleep. She tore off a piece of her skirt, mopped up the urine, and then threw the sopping material into the darkness of a far corner of the room. She was sure she would find a way to kill her husband when next he came back.

The sun was now up over the bay, although the air held its night chill. The orioles had resumed their song, encouraged by the morning light. Their whistling wrenched Dave from the memory of the woman and her daughter. He could now see where the birds were in the birch tree behind the ash. Flashes of bright yellowish orange darted among the leaves, and the thin branches dipped as the orioles landed. And then, after five or ten minutes of sustained but inscrutable activity, they flew off, two larger shapes of the adults followed by the smaller fledglings, toward the bay. They disappeared in the now brilliant rays of the sun. With their departure, Dave felt a moment of relief, as though they had taken with them the memory of the woman and her daughter.

He studied the quiet and still tree where the birds had perched. He recalled occasional trees that lined the street that ran by the house where the woman and her daughter lived. Those maples once shaded brownstones, before the houses were torn down and replaced by the projects. Now those maples gave the block a specious feeling of rustic serenity belied by shouted curses and occasional bursts of gunfire.

It was beneath one of these trees that Dave next saw the woman. It was a month or so after he'd obtained the order of protection for her. He had not heard from her, and when he tried to call, he discovered her phone disconnected. On an urge, he walked to her block, not too far from his office. As he neared her house, he saw a family approaching—a man, a woman, and a child. It was the woman, and her husband and their daughter. She did not look at him as she passed him by. Dave was about to speak to her, when he saw the new swelling of her stomach and then the tightening of her lips as her eyes followed his. The little girl's face wore the expression one sees on an elderly person whom life has worn down. Dave smiled at her, as one would at any child, but the girl retreated behind her mother. The man, though, grinned, as if to apologize for his daughter's bad manners, and that smile more than anything else haunted Dave's sleep for many weeks thereafter.

Dave figured the man would violate the order of protection, and he knew the police would be unable, or unwilling, to keep him away from the wife he was abusing. Dave had not, in his innocence, understood that she would have tossed away her hatred, like the urine soaked piece of her skirt, that she would throw it into a corner of her consciousness, so far removed from thought that she could invite him back not only into her life, but into her bed. He did not know, then, when he saw the smug grin on the man's face that the woman had buried her hatred only to nourish it. A year later, with her infant son sleeping in the crib and her daughter staying at her grandmother's house, the woman obtained a shotgun. The police found the man, his face blown away, and the front of his skull several feet behind him, lying naked on his back on the bed. The infant son was crying in his crib. Next to him lay his mother sobbing. She told the police that she had intended to kill the baby and then herself, but with only one shell left she could not decide what to do. She hated the sight of the child because of his father's blood in his veins, but she could not bring herself to pull the trigger after she propped the heavy weapon on the rail of the crib. Nor could she imagine letting the child grow up motherless. So she did nothing, just lay on the floor, the useless shotgun at her side, until the police came.

Dave was no longer her attorney when her case came to trial. He obtained permission from her new lawyer to talk with her, but when he did, she did not seem to recognize him. When she finally did, she asked him if he could get her another order of protection against her husband. The old one, she thought, must have expired by now.

A jury found Bonita Mercado competent to stand trial, and she was convicted of second- degree murder. She was sentenced to life in prison, and her children were placed in foster care.

Dave waited for the orioles to return, but they did not. It was as though they had sung the woman's story for him, and then, their task completed, had abandoned him to greet the sun alone with his memory, mixed as it now was with the image of the girl who had come to him the night before, saying her mother had gotten a gun.

Dave stood up and stretched. He had been sitting in that chair long enough to travel back to Brooklyn and another time in his life. Maybe this time he would get it right.

CHAPTER FIVE

DAVE and Kelly stood in front of the gift shop at a quarter to nine. Early or not, Dave had the uneasy feeling that they were already too late. In blunt block letters, inscribed by a pencil, a sign on the window stated, "Closed."

They peered through the front window. All looked as it had when they were there yesterday, but there was no sign of anybody getting ready to open for business. They walked around the building and found that the rear door was locked. Dave knocked, but nobody responded. He checked the parking lot again, and saw only the Caddy.

"Let's see if we can rouse somebody in the Administration Building," Kelly said. "Maybe we can get an address for Robin."

As they started to walk across the parking lot, they heard the rumble of a truck engine. Dave turned in the direction of the sound. The angled rays of the sun blinded him. He shielded his eyes, and after a moment he could again see the Caddy. It looked like it was glowing. A bulky shape pulled up next to it. Dave squinted until his eyes were nearly shut, but he could see only the outline of the vehicle. It moved toward them for a few feet, paused as though the driver noted them standing in front of the store, and then it spun around to disappear into the low hanging ball of the sun.

"Could you make out anything?" Dave asked.

Kelly shook her head.

"Not much. It sounded like the truck that came to our house last night, but there are hundreds of pickups around here with engines like that, and I couldn't even see the driver."

"Hard to miss that guy, if that's who it was," Dave said. "Whether it was or not, he seemed to have been spooked by something."

"Us?"

"I don't see anybody else."

The receptionist at the Ojibwe Tribal Administration Building was sipping coffee from a Styrofoam cup. She was an attractive young woman with her hair pulled back into two long braids, fastened by beaded ties. She put the container down and glanced up shyly at Dave and Kelly as they approached the counter. As a hunched figure of a man entered the receptionist's area from a rear door, she became nervous. He picked up the wastepaper basket and emptied it into a trash cart, just visible through the door. As the man re-entered to return the basket, Dave could see gray stubble on his face and a black patch over his left eye. The receptionist waited for him to leave before she asked if she could be of help.

"We were just across the way at the gift shop," Dave said, "and there was a sign on the door that said it was closed."

She glanced at her watch.

"It is a little early. Maybe Frankie hasn't come in yet. Sometimes she has a problem getting a ride to the store, when her husband is using the truck."

"Then who would have put the sign up?" Kelly asked. "And we saw a truck leaving the parking lot." Her tone was contentious, and the young woman recoiled.

"I don't know. Trucks pull in and out of here all day."

Dave took out a business card and handed it to the woman. "I had an appointment to talk with Frankie. Do you know where I might be able to get in touch with her? An address? Phone number?"

The woman studied the card as though it contained a foreign message, and then she placed it carefully on the counter.

"Maybe you'd better wait until my boss comes in." She nodded toward a couch and a chair near the front door. "I don't think I can help you with your business."

"When do you think your boss might be available?" Dave asked.

"Soon, I think. But sometimes he has other things to do before he comes in," she replied.

"Does he have a name?"

"Of course."

"Could you tell it to us?" he asked.

"John Leaping Frog."

"Would you tell Mr. Leaping Frog that we're waiting for him?"

She lifted her coffee cup and nodded in a way that said, "I hear you, but I don't know who you are, or what you want, and I have my job to think about."

Dave and Kelly sat on the couch for ten or fifteen minutes before Kelly spoke.

"Your business card impressed the hell out of her," she said.

"I was reading in the local paper about some scandal at the casino. Perhaps she thinks I am connected to the investigation, and she's protecting her boss, and herself, for that matter."

"Maybe she just doesn't like lawyers," Kelly offered. "I've heard some people don't."

"So have I. But I've never understood it."

He expected another quick retort from Kelly, but she seemed not to have heard him. After a moment, she said, "Sorry, I was thinking about Allie."

"Why not call her when we get home?"

"Yes, I could do that," she replied. "As soon as I figure out what I would say to her."

"About her father?"

"Yes."

The hunched figure who emptied the trash crossed toward them, his good eye fixed on magazines and newspapers on the table. He busied himself placing periodicals in neat stacks, newspapers on one side, and magazines on the other. Then, he muttered something.

"Pardon?" Dave asked.

The man did not respond, but seemed concerned that the pile of magazines was not quite neat enough. He placed his palms on either side of the stack and straightened them.

"That Leaping Frog, you gonna wait a long time for him."

His voice was barely audible, so Dave leaned over as though to select a magazine. The man placed his hand on the pile as Dave was about to pick up the top magazine.

"Maybe you're thirsty," the man said. He motioned with his head toward a water cooler down a corridor, and out of sight of the receptionist.

"Sure," Dave said. "I think I am."

The custodian pushed his cart down the corridor, past the drinking fountain. Dave picked up the magazine, a six-month-old *Time*. After glancing through the pages, he replaced the magazine, got up and made his way to the fountain. The custodian waved him on to the end of the corridor. When Dave got there, the custodian was gone, but he saw a door ajar leading to a field behind the building where the custodian stood.

"I think you've been watching too many movies, my friend," Dave said.

The man shrugged, and then he gestured toward his patch-covered eye.

"Cue stick," he said.

"I thought the idea was to use the stick to hit a little white ball against colored balls—you know the ones with numbers on them—into those holes on the side of a table."

"Charlie Williams was on the other end of the stick, when he shoved it into my eye."

"I'm interested in a woman named Frankie."

"Frankie Asebou, that's Charlie's wife."

"Big man, with a bigger belly?" Dave asked.

The custodian nodded.

"Then talk to me," Dave said.

"I still got one good eye."

"And you want to keep it. Understood. I'm on Frankie's side."

"I ain't on nobody's side, except I wouldn't mind payin' that bastard back."

"I'm listening."

"All I got is where she lives. That's more than that cigar-store Indian Leaping Frog would give you. You wouldn't get the time of day from him. He's the one about to go down for using the casino as an unofficial kind of bank for people who have lots of unofficial kind of money."

Dave took out a twenty dollar bill, but the custodian shoved his hand away with some force.

"I told you what I was after," he said. "That'll be payment enough if I can see that lard belly sittin' in jail where he belongs."

"Fine, the address?"

"Ain't no address, so to speak. Their place is out off the county highway. A two track a couple of miles north of here. There's a falling down barn at the corner. Make a right. It's the only house on the road, and then it ends." The man turned to his trash wagon and pushed it toward a dumpster at the far end of the building.

"So let's check it out," Kelly said. "I think I know the road he's talking about."

"I'm just going to say good-bye." Dave replied.

He walked over to the receptionist. When she looked up at him, he offered his best smile, the one he knew would be read as a condescending insult by the smart ones, or accepted as the mindless blandishment of a used car salesman by the others.

"Please tell Mr. Leaping Frog we couldn't wait any longer, but perhaps he could give us a call. The local number is handwritten on the back of the card I gave you."

The woman turned the card over and glanced at it. She nodded.

"Thanks," Dave said. "I do appreciate the courtesy." Apparently, the receptionist had decided that she wouldn't buy a used car from him.

With Kelly behind the wheel, they found the road the custodian described. It branched off the highway just after the casino. The houses near the casino were modest modular prefabs, mostly well tended, with small but neat lawns in front. They turned off the highway onto a dead end dirt road, leading to a lone house at the end.

"I guess the revenue from the casino goes only so far," Kelly said.

The house was more like an oversized, square box, with exterior walls formed of rough hewn planking interrupted in the front by a crooked door and a window propped open by half a broomstick. A pipe extended above the shed roof, and Dave imagined that it descended into a stove inside the house. Next to the pipe, wires led back to a pole on the road.

The front lawn was overgrown with uncut grass and weeds, two or three feet high, and no sign of any attempts at landscaping. Tracks, the width of a pickup truck, ran along the edge of the high grass toward the side of the building. On one corner of the house hung a basket of fuchsia, offering bright red blossoms to the morning sun. They found the grass beaten down, making a path wide enough to accommodate one person leading to the front door. Near the hanging basket, they saw a number of empty fruit crates arranged to form steps. A child's plastic watering can, half full, sat on the top crate. A small, black beetle seemed to be swimming leisurely across the surface. Dave nudged it and found that it was dead.

The tire tracks led to this side of the house, but curved slightly as they passed the basket. Dave followed the tracks to a rectangular patch of dirt where, apparently, the truck was ordinarily parked. In the middle of the patch was a pool of black oil. He leaned down to dip his fingers into the pool.

"It's still warm," he said.

Nobody answered Kelly's knock. Part of the door frame had been torn off as though somebody had forced it open while locked. It hung permanently ajar. Dave knocked once more, loudly, and then he pulled the door open. It swung heavily on its bent hinges.

They stepped inside. The sun fully illuminated the tiny living room through a bare window on the east side of the house. A jagged crack formed a vertical line in the window, ending where a pane was missing. The stove sat in a corner of the room, next to a sofa that sagged badly on one side, perhaps where Charlie Williams sat. A portable television connected to a cable box rested on a small wooden table, and a couple of steel folding chairs were lying on their sides next to the table. Glass shards from a broken whiskey bottle littered the floor in front of the sofa. The television was turned on, showing Big Bird's clumsy figure leaning over Oscar's trash can. Dave switched the set off.

Kelly walked ahead through a doorway to a narrow hall that led to a bedroom. Dave heard her catch her breath. He came up behind her, and over her shoulder he saw a figure on the bare plank floor next to a bed with a stained and lumpy mattress hanging over the side of a metal frame. The woman's hand held this piece of the mattress, as though she had tried, and failed, to raise herself from the floor.

Dave leaned over her, and he saw her chest move.

"Thank God," he said.

Frankie shifted her position and groaned. She opened her eyes for a moment and tried to focus on Kelly.

"Robin?" she said. "Is that you?" Kelly began to respond, but Frankie closed her eyes again.

"I thought we were too late," Kelly said. "From the looks of her, we almost were."

Frankie's face bore new evidence of a heavy hand. The bruise under her left eye was now balanced by the swelling over the right. Her nose was puffed, and dried blood sat on her upper lip. She was wearing a thin cotton robe, which was undone and revealed her breasts, belly and groin. The skin on one breast was black and blue near the nipple. Deep scratches ran across the insides of her thighs, disappearing into her matted pubic hair. Blood had dripped down her legs between the scratches, and in greater quantity than the scratches themselves would explain.

"The bastard," Kelly muttered.

"We'd better check the rest of the house," Dave said.

"You go. I want to see what I can do for her."

Checking the house took no more than five minutes. There was one other bedroom, apparently Robin's. A cot occupied most of the space, and it was neatly made up with a ragged teddy bear lying against the thin pillow. Dave looked in the closet and saw a pair of jeans, a sweatshirt, and the smock Robin had been wearing in the gift shop.

In the kitchen he found a few unwashed plates and cups in the sink, and the bathroom looked as though it had not been cleaned in some time. A stale stench of urine wafted up from the toilet, and a rust stain circled the drain in the sink. Dave located a back door that led outside. Kelly joined him, and they looked out on a narrow meadow that gave way to a wooded hill.

"I can't do much more than wipe off the wounds with a cloth," Kelly said. "And I can't get the water turned on in the bathroom sink, and the one in the kitchen is crawling with roaches. We'd better get her to the hospital."

"Right," Dave said. He started to turn back into the house, but he stopped to look back over his shoulder at the hill.

"Do you know where we are, in relationship to Peterson Park?"

"That's on the other side of the peninsula, not too far, maybe five miles. I used to go there when I was a kid. Why?"

"Isn't that the beach covered with fossil stones?"

"Sure. Why do you ask?"

He began to reply when he realized that he didn't know why he asked, so he shrugged. Kelly studied his face for a moment, and then she walked back inside.

"I'll see if Frankie needs help getting into the car," she said.

Frankie was sitting, legs splayed, and examining the black and blue mark on her breast.

"Shit," she said. "That son of a bitch." She started when she saw Dave and Kelly standing in the doorway, and she pulled her robe closed over her chest. "What are you doing here? Where is he?" She looked around the room "Where's Robin? And the gun?"

49

"We came out to talk to you," Dave said. "To see if we could help stop this from happening."

Frankie looked confused.

"How did you know? I mean before you came out? Have you seen him?" She stared toward the front of the house. "He's in the living room. That's where I left him."

"There's nobody there," Kelly said.

"The hell you say." Frankie struggled to her feet, and took a step toward the doorway. "I mean I shot the son-of-a-bitch last night. Right there in the living room. That was after he beat me, raped me, and when he was through, just to show me there was no hard feelings, he offered me a drink. To celebrate our reunion, he said. I cracked the bottle over his head, and then while he was staggering around, I shot him. I saw him fall against the window, and then onto the damned floor. And then I ran into here. Robin was in her room. In bed."

"Her bed doesn't look like it's been slept in," Dave said. "And your husband is not in the house."

"Then where the fuck do you think he is?" She broke into a crooked grin, as though she had just caught the joke. "You don't think that his manitou came during the night and carried him off, do you? He's too fuckin' heavy for an army of manitous."

"Maybe," Kelly said, "you'd better sit down, and tell us everything again."

"Robin," Frankie said, her voice tinged with terror. "I must find her."

"Talk to us," Dave said. "And we'll do our best to help you do just that."

Frankie looked hard at him.

"What is all this to you? I can't pay you."

"You don't have to."

"Why?"

"I have my reasons. Maybe you remind me of somebody. Just let us help you."

The emergency room at Community Hospital was quiet when Dave and Kelly walked with Frankie between them. She had been unable to add much information to the events of the preceding night. She was only clear on two things: She had shot her husband, and she must find Robin.

Kelly sat down with Frankie, and Dave introduced himself to the admitting clerk as Mrs. Asebou's attorney.

The clerk, a woman in her thirties with light brown hair cut short, and wearing pink toned spectacles, eyed Frankie through the thick lenses of her glasses.

"Does she have insurance?" the woman asked.

"I don't know," Dave replied. "Why don't you have a doctor look at her while I take care of the paperwork. I will be responsible for the bill."

"Do you?"

"Pardon?"

The woman's face soured into exasperation.

"Have insurance?"

"Yes, but what's the point? It won't cover her. I'll pay your charges by check if that is satisfactory." Dave had expected this routine, but he felt his patience begin to wear.

The woman stared hard at Frankie.

"She live over at Peshawbestown, on the reservation? If she does, she might be covered."

"Yes," Dave snapped. "Do you think you could get a doctor to look at her? She may have internal injuries. She's been beaten."

"Who by?"

"Does that matter?"

The woman looked at Dave as though he were a backward child. Then she nodded, a slow, studied movement of her head.

"Of course it does. We have to report certain kinds of things. You should understand that."

"I do. But can you please just have a doctor examine her?"

"Surely," she said. "I am just doing my job." She handed him a clipboard with a form to be filled out, turned on her heel, and disappeared through a door into a corridor flanked by small examination rooms. Within moments, a young intern came through the door.

"Mr. Abrams, I am Dr. Wiley. I can see your client now," she said.

Kelly helped Frankie to her feet and led her to the door leading to the treatment area. Dr. Wiley took Frankie's arm.

"I'll take it from here."

Kelly began to protest, but the doctor smiled and closed the door.

Standing in front, catching his breath after hurrying down the corridor, was a young Native American wearing a deputy sheriff's badge.

"Is that all you know, Mr. Abrams?" The deputy sheriff screwed his boyish face beneath his straight black hair into a frown. "It doesn't make a lot of sense."

"That's it Deputy Crow. She says her husband attacked her, and," he paused, "then there was a struggle. She passed out, but she remembers seeing him on the living room floor."

"But he wasn't there."

"No, he wasn't. Nor was her daughter. Look, deputy, she probably doesn't know what she's saying. Maybe she's in shock, or delirious. But it's clear she's been beaten, abused, probably raped."

"By her husband?"

"Yes," Dave said, "although I think they were separated."

"You say there was a broken whiskey bottle on the floor?"

Dave nodded.

"Yes, deputy. Just what is the point?"

"No, point, Mr. Abrams. I'm just trying to gather the facts."

The door to the treatment area swung open, and Dr. Wiley stepped into the waiting room. She held a clipboard, and beckoned to Crow, who took the clipboard from her. After a few moments studying the report, he raised his eyes to Dave.

"Dr. Wiley says your client keeps insisting that she shot her husband."

"She's not competent to know what she's saying at the moment," Dave said.

The deputy studied the report again.

"Says here that her blood alcohol was .08. No wonder she isn't making much sense."

Dave checked the anger rising from his belly. This was not Brooklyn, and this young deputy was just reporting what he was seeing.

"What else does it say, deputy?'

Kelly rose from her seat and strode toward the doctor and Crow. She paused for a second as she reached the door.

"Any objections?" she asked. "I'd like to comfort the victim."

Dr. Wiley glanced at Crow, and the deputy nodded. Dr. Wiley followed Kelly into the treatment area.

"It says," Crow continued, "what we already know. Fresh contusions on her face, abrasions and contusions on her breasts and thighs. And," he paused, "lacerations of her vagina, and traces of semen, indicating recent intercourse."

"Thank you," Dave said.

"All that glass on the floor," Crow muttered.

"I don't think she sat on it," Dave said..

Crow started to reply, but then caught himself.

"I'll turn in my report. You may be hearing from Mr. Heilman, the prosecutor. But with only a crazy story like this, and the fact that whatever happened, happened on tribal land, well, I don't know. Maybe you should get in touch with the tribal court. They usually handle domestic disturbances."

"I don't believe that is what we are dealing with," Dave said. "Rape is covered under the Major Crimes Act, giving the federal government, if not the state, jurisdiction."

"You're the lawyer, Mr. Abrams. I don't know about that," Crow replied. "But murder is murder. If a body turns up."

"Does your department handle missing children who might be at grave risk?"

"Sure. You mean Robin, sweet kid. Look, I see how concerned you are. And so am I. But understand I know Frankie from the rez and Charlie, too. Been to their house more than once, cleaning up their mess, trying to find out who did what to who. You know what I mean? You're from New York. You know what I'm talking about don't you?"

The name of Bonita Mercado formed on Dave's lips, and he nodded.

"Yes, deputy, I do. And that is why I seem so exercised by this case."

"I understand," Crow replied. "By the way, did you happen to find a shell casing? In the living room where Frankie said she shot him?"

"No," Dave said, remembering the missing window pane.

"Could have been a revolver," Crow said, "if anybody shot a gun."

And maybe she did and missed, Dave thought.

"The doctor says her wounds are superficial, that she'll be all right even though she will have some trouble walking or sitting for a while. Isn't that far-fetched?" Kelly's face showed her disbelief. "And that, from a woman doctor, too." She pointed at Frankie. "Just look at her. Does she look okay to you?"

Frankie was lying on her side on the sofa in her living room. Her eyes were unfocused, staring out the window. The basket of fuchsia hung next to that window, and Frankie had paused on the way in the house to pick up the little watering can. She now clutched it to her chest, unaware that water dripped from the spout onto the robe she still wore.

"She's waiting for Robin to come home," Dave said.

"Maybe I'd better stay with her," Kelly said.

Frankie roused herself and turned to Kelly.

"You go home with your husband. I need some time to rest. Then, when I'm feeling a little better, I'll water her flowers. She'll be home, soon. If not, then I'll go out to look for her. I know where she might be."

"Dr. Wiley said you should stay in bed for a couple of days."

"Is she going to find my daughter? Is she going to pay my bills if I keep the shop closed?"

"It'd be no trouble for me to stay with you," Kelly said.

Frankie's expression softened.

"No, it would not be a good idea. What if he comes back and finds you here?"

"Comes back?" Dave asked.

"I know. I shot him," Frankie said. "I just forget."

"Are you sure?" Kelly tried one more time, and Frankie nodded. She turned her gaze to the window, much as she had stared out of the window of her shop the day before.

"We'll keep on the police," Dave said, "to make sure they look for Robin."

Frankie snapped her head back toward Dave.

"No use there. Eddie Phillips. He's the head of the tribal police, and he is Charlie's uncle."

"I meant the sheriff's department," Dave said.

"Less help there," Frankie mumbled.

"Maybe," Dave said, "you can tell us where you think she might be." Frankie, though, did not reply. Her eyes closed now, as she clutched the plastic green watering can and continued to look through the window for her daughter.

Hooper greeted them at the door with a look of recrimination in his mournful eyes. Dave leaned down to scratch the dog's head. "I know," he said, "you're waiting on your supper."

"I'll feed him," Kelly said.

"Excuse me?"

"Don't misunderstand. I'll feed the dog, if you'll fix something for us. It's a trade."

"Ham and eggs for us?"

"Sounds good."

Dave had just cracked the last egg, and Hooper was contentedly belching beneath his feet while staring up hopefully at the slices of ham next to the frying pan, when the phone rang. Kelly picked it up.

"Allie," she said, "I'm so glad you called. I was going to, but I thought I should wait."

Dave tracked the changing intonations in her voice, from apprehension to relief. He set the table and then leaned into the refrigerator looking for the bottle of Riesling from the local winery. The wine was at the rear of the top shelf, behind the milk and soda. He grasped the bottle by its neck and started to pull it out, when he realized the happy enthusiasm had disappeared from Kelly's voice, replaced by a series of concerned murmurs. He eased the bottle out, uncorked it and poured it into two glasses, and turned toward Kelly. Her face was dark, and her eyes anxious. She pushed a wisp of hair back from her forehead, and then brushed at it again as though it were a fly buzzing about her head.

"Well, she is your friend, isn't she? Maybe that's all he meant," she said. The words offered assurance, Dave thought, but the tone was hollow.

"No, I don't think so," she said. "But I'll call you later." Kelly held the phone for a moment, her eyes distracted, and then placed it on the receiver.

"She's not having a very good time," she said, as she sat at the table.

"Anything particular?" Dave asked.

"No, not really. Just something he said that upset her, and now she wants me to come pick her up. I told her I couldn't, not right away, anyway." She scooped a slab of the ham and eggs onto her plate and took a sip from her wine. "He insisted that she invite her friend Grace to sleep over. She had come over, and apparently Michael spent more time talking to her than to Allie."

"Is Allie being a bit sensitive?"

"Perhaps," Kelly replied, her lips pulled back from her teeth. "When Allie was a baby, we had this sitter. What Allie just told me reminded me."

"Go on," Dave said.

"It was just the way he looked at that girl. She was Allie's age now, so, I made it my business to do the picking up and dropping off."

"That's all?"

"Yes." Kelly took another sip of wine, and then stared at her glass. She put the glass down hard.

"Do you want to go back and get her? Or we could buy a ticket for her," Dave suggested.

Kelly's face relaxed just a little.

"Not yet," she said. "But I'll let you know."

"Does Allie know why her father was in jail?"

"For kiting checks? She was young at the time, and for her own reasons she didn't seem to want to know any details. I just told her that her father had done something dumb, had cheated people, and he had gotten caught. The only question she asked was when he would be coming home again."

They watched PBS until its broadcast day was over, but neither turned the television off, and the screen had now been blank for more than an hour. Kelly finished the bottle of wine, one slow, determined sip after another, and Dave busied himself with a crossword puzzle book. Neither suggested that they go up to bed. Then the phone rang, and Kelly started to reach for it.

"It may be Allie," he said.

"I know," she replied, but she still let the phone ring another couple of times. Then she picked it up. He watched the tension lessen in her face as she heard the voice on the other end.

"Yes, he's here," she said, and held her hand over the mouthpiece of the phone. "It's Heilman."

"Have you got anything yet?" Dave demanded.

"Yes," the prosecutor replied.

"You found the girl?"

"That's right. Found her not twenty feet from her father's body, which was lying in the shallow water by the beach at Peterson Park." Heilman was silent for a moment. "Just about now, Deputy Crow is taking your client into custody, charged with her husband's murder."

"She was violently beaten and raped."

"Save that for the hearing, counselor. What we got here is a dead body with two bullet holes, one in his belly, and one in his neck. And we've got the woman's statement to the doctor who attended her."

"That is privileged."

"Tell it to the judge, Mr. Abrams. I'm sure he'll want to hear everything you have to say."

Dave hung up the phone.

"I heard," Kelly said. "What can I say? We'd better take a look."

_CHAPTER_SIX

FROM the top of the cliff overlooking the beach, Dave could see the body. Somebody was shining a powerful flashlight beam on the white shirt that curved over the belly. At the top of the curve, a bright rust colored stain stood out against the fabric. The beam played over the body, moving from the feet and then up to the head, which faced the shallow water where the body lay. One arm was thrown across his chest as though he had tried to move himself into a ponderous roll that would have carried him to dry land. He hadn't found the strength.

Dave and Kelly were at a railing next to the stairs that led down to the beach. About ten feet from the entrance to the stairs the railing was broken, as though something had crashed through it. Dave examined the jagged wood.

"Looks like he might have started up here," he said.

"We'll want a closer look, won't we?" Kelly asked.

"They've probably checked him out as much as they can down there," Dave replied. "And now they're figuring out how they're going to hoist him up to here."

"I can see why they're taking their time on that one."

"Maybe they'll bring in a boat."

A full moon shone through the cedar trees that clung to the sandy soil of the cliff, casting gigantic shadows on the wooden platforms that served as steps, creating pools of yellow light against the black background. About halfway down the steps, Kelly paused and stared to her right. She leaned over the rail and extended her arm.

"Look at this," she said. Dave peered at a cedar branch that she was holding. Kelly pulled the branch toward them.

"Here, see. I don't want to pull too hard." She pointed toward a gash in the middle of the branch, and to its end where the needles had been stripped.

"Odd," Dave said.

"Yes, isn't it."

"Let's see what he looks like."

Kelly started down, but a flash of white caught Dave's eye. He reached over and picked up a piece of paper. It appeared to be part of a store receipt, but the top, where the store's name might have appeared, was torn off. In the middle of the paper was the number 201, written and circled in heavy pencil. He studied the paper for a moment, and then caught up to Kelly.

Night air condensation layered the beach rocks with a pale, opalescent film, which appeared in the moonlight as though it had been left by a gentle rain. They stepped carefully over the stones toward the cluster of men surrounding the body. The darkening blood stain on the man's shirt and the unnatural angle of his head argued against the specious charm of moon, water, and beach. He was wearing a thin windbreaker, which was falling off his huge shoulders. His eyes were open and staring as if in disbelief. His right fist, the one toward the water, was clenched as though he had been holding onto something. Dried blood etched a wound on his neck. As Dave and Kelly approached, a man turned to greet them. He was wearing a tuxedo.

"Mr. Heilman," Dave said. "At first I thought you must be the mortician."

The prosecutor extended his hand, but he did not smile.

"I was at a thousand-dollar-a plate-dinner when the call came."

"Right," Kelly said, "the governor is in town."

Heilman shrugged.

"One does these things."

"The girl?" Dave asked.

Heilman pointed toward a shadowy cedar tree at the base of the cliff.

"We found her over there."

"And now?"

The prosecutor took a deep breath that stretched the stiff front of his shirt uncomfortably over his stomach. Dave studied the fake pearl button that seemed about to pop from the pressure. Heilman placed his hand over the button. He was wearing a pinky ring, a sapphire in a heavy silver setting.

"We woke up a county social worker, who took her to the hospital, to be checked out. The child was out of it, in shock. They gave her a sedative, and she's sleeping."

"Are you going to let her see her mother?" Kelly asked.

Heilman turned his cold, blue eyes toward her.

"In time, perhaps," he said. "Let's not forget that her mother murdered her father."

"Aren't we getting a little ahead or ourselves?" Dave demanded.

"I'm sure you think so. We don't."

"Another matter for time to take care of," Dave replied. "Do you have the weapon?"

Heilman glanced down the shoreline where dim figures moved like ants across a huge, petrified piece of stale white bread. Among them was one large man who was waving his arms, as though to direct the others.

"The sheriff has got his men looking," he said. "We'll find it. If not here, then someplace."

"It must be tough," Dave said, "to be called out on nasty business like this in the middle of the night. You'd think these Indians would be more respectful, what with the governor in town, and all."

Heilman's face showed that he was about to take the bait, but then he relaxed his jaws into a sigh.

"We're both here," Heilman replied. "Taking care of business."

"Yes," Dave said. He shook Heilman's hand and squeezed it so that the pinky ring would dig into the prosecutor's flesh. It was a heavy ring, and Dave could feel the engraved surface of the setting. Heilman stifled a wince, and returned the pressure of the handshake.

"Always a pleasure, Mr. Abrams."

It wasn't that Dave disliked the prosecutor. Two summers ago, Dave defended one of John's workers in a case prosecuted by Heilman. The young man, a migrant worker from Mexico, celebrating the end of the cherry harvest, drank too much and muttered curses directed at the fruit he had just labored sixteen hours to gather. A woman walking with her little girl overheard the young man's profanities, and complained to the police. Heilman first checked to find out if the young man was in the country legally. When he found that he was, the prosecutor dusted off a nineteenth century ordinance against speaking obscenities in public and brought charges against the young man. With great effort, Dave managed to have the charge dropped. While Heilman was technically correct, Dave came away from that encounter with a decent respect for Heilman's competence, but questioned his priorities, if not his judgment.

Kelly had been staring at the ant-like figures down the beach.

"Looks like they'll be at it for a while," she said.

"Something tells me that they're not going to find it, not tonight, or tomorrow," Dave said.

"You're not proposing that we join the search, are you?" Kelly asked.

"No," Dave replied. "but maybe we could be a little bit smarter about it."

"Meaning?"

Dave looked up to the cliff, but Heilman shook his head.

"We don't think he fell from there. Kids use this place for parties. There's been a lot of vandalism, but we'll check it out."

"Do you mind if I borrow your light?" Dave asked the officer who had been shining his beam over the dead man's body.

Glancing at the prosecutor, the deputy held out the heavy flashlight. Dave played the beam over the body, as though looking for nothing in particular. Heilman had resumed his conversation with the officer, and Dave knelt beside the body. The windbreaker pocket was turned inside out. He shone the light on the clenched fist. Kelly leaned over and pointed.

"Do you see it, there in his fingernails?"

"Something green," he said.

"Like a small piece of cedar."

"Find anything interesting?"

Heilman had padded over to them. His voice was unnaturally bland. Dave and Kelly straightened up.

"Not much, except his nails could have used trimming."

Heilman took the flashlight from Dave and examined the man's fingers.

"Could be anything. The lab boys will tell us," the prosecutor said. "They like to check these things out, put their little bits of stuff under a microscope."

"You don't sound too interested," Dave said.

"I've got a confession and a body with wounds that fit the statement. I'm in pretty good shape."

"Except the confession is probably tainted, and anyway it has the body in a house miles from here."

"She dumped it," Heilman replied.

"You're going to need a crane to hoist that man out of here," Kelly objected.

"Adrenalin," Heilman replied, "can do wonders. Maybe the girl helped. Or friends and relatives. You never know."

Back in the Caddy, Dave hesitated for a moment, and then turned to Kelly. He took the piece of paper out of his pocket and handed it to her. She squinted at it in the moonlight.

"Looks like the same hand that wrote on your business card," she said.

"Yes," he replied, "and it might have come from his jacket. The pocket was turned out." He took the paper back from her, folded it, and put it in his pocket. "It may be nothing, or it may be something."

The police did not find the weapon that night, and the next morning Heilman's voice snaked through the telephone.

"Look, Abrams," he said, "maybe you can help us with this one. Frankie says she won't talk to us anymore. Unless you're there. The girl is still sleeping. I doubt she knows much anyway."

"You want me to discover some evidence to make your case?" Dave affected a tone of disbelief.

"We all just want to nail this one down," Heilman continued. "It's almost there. The gun will help." He paused, and when he resumed, his voice dripped even more oil. "We know this is an abuse case. We've already taken some testimony to that effect. We might be able to work something out on the charges, if you help us find the gun."

"Happy hunting," Dave said.

"I was hoping you might see the wisdom in being a bit more cooperative."

"Never my strong suit. And in this case, my intuition is talking to me."

"Telling you what?"

"That Frankie did not kill her husband."

"Oh," Heilman said. He sounded disappointed.

"But," Dave said, "if I find out anything that you should know, you will."

"If that's the best you can do."

"It is."

Dave hung up the phone and turned to Kelly.

"Let's see if we can work our way into Robin's room at the hospital before Heilman's investigators do."

The nurse looked up with weary eyes from behind the counter at her station. It was just before eight a.m., and she seemed to be at the end of her shift. She stifled a yawn.

"Excuse me," she said. "I've just worked a double. Joanne called in sick last night, the second time this week, and they asked me to stay." She shrugged. "At least the money will look good in my paycheck."

"We're looking for Robin Asebou, a girl about fourteen," Kelly said.

The nurse checked a clipboard.

"Nobody by that name here."

"She would have been admitted last night. She was sedated."

The nurse squinted at the clipboard, and then shook her head.

"These are the recent admits. Lord knows, I've been on enough to know everybody else. She's not here."

"Try 'Robin Williams,'" Kelly suggested.

The nurse ran her finger down the list.

"There's a Williams here, no first name. Room 314, admitted at 1:30 last night." She put the clipboard down. "I seem to remember her now. She was out like a light when I saw her."

"Thanks," Dave said.

They began to walk down the hall when the nurse's voice trailed after them. "It's not visiting hours yet." The voice was very tired, and they kept walking. Kelly pointed to a sign on a wall that directed them down another corridor, to the left, for Rooms 300-325. The nurse did not follow them.

An orderly, pushing a cart with cleaning materials, stopped to glance at them. He was a young black man, his hair in dreadlocks, one ear heavy with a thick golden hoop.

"Can I help you?" he asked. His voice still carried the lilt of the waves on some Caribbean beach.

"We're looking for Room 314," Dave said.

"I thought so," he replied.

"And why is that?"

"Because there ain't nobody in that room, now."

"Now? There was, wasn't there? A little girl?"

"Whoa, man," the orderly said. "Like I said, there ain't nobody in there now. But there was, a pretty little girl, but somebody must have come to take her away."

"I don't suppose you saw who that was?"

The orderly shrugged, and then squared his shoulders to push his cart.

"I saw her at the beginning of my shift," he said. "Oh, there was a lot of commotion. Doctors and the policemen. I watched, you know, and then they all left, and the little girl went to sleep.

When I come back here later, I look in on her, just like I do with my own little girl at home, but all I see is her bed, made up like she was never there. It makes me to wonder."

"But you did see her," Dave demanded.

"It just made me to wonder," the orderly repeated. He shook his head slowly from side to side, and then fixed his eyes hard on them. "You don't see any other brothers around here, do you? So you see my point, don't you?"

"We just need a little information," Dave said.

"I already told you what I know, and I don't know that anymore. And now I am done for the day, and I think I'll go home and make sure my own little one is where I left her."

"She should be in there," Nurse Hodges insisted. "Look," she pointed at a computer screen. "She's even been punched into the computer." The exasperation on her face transferred to an abrupt energy in her arm as she gestured toward the screen. "There's her name. Room 314. Like I told you before."

"But she's not in the room."

"Did you check the bathroom?"

"Yes," Kelly snapped. "And under the bed, and down the hall in the lounges, and the other bathrooms in the corridor. She's gone."

Nurse Hodges looked at her watch.

"I know," Dave said. "You've worked a double, and now it's past time to go home. But we have a missing little girl."

The elevator door slid open, and Deputy Crow walked out.

"Mr. Heilman said I'd probably find you here, if you hadn't already come and gone."

"You're a bit late," Dave replied.

"You've talked to her? Is she awake?"

"No."

"Is she still asleep, then?"

"Can't say. You haven't asked the right question. The simple fact is that she's gone. And nobody here seems to have a clue as to what happened."

Crow turned to the nurse, who offered a weary shrug.

"She's in the computer," she said. "I didn't see anybody come or go, and Lord knows, I've been here all night."

"You might try the orderly who's around here pushing a cart someplace, if you can catch him before he goes home," Dave suggested.

"Did he see anybody?"

"He saw the girl last night. But not this morning."

"Doesn't sound too helpful."

"It's the best I can do."

"We've searched the floor," Kelly added.

"I'm obliged," the deputy said. "But I'll take a look myself. Then I'll call Mr. Heilman."

"Any ideas?" Dave asked.

Kelly did not respond. They were standing in the parking lot in the back of the hospital.

She seemed to start, as though his voice had brought her back from a distant and troubled place. Her face was drawn, and her hand trembled.

"It's Allie. I keep thinking about how she sounded on the phone." She put her hand on his mouth as he began to offer a word of comfort. "Don't say it."

He removed her hand and held it between his.

"Why don't you call her as soon as we get home?"

She lifted her cell phone out of her pocket.

"I already tried. While you were talking with the deputy. Her cell doesn't answer. Get a message that it 's not available." She shook her head in frustration. "That child. She never remembers to keep the damned thing charged."

"Do you want to call the house?"

"Michael told me he doesn't have a land line phone. Only a cell. And, yes, I did dial it but only got his voice mail. And, well, I just couldn't think how to frame my question, so I just left a message, asking that he have her call me. I've been walking around with my cell on, but it hasn't rung. I can't just sit here waiting any longer. I'm going crazy."

"I do need you here," Dave said, the words rushing out of his mouth before he could stop them.

"So does she."

Reading the concern in her eyes, Dave said, "I can come with you. Let the police here do their job without my help."

She shook her head.

"I know how you are making this case into another Bonita. And you may be right. Stay here and do what you have to do. I'll be back as soon as I can."

"With Allie?"

"I don't know. Maybe."

With its bloated fuselage hanging beneath ridiculously flimsy wings, the turbo-prop plane looked, Kelly concluded, as though Snoopy should be its pilot. She amused herself with this thought, while avoiding what she knew she had to get straight in her mind, the question of why she had not told Dave what was troubling her. The quick reply was that she had been unable to find the right words, but she knew the answer lay much deeper.

Her flight to Chicago was called, and she joined the dozen or so passengers as they queued up before the gate. She found herself standing behind a young couple, and in front of an old woman. The couple had their arms locked behind their backs, and their hips rubbed together as they walked. The young man slid his hand to cup the woman's buttock. Kelly realized she was smiling, then heard clucking coming from the older woman behind her, who murmured, "Why, I never, just look at them." Kelly turned to the woman and offered a shrug, but the woman's face hardened and it seemed the thick powder and rouge on her cheeks would crack like stained glass under the weight of her indignation.

On board the plane, Kelly sought a seat by herself in the rear of the tiny passenger cabin. She buckled herself in and surveyed the other passengers. She noted that the old woman was behind the couple. She was wearing a black, straw hat with a pink band around the crown, and it seemed to float from side to side as the woman shook her head in constant motions of disapprobation. The flight attendant offered the old woman a magazine, but she declined with an irritated jerk of her arm, which was laden with cheap, costume jewelry bracelets that clanked dully.

The lovers, obsessed with themselves, were indifferent to the world's clucking disapproval, just as, Kelly thought, she and Michael had been years ago. She picked up a magazine out of the pouch on the back of the seat in front of her, and stared at its cover. It was one of those in-flight publications that airlines provide to motivate their customers to fly to exotic places where everybody is smiling beneath a brilliant sun. She opened it up and flipped some pages, stopping on one that featured a line of tourists on horseback on a beach somewhere. The people were silhouettes, dark shadows against damp sand and foaming surf. She leaned her head back and closed her eyes. She tried to listen only to the surf and the muted thud of the horses' hooves.

But, instead, she heard again her husband's hand slap against her cheek, not once as she had told Dave, but several times in rapid succession, each one harder than the last until she was on the floor.

She had come home late from her class to find Michael sitting at the dinner table behind a row of beer cans. Each one had been squeezed into a crude hourglass. He drained the can in his hand as she entered the room. He turned his eyes, hard and hostile, towards her, then slammed the can onto the table, causing a sputter of foam. With slow and deliberate motion, he wrapped his hand around the can and squeezed. She could see the veins stand out in his forearms, and she heard the grunt he expelled between his clenched teeth. It sounded something like the noise he made when he came during lovemaking. She had always thought that sound held more anger than love.

"I'm hungry," he said.

She felt the guilt, like his hard hand, press against her stomach. She had stayed after class to discuss her research project with her teacher. She really did not need the help, just a minor point or two of clarification. The professor was her age, no more than twenty-five, and his eyes lit up when she approached the desk with her question. Afterwards, she realized that she knew he would smile at her that way, and she wondered if that is why she chose to ask the question. And as the professor spoke, providing much more detail than she needed on an obscure point of bibliographical strategy, she had felt her belly tighten with the thought that Michael would be waiting for his dinner. Yet, she asked another question, and then another, until perversely she had made herself hopelessly late, as though she knew and welcomed the scene that would confront her.

Now, without thought, but as if she had memorized the line, she said, "Well, I'm going out to pick up a sandwich from the deli. Would you like one?"

She thought she knew before she spoke what his answer would be. And she was mostly right, only she anticipated words, not the blows that fell on her face. She sat on the floor in stunned disbelief, and when she rose she shocked herself by saying, "I'm sorry."

That statement haunted her for all these years. She did not care to remember Michael's sneering response. What she could not forget was that she had tried to will her legs still to prevent them from carrying her into the kitchen, and her hand from preparing a supper. And finally, she could still feel Michael's weight bearing down on her in bed, expressing his forgiveness, which she accepted, with each thrust of his hips, and with his pained grunt of pleasure.

She opened her eyes and looked around the warm plane, closed the magazine and then her eyes again as the plane taxied. The plane hit turbulence as it worked its way down the shore of Lake Michigan toward Chicago. With each sudden drop, she was jolted back to the present, and with each ascent into the bright sky she was carried back to that night so many years before.

And now torn between anger and shame, she was flying back to New York, leaving Dave to try to locate one abused and missing child, while she sought to assure herself that her own daughter was safe with the man she had never stopped fearing. But, as she had finally come to realize, along with her fear lingered an irrational guilt that she was somehow responsible for Michael's abuse of her, and more than that, the man he seemed to have become. At certain times, she could not free herself from the thought that she had knowingly provoked his anger, even though her acts were provocative only in the sense that they violated Michael's unreasonable restrictions and expectations, born of his resentment that his wife was leaving behind her the bars and pool halls of Red Hook where they had both grown up and was finding her own way into a career as a librarian while he floundered, failing in one business venture after another, as a jewelry wholesaler, as a caterer, as an importer, in each case revealing a positive talent for bungling his opportunities just on the cusp of success. His frustration at his failures turned on himself and then on to her.

Rationally, she understood this deflection. But her heart did not forgive herself. Their marriage bed turned cold, their intimacy transformed to physical confrontations, and through it all she wondered what she should have done differently. When she divorced him, her devout Irish Catholic family distanced themselves, leaving her alone with her irrational guilt.

Maybe, she thought, she had acceded to his wish to have Allie spend part of the summer with him only because she felt she owed him an opportunity for redemption. The horror of that idea had propelled her to the airport, and now held her in its chilling clench as she watched without seeing the puffy white clouds, as innocent as lambs, through the grime-encrusted window of the tiny commuter airplane.

CHAPTER ‾SEVEN

DAVE felt Hooper's head press against his calf, and he reached down to pet the dog's broad, wrinkled forehead. Hooper groaned, wagged his stump of a tail, and then lay down, his eyes closed while Dave's fingers continued to scratch him. Hooper's head pressed up against his hand, and Dave offered one more, cursory, scratch. Kelly was tending to her own, necessary business, and he would have to take care of his. Uncle John would be as good a place to begin as any.

Uncle John was really Kelly's father's cousin. His family had been poor potato farmers in a village in County Armagh, Ireland. As a boy John vowed he would not die with dirt under his fingernails, as every male progenitor had done for generations. He stowed away on a steamer to New York when he was twelve, in the 1920s, became a naturalized citizen, and moved on to Chicago where he joined the police force. The defining moment of his career found him crouched behind a car facing a darkened warehouse, taking careful aim at his adversary. He squeezed the trigger, anticipating the usual shock against his palm, running up his wrist to his forearm, but nothing happened. His adversary had seen him, and was emptying his revolver in his direction, bullets thunking into the heavy steel of the sedan. John squeezed harder, and his gun blew up, taking off his three middle fingers, leaving him his thumb and pinky. He saw the revolver lying some ten feet away on the street. He went to pick it up with blood spouting from his amputated fingers. He always concluded the story by saying that maybe the gods of potato farmers were paying him back for foreswearing his vocational heritage, but at the least, he had fewer fingernails for dirt to lodge beneath when he was laid out in his coffin. He never did explain what the man who was shooting at him was doing while he stared in wonder at his fingers, which still looked as though they could curl around a coffee mug, as they lay next to an empty pack of Camels on that dark Chicago street.

John seemed to have a decent pension, and when he retired after his accident, he had enough capital to buy a small farm out on the peninsula. "What else was I to do?" he said then. "The only things I knew were being a cop and farming." When Dave first met him, several years ago, John was looking toward a second retirement, this time from cherry farming. Dave heard rumors from neighbors that John occasionally did some "unofficial" police work—some said it was for the sheriff's office, others the Coast Guard.

Dave pulled out his cell phone and flipped it open to see if Kelly had called during his ten-minute drive to John's farm. There was no message or indication that a call had been missed. But the indicator for the battery showed it was low. As he slipped the phone back into his pocket, he saw John directing a crew that was shaking a section of orchard near the house. The profile of the shaker rose in a semi-circle from its back to the cab where the driver sat atop the engine controlling the arm, whose padded clamps grasped the trunk of a tree, and as its engine revved, the arm vibrated, spilling the fruit into the tarps spread below. Dave watched as the crew lifted the tarp and fed it onto a conveyor belt beside the catching frame, and the belt dumped the cherries into a large water-filled tank. In the meantime, the shaker driver guided his vehicle to the next tree. John waved to Dave and motioned him toward the house.

John's front porch offered a marvelous view of the bright blue waters of the bay, now darkening as the sun slid behind the trees. Dave watched John walking, slightly stooped, towards him. He was over eighty, but his hair, a shock of wavy, thick silver, and his broad shoulders and muscular forearms, testified to the powerful man he must have been in his youth. John glanced over his shoulder at his crew, shrugged, and then joined Dave.

"That'll about do it for the day," John said. He sat next to a redwood table where a bottle of Johnnie Walker Black Label beckoned. He held the tumbler in his good hand, and the stump of a cigarette between the thumb and pinky of the other. In order to bring the cigarette to his mouth, John turned his palm toward his face, so Dave found himself staring at three middle knuckles and no fingers. Dave sat down on the chair on the other side of the table.

"Care to join me?" John asked. Without waiting for an answer, he poured a double into the extra glass he always had out in case company came. With the cigarette between his teeth, and its ash glowing perilously long over the whiskey glass, John poured with a careful eye. Just as the ash was about to drop, he moved his head, and a second later, the ash dropped into the ashtray on the arm of his chair. He took a puff, and lifted his glass.

"To your health."

Dave took a good sized gulp. The Scotch was smooth and warm.

John settled back in his chair. Dave knew he was wondering where Kelly was.

"She's gone back to New York, for a while," he said. "She's worried about Allie."

John nodded, ground out the cigarette and took another sip from his own glass.

"She's got to make certain the girl is okay, always did, ever since the trouble with her first husband." Dave noted that John never spoke of Kelly's "divorce," but always "the trouble," the way the Irish refer to difficulties in their homeland. "You know she came out here that first summer," he paused, "the first summer she was alone. Allie couldn't have been more than four or five."

"Did she tell you much?" Dave asked. "About exactly what happened?"

John shook his head.

"No, and I didn't see it as my business to ask. She came out here for the quiet, like she used to when she was a kid. Just took a lot of long walks with her daughter." He held out his right hand. "It's a funny thing with kids, you know. Allie asked me where my fingers were, and I just said I lost them a long time ago. She looked at me puzzled, and then she said she'd help me look for them. And that's what we did, for a while, until she got bored. We'd walk all over, picking up leaves and poking into bushes, or whatever. Finally, she said that I seemed to be doing okay without them, and maybe she'd help me look again next time her mother brought her out. Of course, we never got the chance because Kelly didn't come again for years, and the next time she did, she had you with her, and Allie was off in summer camp somewhere."

"She's worried, really worried," Dave said. "She's not sure she did the right thing leaving Allie with Michael for a couple of weeks."

"A father should be able to spend some time with his daughter, no matter what happened between the mother and the father." He paused as though uncertain whether to continue. "I liked the Michael I knew, years ago, when he came up here with Kelly. City boy, like you, but he learned how to pull the tarp on the catching frame, and even how to handle a tractor a little."

Dave took out his phone again.

"I didn't hear it ring," John said.

"It didn't. I'm checking for a message from Kelly. But my battery is dying."

"That's why I don't bother with them," John replied.

A young man, his face darkened with sweat and grime, approached the porch. Red cherry juice stained his shirt and the white bandana wrapped around his neck.

"We're through for the day, Mr. O'Brien," he said.

"Well, Hank, I think we finish up tomorrow." He nodded at Dave. "Then maybe Mr. Abrams over here might have some work for you to do at the old Wilson place."

"Those Napoleons will be ready real soon," Hank said.

"We'll be in touch," Dave replied.

John kept his eyes on Hank's retreating figure.

"There are a lot of men in jail," John said. "Some of them belong there, and some don't, and then there's those on the street who should be. Sometimes it gets hard to tell who's who. Michael probably said he was framed. Never knew one inside to say anything different."

"Actually," Dave replied, "Michael freely admits his guilt. Says he's rebuilding his life, clerking in a shoe store. Look," Dave said slowly, measuring his words against his understanding of John's traditional views on marriage, "the other day we were in the Ojibwe Gift Shop, and we saw the badly bruised face of the woman behind the counter there. We both saw her, but Kelly, I think, saw herself. And since then, I've not been able to talk to her very easily. This afternoon she just told me she had to get on a plane. She didn't want me to go with her. Said I should stay here."

"Because of that woman in the gift shop? Now would she be the one whose husband was found on the beach at Peterson Park?"

"The same."

"Can I help you in some way?" he asked.

"You do have an expertise I could use."

"You want to find the wife?"

"She's no problem. She's in jail, accused of murdering her husband."

"And you're defending her?"

Dave nodded.

"Right now my problem is finding her daughter who disappeared from the hospital."

"Well, I'll make a deal with you. I'll let Hank finish up tomorrow. I only hang around, getting in his way, to convince myself that I'm still useful. I'll stay at your place, in case Kelly calls there because your cell phone is dead."

"You don't have to do that."

"At my age, I don't have to do anything I don't want to, except take care of my farm, and for that the season's just about over." He shook his head slowly from side to side. "That's the wonder of old age. I just do what I want, but I hardly ever have anything I want to, or need to do. I know you're worried about her. And in return for letting me visit at your house, and keeping company with that thing you insist on calling a dog, I think I can tell you where to start looking for this child." He picked a cigarette out of the pack on the table, using his thumb and pinky like pincers, and lit it. "If you catch Livonia early, she'll probably be in a better mood. Try calling her O-ko-mes-se-maw. Maybe she'll look at you like you're crazy, but maybe she'll talk to you. Never can tell with that woman."

"We met yesterday."

"I'm sure she'll remember," John replied. "Anyway, if anybody knows where that child is, Livonia will."

Dave drove slowly around Route 22 toward Peterson Park. Not far from the park, John had said, he would find Livonia's roadside fossil stand. As he headed north, the sun gilded the waters of Suttons Bay to his right. The highway took him through the town, several blocks of stores that offered the summer tourists everything from lunch served in a converted firehouse building to antiques culled from area farms.

Dave left the town, and the Caddy's wide carriage filled the lane on the curving road, and the breeze felt warm on his face. At one place, a squat, masonry building sat almost on the road. It looked like it was a guardhouse on a medieval manor, except there were no walls extending from its sides, and no moat. Instead, the structure seemed to have been built over a dried creek bed, and Dave concluded it must have been some kind of mill, perhaps a sawmill. Behind it was a barn with gaping holes in its walls, and half its roof gone. Beside the barn was a stone silo.

He heard the thudding hum of a marine diesel, and turned to see a trawler, its nets hanging over the side, cutting across the bay. He thought he saw the figure of a child above the net, and strained his eyes against the sun, but saw only a bright blur.

The shore was heavily wooded. So many places, he thought, for a young girl who knew her way around to hide. She was undoubtedly scared, and why not, after having huddled on that beach that night, not twenty feet from the dead body of her father. Dave remembered her thin frame, the young eyes that had already seen too much, and how she had marched bravely back to the pickup after returning his business card to face her father, his thick arm gathering her frail shape into the cab of the truck, not with violence, but with cold menace, and then to sit a silent vigil through the long darkness as her father's body stiffened in the chill lake breeze. Of course, she would run, and he knew he'd never be able to track her without help.

Seeing Livonia's wooden structure ahead on the roadside reminded him of his best hope of getting that help. He slowed the Caddy and brought it to a stop next to the stand. It was no more than a couple of boards supported by two stacks of empty fruit crates. A cloth banner, tacked across the space between the crates, announced in bold, red letters, "Fossil Stones, Etc." Behind the stand sat Livonia, her wrinkled face in the shadow of her oversized straw hat.

He approached the stand and glanced at the wares displayed on the boards. There were beaded necklaces, woven baskets, and what he had learned were dream catchers, circles formed from reeds, holding a web made of deer sinew, with a feather in the middle. Most of the counter's surface, however, was occupied by the irregularly shaped stones. Some had been polished so they glowed a charcoal black, others were a matte ashen gray. All were pitted, and in the indentations were outlines of the shells of marine animals. The polished stones sat behind a sign that said five dollars; the natural ones cost two dollars, or three for five dollars. Dave picked up one of the polished stones. It looked like the one on the counter of the gift shop.

The old woman seemed not to notice Dave, but then her lips started to move, as they had before she started telling her story at the pow wow.

"You are not here to buy a stone," she said.

"I saw a stone just like this one at the Ojibwe Gift Shop," he said.

"The beach is covered with stones, but I gather only certain ones. And they are not stones at all."

"O-ko-mes-se-maw, tell me what you mean."

Livonia's eyes narrowed for a fraction of a second, an almost imperceptible lowering of her lids. Again, she moved her lips several times before offering her words.

"Kene-se-to-tow-naw?"

Dave felt as though he had rolled the dice and had come up craps.

"Excuse me?" he said.

Livonia pulled back her lips in a toothless smile.

"So," she said, "you have learned one word. You learned to call me 'grandmother.' Maybe John taught you that?"

"He did."

"How long have you been practicing it?"

"Not very long. I learned it last night."

"Good. Maybe tonight you will learn another word, and then another."

Dave looked for a sign of mockery in her eyes, but found none.

"I'm looking for a young girl, " he said. "Robin Williams, or maybe Asebou. I saw a stone like this in the gift shop owned by her mother."

"Her father, ne-bou."

"Pardon?"

Livonia motioned vaguely in the direction of Peterson Park.

"He bought the farm," she said, "over there, on the beach."

Livonia's switch to his slang startled Dave.

"Look, Grandmother..." She frowned, and he caught himself. "Then, Livonia," he continued, and she nodded. "I thought I was the fisherman, but now I find a hook in my mouth."

"You are learning, then, and if you learn more than the words, you can call me O-ko-mes-se-maw."

"Fine," Dave said. "That man, Charlie Williams, who bought the farm on the beach, his wife is in jail, accused of the murder, and the girl has disappeared from the hospital. I need to find her. So I can help her mother."

She reached across the counter and picked up a stone.

"You heard my story about these stones, didn't you?"

"We were talking about finding Robin."

"And that is what I'm talking about. You must learn to listen. To me. To the stone. To everything. That girl loved to hear me tell the story about these stones." She put the stone into his hand. "Take that home with you."

"And listen to it?"

"Yes."

He began to say something about listening to the ocean in a seashell at Coney Island Beach, but he caught himself. This was not Brooklyn, and Livonia was certainly not a wisecracking assistant district attorney. He reached into his pocket and took out a couple of singles. Livonia waved his money away.

"My gift to you. For learning your word."

Dave reached across the counter and picked up one of the dream catchers.

"My wife has wanted to get one of these." He looked at the sign that said the dream catchers cost ten dollars, and he fished in his pocket for another bill. "You are a businesswoman, after all, and I want to make our conversation profitable for you."

"That'll be twelve dollars," she said without missing a beat.

Dave understood. He handed her a ten, and the two singles he had intended to use to pay for the stone.

"After all," she said, "business is business." She motioned to the dream catcher in his hand. "Do you know how to use that?"

"No."

"Hang it over your head where you sleep. The feather will guide good dreams through the hole to you, and the web will catch the bad ones, and hold them until they can burn off in the morning sun." She fastened her dark eyes on him. "Maybe you will need that until your wife comes back to you."

Dave started, began to protest that Kelly wasn't really gone, but then he simply nodded and turned back to his car.

The next morning when he awoke before dawn, he flicked on the light and examined the dream catcher hanging over his bed. He expected to see the web sagging under the weight of bad dreams, for certainly a number had found their way through the catcher into his sleep. He could remember only fragments, now, images of Kelly dressed in black, and a coffin, small enough to hold a child, and a man's leering face, which might have belonged to Michael, or Charlie Williams, and then another one, or more properly, the torn flesh that had been the face of Bonita Mercado's husband.

Something else also had come to him as he slept, not a dream exactly, but a certainty. He picked up the stone from his night table and squeezed it into his hand, and again he felt the clarity he remembered from his sleep. At the same time, he experienced a chill, and he realized he was perspiring heavily. He sat up on the bed, and put the stone on the rumpled pillow. He stared at it.

How could Livonia have known? And now Dave knew the same thing. She said nothing but listen to this stone. And the damned thing had spoken to him. Most shocking was the realization that he and Livonia had tapped into the same inspiration from an unknown source. He went to her for information, and she handed him the stone, with the admonition to listen to it. He thought Livonia knew where Robin was, but this morning he realized she did not but the stone did. It had spoken to her before she placed it in Dave's palm.

CHAPTER EIGHT

KELLY fought against the shudder that gripped her shoulders as the cab worked its way down First Street. She sat rigid in the back of the cab, telling herself her fears were magnified, if not groundless. She forced herself to imagine how Allie would greet her with a look of adolescent annoyance at an intrusive parent. Allie would insist that, of course, everything was all right. Michael would be sitting in a chair, looking professorial, as she knew he sometimes did, and lift his eyes from the book he was reading, and make a lame joke about how some mothers had to learn to let go of their daughters, if only for a short time. There would be classical musical playing on the stereo, probably something by Mozart. The father and daughter would have spent the day at a museum.

She manufactured these images against her fears, but the fears gave way to others, bred of anxiety, that forced themselves into her mind like pictures from a double-exposed roll of film, the darker imaginings sliding over and finally replacing the brighter ones. In these she saw Michael as the man she remembered from the end of their marriage, eyes bloodshot, beard unshaven, an arrogant smirk on his lips. And Allie was huddled on one side of the futon, clutching the now very raggedy Pooh Bear while on the other end with a knowing look on her face sat Grace. Or maybe Allie herself, catering to her father, skimpily clad in low slung shorts and scoop neck top, smiling, an ugly knowing smile, telling her to go back home to her new husband. She shut her eyes tight against these images of Allie, the one suggesting a trauma caused by her failure of maternal judgment, the other a tawdry conspiracy between her daughter and her father, opposites but both setting her on the other side of an impenetrable wall, fearing she had lost her daughter forever. She started into an awareness that the cab was no longer moving, and glancing out the window she saw that they were stopped outside of the century old brownstone where Michael lived. She forced herself to stare at the meter.

She had not spoken to the cabbie since the airport. He turned to face her now. He had a swarthy complexion, pocked with acne scars, and when he opened his mouth to talk, his gold front teeth caught the reflection of the streetlight. He glanced at the meter.

"Fifty dollars," he said.

She studied the meter, and saw it was turned off.

"You remember, don't you?" the cabbie said. "What I told you at the airport. That I was off duty. You remember how you sat in my cab, even though my off duty light was on, and wouldn't get out?"

"No," Kelly replied truthfully. "I don't remember doing any of that."

The cabbie shrugged.

"Look you want to rip me off, what am I gonna do? Call a cop? Look at me, and look at you, the way you're dressed in them fine lookin' clothes. You some kind of lady lawyer or something, and what's the cop going to do?"

"Wait a minute," Kelly said, feeling a rush of anger. "I didn't say I was going to stiff you. I said I don't remember this conversation."

"Well, I told you, like I just said, me bein' off duty and all, and you havin' to get home to see your daughter, that I'd take you there on my own time. For fifty dollars."

"Fine," Kelly said. "Just a second."

She fumbled into her purse and found her wallet. She took out two twenties, and began to hand the bills to the cabbie before she realized her mistake. Then she added a ten and held out the money for him.

"Good, lady, that's good. You can forget the tip."

Kelly felt herself redden.

"I'm sorry. I wasn't thinking." She started to reach into her wallet again.

"Please, lady. Just let me get on home. Forget it." He studied her face for a moment. "Whatever your problem is, I hope it ain't as bad as you think it is."

She stood on the sidewalk next to the streetlight and watched the cab pull away. Glancing down at her hands, she realized she was still holding the bills she had intended to give the cabbie as a tip. She stuffed the money into her coat pocket, and turned to Michael's building.

All she had to do, she told herself, was open the wrought iron gate, walk down the two steps that led to his private entrance, and ring the bell. She looked at her watch to see that it was eight-thirty. She didn't remember the times of her flight from Traverse City down to Chicago, or how long she waited at O'Hare, but at any rate, it was not very late now, so she would not be disturbing anybody. She caught herself, wondering why she cared about upsetting anyone. The only person she wanted to see was Allie. She hadn't given herself a chance to think about what she might say to Michael if he answered the door.

She peered at the window next to Michael's front door. She remembered that the room behind it was his living room. She recalled how bare it was the day they dropped Allie off. As she looked at the window now, all she saw behind the glass was darkness.

She willed her legs toward the gate. She fumbled with the latch, but could not make it open. Her frustration mounted, and she thought she might have to climb over the fence. It was no more than three-feet high, but she was wearing a tight-fitting skirt. The situation, she realized, was ridiculous, and yet she felt her eyes moisten. She pushed again at the latch, and then leaned against the gate. It opened.

She took a moment to collect herself, and peered again toward the darkened window. It made no sense that they would be asleep. Perhaps they had gone out to a movie. Again, the contradictory images of Allie struck her but quickly she chastised herself for foolish and exaggerated imaginings. After all, Michael had once been a kind and loving father, he could still be, and as for Grace, yes she had a wild streak, but Michael, well, in spite of everything he must recognize the boundaries. She realized she would lose that argument with herself. She started to reach into her purse. She could not decide if she was looking for her compact mirror to check her face before confronting her ex-husband or searching for a gun she did not have to shoot him.

She stepped to the door and found the tarnished brass knocker. She pulled it and let it fall. It struck with a barely audible thud. She lifted it again, and this time she brought it down with some force. The sound seemed to echo into the street. She listened for movement in the house, but heard none. She brought the knocker down once more, even harder, but still there was no response. She waited a few moments. Then she slammed the knocker against the door again, and again, in a rising crescendo of sound, each time slamming it harder, even when she knew that she had reached the limit of her strength. Her hand and arm ached from the effort.

She heard movement finally, but it was not coming from Michael's apartment. Somebody was in the hallway on the floor above his, fumbling with the main entrance door to the building. She stepped back and saw a figure emerge, standing on the cement stoop above her and peering through the darkness.

"There's nobody home, lady," a reedy male voice said.

A maple tree's branches blocked most of the illumination from the streetlight, casting the stoop in shadows. She could just make out a plump figure. The figure's feet, wearing sandals, were clearly visible. A ray of light reflected off the polished and manicured toenails.

"Just a second," the man said, "and I'll be right down."

The sandals flopped against the cement steps, and padded toward her. She could see that the man was shorter than she, and that he was dressed in jeans and a T-shirt that displayed the bushy hair and face of Albert Einstein. He wore wireless spectacles, in the fashion of the sixties, and his brown hair, streaked with gray, was pulled back from his round face in a pony tail.

"I'm Jim Holt," he announced. "I own this building." He drew himself up to his full height for a moment, and then, as though wearied by the effort, permitted his shoulders to fall back and his chest to slip toward his belly.

In the half light, she studied his face, which appeared unhealthy, very pale, as though Mr. Holt did not often venture into the sunlight. It also seemed a bit bloated, and Kelly remembered how alcohol had puffed her father's face while it destroyed his liver. She guessed Mr. Holt's age at about fifty, and judging from his complexion, not a man she would want to sell life insurance to.

"I'm Kelly O'Brien Abrams," she said rolling the disparate names out of her mouth as she did when confronted by a class of bored freshmen whose instructor had brought them to the library for a session on research. "My daughter has been staying with my ex-husband, Mr. Gallagher, in this apartment." She motioned toward the darkened window of Michael's living room. "I..." she began, and then caught herself.

"Yes?" he encouraged. He stepped closer, and held the sibilant sound, as though he were hissing. His breath carried the pungent sweetness of pot.

"I just stopped by," she said, "hoping to surprise them."

"Why on earth would you want to do that?" he asked. His eyes remained unfocused, but his voice now had an ironic edge. "Did you think they forgot you?"

Kelly's patience ended.

"Look, I've been on three or four different planes today, and I just got driven here by a cabbie who found every pothole on the Brooklyn Queens Expressway. My bladder is so full and shaken that I might pee right here in front of this door. And to answer your question, I have reason to believe that my ex-husband might be sleeping with my daughter's under age friend. In his apartment. In your building."

The man covered his face as though the fury in her voice were beating against him, and as she finished he put his hands over his ears.

"Well, really, I had no idea," he managed to say. "Why don't you come upstairs to my apartment. I'll make you a cup of tea to calm yourself. Of course, you can use the bathroom first, you wouldn't want to explode." His face cracked into a crooked smile again, and she could see him working his jaw muscles to reform it into a look of concern.

"You said you own this building," Kelly said, her tones now flat.

"Yes, I did. I inherited it from my mother. She died six months ago."

"I'm sorry," Kelly forced herself to say.

"Yes, well," he muttered. "I've taken the top floors for myself." He glanced down at Einstein's face on his T-shirt. "I like to be above things."

"Then you have keys."

He fumbled in the pocket of his jeans, and shook his head.

"Upstairs? In your apartment?"

He brightened.

"Of course. And you'd like me to let you in? So you can kind of check things out. Even though they're not here, like I told you. As a matter of fact, your ex-husband does travel a lot."

Kelly fought the surprise from forming on her face, and instead she set her jaw.

"I wouldn't know about that. Maybe I'll just use his damned bathroom, if you can get a move on."

He nodded vigorously, turned on his heel, and disappeared back into the shadows. She heard his sandals slapping against the stairs, and then the door opened above her and he was gone.

While she waited for his return, she paced to and fro in front of the door to the apartment. Once she stumbled over a deep crack in the cement and threw her hands out to catch herself. She felt metal beneath her outstretched palms, and sensed something brush by her side before hitting the ground with a flat sound like that made by a magazine. She ran her fingers over the object beneath her hands, discovering a lid, and then she realized that she was holding onto a mailbox attached to the wall next to the door.

She lifted the lid and groped inside. It was stuffed with paper, too much to get her hands around. With some effort, she removed the top pieces and she struggled to grasp the remainder. Somehow, this pile of mail, sitting in a rusted box next to Michael's apartment, seemed very important to her, although she didn't know why. She tried to read return addresses on envelopes, leafing through them even though the light was too feeble to make out anything. Her foot slid on something, and she knelt down to scoop up two or three more pieces of fallen mail. A beam of light blinded her for a moment, and then it moved to illuminate the letters she was holding. She looked up to see Jim Holt, staring at her with a bemused expression on his puffy face.

"I don't know if you should be looking through his mail, you know," he said.

Kelly stacked the envelopes in her hand.

"I'm looking for my daughter," she said. "I don't give a damn about his mail. Did you bring the key?"

He nodded but made no motion to open the door.

"I said I'm looking for my daughter," she repeated, honing each word as though it were a knife that could cut through the landlord's confused indifference.

"She's not there," he mumbled. "I told you that."

Reaching into her purse, she pulled out her cell phone. "I need to make a call. To a cop friend who would just love to bust your fat little ass for the dope you must have stashed in your apartment." She squeezed his arm and brought her face within inches of his. "Am I getting through to you Mr. Holt? I want to see the inside of that apartment."

He pulled his arm from her grasp and buried his hand into the pocket of his jeans. He withdrew it, holding a key. She stepped aside as he inserted the key into the door.

"She's not inside," he said yet again, but he turned the key and opened the door.

Kelly pushed by him and entered the hallway. She groped on first one side of the door and then the other until she found a light switch. She flicked it but nothing happened. Holt followed her into the apartment. "The bulb must have blown," he said. "I remember seeing it on late at night for several days."

She didn't know if he was consciously trying to heighten her anxiety. More likely, she concluded, he was just being a jerk. "You can go now," she said.

He turned to leave, but then stopped.

"I'll lock up on my way out," she said.

"Then you'll need the key," he replied. "I really don't have much stuff upstairs, anyway." His voice aspired to bravado but came out a sad whine.

"It doesn't take much," she replied. She put her hands on his shoulders and pushed him back toward the door. "I'll leave the key in the mailbox."

"You weren't going to call anybody were you?" he asked. "You probably don't even know any cops."

"Maybe not, but then again, maybe I'm one myself. Or worse, perhaps I'm an assistant DA whose career could use a boost. You don't have to know any of that. What you do have to know is that I'm a woman whose daughter has apparently disappeared from the building you own."

"I'm not responsible for that."

She pushed him out of the door.

"No," she said, "but just keep out of my way."

She watched him retreat, shoulders hunched and feet slapping the pavement, and then she heard his door shut.

She took a deep breath.

"Now, Allie, where the hell have you gone?" she said, and then she strained her ears against the darkness as though it would answer. All she heard, though, was the hum of the refrigerator from the kitchen as it cycled on.

She could just make out the bulky outline of a futon, opened into its bed position. There was a white covering on it, perhaps a sheet, and for a moment she thought she saw Allie's thin shape beneath it. She wanted to rush forward and pull the sheet off and crawl in next to her daughter. She closed the distance to the futon in a bound. As she reached it, she thought she saw a shape huddled under the sheet near the pillow, too small, she thought, to be her daughter, unless of course, it was only her head, or her torso. Her imagination assailed her with pictures of all the cut-up bodies of young girls she had read about. The refrigerator's hum seemed even louder, as though it were laughing at her, saying "You'd better come here and open up the door, open it slowly, and then you'll see."

She leaned down and ripped the sheet off the futon. Something flew off into a corner of the room and landed with a soft thud. She groped behind the futon and found the lamp switch. In the brilliant and sudden illumination, she at first could see nothing, and then as her eyes adjusted, she could make out the empty bed, the white sheet hanging from its edge, and across the room in the corner where it had landed, Allie's worn and tattered Pooh Bear. Kelly permitted herself to collapse onto the futon, and then to sob in relief and in pain.

After a while--it could have been a minute or an hour, she couldn't be sure--she turned her eyes back to the stuffed animal in the corner. It had landed right side up and was sitting in its silly red sweater, grinning as though somebody had placed it there. She retrieved it and placed it on the pillow, thinking as she did how Allie had sought comfort from it, stuffing it into her overnight bag after everything else had been packed. Allie must have been too ashamed to admit that she wanted to take it with her.

Somehow the presence of the stuffed animal in Allie's bed comforted Kelly as well. She could not imagine Michael doing anything untoward under the watchful eyes of that toy, which he had bought for her, she now remembered, on her third birthday as an antidote to the child's nightmares. He could not, she told herself, have turned into that much of a monster.

Nonetheless, the thought struck her, however illogically, that the bear could not see into the bedroom. On unsteady legs, she got up and pushed open the door to that room. She felt herself relaxing even before she found the light switch on the wall. In the darkness, the room did not give off any sense of evil. To the contrary, she smelled the faint aroma of Michael's cologne, familiar to her still after so many years, and she knew the room would be innocent. She turned on the light and saw, as she expected, his bed neatly made up. It was an oak, platform bed with a one-shelf bookcase behind it. A newspaper was carefully folded on the shelf, and on it sat a pair of glasses. The room was bare of furniture except for a matching oak armoire.

She did not remember Michael needing glasses, and she picked up the pair from the shelf. She tried them on and discovered that they were reading glasses, providing a modest magnification that did not trouble her eyes. She walked to the armoire and began to open its doors, but then her curiosity yielded before her revulsion at even a second hand intimacy with Michael, and she let her hand drop.

She remembered that she had dropped the pile of mail when she tore the sheet off the futon. She turned off the bedroom light, returned to the living room and picked up the envelopes. She started to sit down on the futon, but realized that the thought made her uncomfortable. For a moment, she was perplexed. The idea of returning to Michael's bedroom was equally impossible, but she also felt suddenly exhausted.

She heard again the hum of the refrigerator, and she made her way into the kitchen, fumbling to find the light switch. When she did, she sat down at the small, Formica kitchen table. One mug sat on the table, containing an inch or so of coffee. A dead fly floated on the surface of the coffee. Before she realized what she was doing, she had rinsed the cup out in the sink, watching as the dead fly rode the swirling water into the drain.

She sat down again at the table and sifted through the mail. She did not know what she was looking for, and she found herself scanning the return addresses so fast as not to be able to fully process whatever information they might contain. Most were junk mail advertisement, a few were bills, and a fat envelope seemed to be a banking statement.

Her hand stopped on the only piece of mail that looked like a personal letter. She looked away and then back to the envelope. Allie's still childish handwriting, with circles for dots over i's and large, longing loops on her letters, was unmistakable. The sight of her daughter's script brought a brief smile to her face, recalling how her daughter, with her talent for drawing, still loved to actually put pen to paper, enduring, good naturedly, the taunts of her peers who were busy text messaging each other.

The letter had been addressed to Kelly at the Wilson place in Michigan. It had been returned for postage. Allie, apparently, had forgotten that the postal rates had just increased. As she read, she shook her head.

"Oh, Allie," she murmured, "what are you doing? Why didn't you just call? I would have come right away."

Walking back into the living room, she saw something protruding from behind Pooh Bear. She picked up the stuffed animal and saw the cell phone. When she pushed the button to turn it on, nothing happened. For a moment, she could not decide whether to put the phone back where she found it, after all Allie and Michael might have just gone out for ice cream, but then she remembered what the letter said, and she shoved the phone into her purse, taking out her own, and dialed their number at the Wilson house. With each ring of the phone, she became more frustrated.

"Where the hell are you when I need you?" she muttered into the mouthpiece.

For answer, the phone offered another unanswered ring.

CHAPTER NINE

DAVE drove up to John's place with one hand on the steering wheel, and the other holding the fossil stone. When he knocked on the front door, he realized that he would not be able to explain to John the certainty that had gripped him since he woke up that he would find Robin in that old stone silo he passed the day before on his way to talk with Livonia Walkingstick.

John answered the door with a morning frown on his unshaven face that immediately dissipated into a smile.

"I thought it must be you," he said, "when I heard the car drive up."

Dave felt that he had reached his tolerance for psychic information.

"You recognized the Caddy's engine?" he asked.

"Nope, can't say that I did."

"Then what?" Dave realized his tone was more troubled than the circumstance warranted.

"What's the problem?" John's face registered his surprise. "It's not very complicated. Kelly just called here. She said you didn't answer your phone at the house, or your cell, so I figured it was your car coming up my drive."

Dave pulled out his cell and glanced at the display.

"Missed call," he muttered. "I had it on but it didn't ring." He slipped the phone back into his pocket.

"She was very upset," John said. "Just about beside herself."

"Tell me about it. I suppose she didn't like what she found when she saw Allie." Dave said.

"Worse than that. The problem is she didn't find Allie. Just a letter that came back in the mail. From Allie to her." John took his arm. "Come inside. I'll fix you that cup of coffee, and I'll try to be a bit more coherent, although Lord knows, your wife wasn't just now on the phone."

John's kitchen offered the tidiness that some older men, who have lived a long while by themselves, find necessary. Mugs were stored on a rack above the sink, pots hung on hooks over the stove, and a coffee maker sat on the shining counter. No other dishes, or utensils were visible, except for a sugar and creamer next to the mug of coffee John had been drinking when Dave arrived. He poured coffee for Dave into a mug bearing the Chicago Cubs logo, and he set it on the table along with a spoon. He motioned toward the sugar and creamer, and waited while Dave spooned in sugar and added a splash of milk.

"Beside herself," Dave said, as though their conversation had not been interrupted. "Allie wasn't there? What about Michael? Where the hell was he?"

John took a sip of his coffee.

"One at a time," he said. "She was very upset because Allie was not in the apartment. She had to con her way in to the place. Got the landlord to believe she was an assistant D.A. who could bust him for the weed he was smoking."

Dave permitted himself a quick smile at the thought of Kelly cowing some poor sap, but he also noticed the old policeman's hard edge in John's remarks, something Dave had heard only once or twice before.

"Anyway, she got in and nobody was there. I asked her if anything looked wrong, and she said something about a Pooh Bear, a stuffed animal I guess, and a dead cell phone, but she couldn't really see anything out of place, except for the letter."

"Addressed to her? Out here?"

John nodded.

"Allie didn't put the right postage on it, or the stamp came off. It was returned for lack of postage. Of course, she opened it, and whatever it said upset her to the point that she's on the road trying to find Allie."

"Didn't she tell you what it said?"

"In a manner of speaking. Like I told you before, she was hard to follow. The best I can understand is that something was on her friend Grace's computer."

"Grace," Dave repeated. "Oh yeah. I think I know her. Sharp black kid, Allie's age but much older, if you know what I mean."

"Sure. But what the hell is My Space?"

"It's a web site. You post stuff about yourself and it goes out on the Internet and people get in touch with you..."

"I see. Well, Grace met some guy, who said he was in Michigan, so Grace..."

"Was ready for an adventure," Dave suggested.

"Right. And Allie wanted to come out here anyway. So, I guess they're on their way here. But here's the bad news. Kelly thinks Michael is on their tail."

"Concerned father?" Dave asked without conviction.

"Or he's the guy Grace met. Kelly looked for Michael's car. Couldn't find the car, a '01 or '02 Camry. Gray I think she said. She was very clear on that, almost as though she expected me to keep an eye out for it."

"She probably did. She knew where he worked, as a shoe salesman."

"Yep. In the Runners Shop in the South Street Seaport Mall. Checked there. Michael had called in sick the day before. Didn't say when he would be back."

"So she's following him, and Allie and her friend."

John leaned back in his chair, coffee mug held between the thumb and pinky of his mutilated hand. He took another deep sip.

"Allie had given her the route in the letter. Said they were going to take the Thruway up to Buffalo, and then across Canada, and into Michigan at Port Huron."

"That's a lot of road," Dave commented.

"If they're on it," John said. "she'll find them."

Dave drummed the table, hard, with his fingertips.

"What the hell am I supposed to do?"

"She was clear on that point. She said not to worry, and she'd keep in touch. I told her that I would be staying at your place, like we agreed, while you tracked down Robin." He got up. His face betrayed an anxiety that he tried to suppress. "I suppose I should get over there. Your dog is probably waiting for me." He caught himself. "You never told me what was bothering you."

Dave downed the last of his coffee, and stood up.

"I'll tell you on the way out to the cars. I was going to ask for your help, but I'd rather you stood by for a call from Kelly. I just need you to tell me what you know about a stone silo next to a falling down barn on Route 22."

"I know the place," John said. "There's a window near the top. Corn was fed through it from an elevator. Door on the bottom, crude, wooden. A hell of place to choose to hide. Mice or rats probably all over the place, and a real good chance of getting trapped in there if that old door jams. How can you be sure she's in there?"

"I just am," Dave had replied. "I'll tell you how when we have more time, but it has to do with Livonia Walkingstick and a fossil stone."

The silo stood next to what was left of the barn. Dave took a quick glance through the gaping holes in the wall of the barn. Among the shadows he could make out the hay loft, stalls and feeding troughs. If Robin were in there, he would have to go in and find her. Instead, driven by the conviction that had arrived unbidden, he walked to the silo, which was constructed of irregularly shaped stones and crude mortar, largely crumbled now. It was about twenty-five feet high and perhaps ten or twelve feet in diameter. Weeds were growing in the cracks in the mortar near the ground, and the whole structure wore a long-abandoned look. The door was facing the road, as was the window near the top.

He tried the door, first pushing on it, then applying his shoulder. It gave a little but then stopped as though blocked from inside. There was an old, rusty iron ladder leading up to the window. Dave placed his foot on the first rung and tentatively shifted his weight onto it. He could almost feel the corroded metal give beneath his step, but the rung held. He studied the rungs above him, each one looking less solid than the one below, and he wondered whether it was worth risking a broken leg or worse to confirm the mystic message carried to him by Livonia and the stone she insisted he take with him. He stood undecided for a moment or two until the memory of his dream at waking made up his mind for him. Later, he would remember two other factors. A pickup truck, passing by on the road, slowed and the driver peered with unfriendly curiosity at him, and as it did, his mind jumped to thoughts of Kelly somewhere on the New York Thruway hunting for Allie. He did not want to be chasing some message from a fossil stone while she might be calling from somewhere. He pulled his own phone out of his pocket and checked to see that it was on and fully charged. It lit up.

He started to make his way up the ladder, rung by rung, clutching the uprights. A fine red dust lifted from every rung. By the time his head came even with the window, his palms were red from the mixture of sweat and dust, and he was breathing hard. He permitted himself a glance down and figured that he would probably survive a fall.

He stepped up to the next rung, felt it start to give, and lifted his foot off it just as it snapped. His motion shifted his weight and the ladder pulled away from the side of the silo. He reached for a ledge beneath the window and steadied himself as the ladder swayed and then clanked back against the wall. He tried the next one and it held. One more rung brought his waist even with the window, where a couple of crooked wooden shutters hung from rusted hinges. Bracing against the side of the silo, he pulled on one shutter. It did not budge, and again the ladder lifted off of the wall. He tried the other shutter and managed to move it out. He peered into the darkness and then reached into his pocket for his flashlight. He flicked it on and played the beam across the floor of the silo. He could see what appeared to be browned corn stalks on the stone floor. Something scurried across the floor, and he fixed the light on a good sized rat, which disappeared beneath a pile of stalks. Next to the stalks there appeared to be a blanket. He leaned into the silo and dropped his arm to bring the light as low as he could. He thought he saw a shape beneath the blanket.

"Robin," he called. "Is that you?"

For an answer, the rat scurried out from beneath the stalks and sat on its hind legs, twitching its nose, peering up at the light, blinded by the beam.

He called several more times, but the only response was the rat's blinking eyes. He flicked off the light and pulled himself out of the silo, hearing the rat's claws against the floor.

He turned to stare out over the bay waters, invitingly blue. They looked cool, and he realized he was dripping with sweat, although the day was not particularly warm.

He made his way back down the ladder, and jumped off as the last rung snapped beneath his weight and he tumbled to the ground landing next to the door. As he stood up, a sharp pain told him that he had twisted his right ankle. It began swelling slightly, and he muttered a curse. Bending down to loosen the laces of his sneaker, his eye caught the slow progress of an ant, tottering beneath what appeared to be a piece of grain. The ant scurried along until it was stopped by a cigarette butt. On the ground, almost in a line toward the door were eight or ten more butts.

Dave picked up one of the butts. It was dry and the paper was still white. He remembered that it had rained heavily a couple of nights before. Somebody had been standing here and ground out a cigarette after that rainstorm. He examined the other butts. Several were sodden but most were still dry. Somebody with a serious nicotine addiction had been coming to this door over the past couple of days.

Just as he was about to get back on his feet, he sensed something behind him. He turned and saw a shadow on the ground to his left. He started to stand, but his ankle gave, and he stumbled. Dave caught a glimpse of a face, and then a jolt of pain exploded against the left side of his head, just above his ear.

"You think you saw a scar on his cheek?

Dave nodded, and John rubbed his chin. He reached over, and pressed an ice pack gently against the swelling on Dave's head.

"He caught you a good one," he said. "You'd better hold that ice on it, as hard as you can take."

"Any ideas who it might have been?" Dave asked. As he moved his jaws, pain shot down the side of his head, and he winced.

John nodded.

"The scar might mean something. I'm going to ask you a couple of questions. Don't talk or move your head. Does it hurt to blink your eyes?"

Dave tried, and forced a smile. Then he shook his head, and an ax cleaved the side of his skull.

"Don't move it, I said." John's voice was stern but his eyes showed his concern. "Looks like you might have a concussion, so let's do this fast. Blink once for yes, twice for no. Now, then, did you get a good look at the face of the man who hit you?"

Dave did not answer right away. He concentrated on recapturing the image of the man's face. For a moment, he could recall nothing but the force of the blow against the side of his head, so real that he thought he had just been hit again. A bright light filled his imagination. Then it dissipated, and in clear focus the face appeared. He saw the jagged white scar running from the corner of the man's mouth towards, and almost reaching, his ear. Dave blinked once, and John smiled.

"Good. I thought you might remember. Such things seem to stick in our minds. I can still see the gun in the hand of that punk as he was aiming it at me. It's probably the last thing I'll see when I die, like it's been waiting to claim what was taken away from it. Did that scar you mentioned run from here to here?" He drew his finger from the corner of his mouth toward his right ear.

Dave began to say yes, but then he caught himself. He blinked once.

"I thought so," John murmured. "Must have been Frankie's brother, Leonard. I thought he was still down in Detroit. Charlie Williams gave him that scar, with a razor. They were both drunk, playing cards. Leonard said Charlie's deck had one too many aces.

Probably did. If they had been using Leonard's cards, it would have been the other way around. Leonard's been straight for some time. Got a wife and kids and a regular job, or did. But he never forgave Charlie for reaching his razor before he could get his own knife out. And he sure as hell wasn't happy when his sister started living with the man who had cut him." John paused to reflect for a moment. "Apparently, one other thing hasn't changed. Leonard always did smoke like a damned chimney."

Dave heard all of this through a ice pack covered dull ache. Each word spoken pounded into his ear. He held up his hand to tell John he couldn't listen any more. John understood.

"You lie down. There's nothing much we can do right now. We'll wait until night, and then we'll see if you're up to an old fashioned stakeout. If not, I think I still remember how to do one."

They parked behind a convenience store about a mile from the silo. Dave's head still ached, but he could not convince himself to stay home, perhaps because he wanted an opportunity to say hello to the man who had hit him as much as he was impatient to find Robin. John had recruited a neighbor, Eleanor Simpson, a retired school teacher, to wait by the phone in case Kelly called him at the Wilson place. Dave was not comfortable with that arrangement, but he told himself that he could not tolerate the thought of sitting waiting for the phone to ring, not knowing where Kelly was nor what John might find out. So, he gulped down a couple of Tylenol and now waited in the car while John spoke with the convenience store owner, an old fishing buddy, about leaving his car where it would not call attention to itself.

"Stan says that I could just as well leave this bomb in the junkyard, but if I want to leave it here behind the store, I can," John said. He leaned over the open passenger window and smiled. "I think he's still upset that I caught that lake trout the last time we went fishing."

Dave swung open the heavy door of the '79 Plymouth Fury and clambered out, pausing for a moment as pain throbbed behind his ear and a ripple of nausea rose from his belly.

"Another year or two," John said, "and this car will be a classic." He ran his hand over the peeling vinyl top. "They certainly don't make them this way anymore. And it's a good thing. But are you alright? You don't look too steady."

Dave pushed himself away from the door.

"Good enough."

"We've got a ways to walk."

"Then let's do it. I know you said that there was no place to leave the car closer, but I do have a question."

"Go ahead."

"What if we see somebody coming to that silo and that somebody arrives in a vehicle."

"How are we going to follow it?" John asked.

"Right."

"We don't. We watch, then react."

"Improvise, huh?"

"Got a better idea?"

"We could just break down that door."

"And she might not be home. Then we would have played our card for nothing."

"Got you. Watch and react."

Dave took a step, waited to feel dizzy, and when he did not, he headed toward the road.

John handed him a brown paper bag.

"Coffee and corn muffins," he said. "It may be a long night."

Dave glanced at his watch, turning it to catch the moonlight. The hands read four thirty. He picked up the coffee and drank the last half-inch. It was cold and layered with grinds. They were sitting in thick undergrowth across the road from the silo, its rounded shape exaggerated by shadows. Sheltered by the thick trunks of two pine trees, they took turns staring at the building, and straining their ears for the sound of an approaching engine. John looked across the road and said, "If they come, it'll probably be soon. Just before dawn."

Dave closed his eyes. His back ached, and his legs were cramped, but at least the throbbing in his head had subsided. Several times during the long night he felt his weariness press against his eyelids, but he had not been able to sleep, even for a few minutes. Now he was both exhausted and wired, anticipating that their vigil might soon be rewarded, and anxious to return home so that he could speak with Eleanor Simpson. He shifted his position to rub the mosquito bite on his back against the rough tree bark. He sidled up and down until the itch was replaced by an ache.

Dave heard the sound of the engine just as John nudged him. Peering around the tree he saw the pickup truck headlights approaching. It cut its lights and its engine, gliding to a stop between the old barn and the silo. For several moments, the driver sat motionless behind the wheel, his silhouette just visible in the moonlight, red cigarette tip glowing in the darkened cab. Then, the door swung open and a short man, wearing a baseball cap pulled low over his eyes, emerged and stared directly at the trees hiding John and Dave. He ground out his cigarette and turned toward the silo, taking a step or two toward the door. Then he stopped. Again, he glanced across the road and headed back to the truck.

Dave and John heard the creak of a door opening. Another person had been in the cab and now walked around the side of the truck, moving slowly and hunched over. The driver lit another cigarette and began talking to his companion. He pointed at the silo door and then at John and Dave, as though he could see them as they flattened themselves behind the tree trunk.

"Time to react," Dave whispered. He felt John's hand grab at his arm, but Dave was on his feet and running, ignoring the pain that throbbed in his head. As Dave approached the pickup, one figure retreated toward the truck's open door. Out of the corner of his eye, Dave saw that John had anticipated that move and was circling towards that side of the pickup. Dave turned his glance back toward the man who was bent over reaching into his boot. His motions were deliberate, and when he straightened up he held something shiny in his right hand. As Dave approached, the man extended his arm, and the moonlight glinted off the knife blade in his hand.

Dave stopped five or six feet from the man, keeping his eyes fixed on the blade, which the man waggled in front of him. Dave shifted his gaze to the man's face for a moment, and he saw the thin white scar, running from the corner of his mouth to his ear. Dave held out his hand.

"Leonard Asebou?" he said in a friendly tone. "I think we met this morning."

The man's mouth twitched, but he did not reply. Instead, he thrust the knife blade towards Dave, and then pulled it back.

Dave stepped back half a step.

"This is getting tiresome, Leonard." He glanced towards the truck and saw that John and another figure were standing next to it. They seemed content to watch, for the moment, as though they were spectators at a boxing match. John turned to say something, and the other person nodded. Then Dave saw the bulky shape of a revolver in John's good hand, and he felt a little more confident. "You cracked my head this morning, Leonard. Gave me a hell of a headache. But I'm a forgiving type, to a point." He stared at the knife. "I draw the line at being cut. I'm trying to help your sister. And to do that, I need to talk to Robin. Is she in the building?"

"We don't need your help," Leonard muttered. "Help from your kind always turns out to be worse than no help at all."

"That's a start," Dave cajoled. "Just put that knife away, and we'll talk about it."

Leonard took a quick half-step toward Dave, swinging the knife in an arc that brought it whistling by his ribs.

"Like I said, we don't want your help."

"That's enough, you fool."

The voice belonged to the person standing next to John. It was a woman's voice, a little hoarse but confident. Dave thought he recognized it, and he felt the stone in his pocket. He removed it.

"Hello, Livonia," he said. He held the stone so she could see it. "I listened to it, and here I am. Now, where's Robin?"

"What's he talking about?" Leonard demanded.

"Put the knife down, and we'll tell you," John said, and took a step toward Leonard.

"Back off," Leonard said. He dropped into a crouch and passed the knife back and forth between his hands.

A loud click from John's direction floated on the still, night air. Leonard looked at the cocked revolver aimed steadily at him. As Leonard's eyes studied the gun, Dave aimed his right foot at Leonard's wrist. There was a solid thump, and the knife spun into the air. It landed between Leonard and John. Leonard sprang to retrieve it, but by the time he reached the weapon, John's foot was on it, and the revolver, still cocked, now pointed down at Leonard's head. John picked up the knife. Livonia hurried to join them, moving faster than Dave thought she was capable of doing.

"Fool," she said again. "I sent him here."

"We don't need his help." Leonard said. "We'll take care of things our own way."

"Your sister is in jail, and your niece is scared out of her wits," Livonia said. "What are you going to do about any of that? Disappear again, like after Charlie sliced your face?" Leonard stared at the ground. "Go ahead, fool, if you want. But you're not taking that child with you." She looked at Dave. "She's in there," she said, motioning toward the silo. "Leonard will knock on the door and I will go in and get her."

"Like hell, I will," Leonard said. He was still kneeling on the ground, and he swung his hand toward John's revolver. "That piece looks ancient. It probably doesn't work."

"Care to find out?" John's voice was sweet, almost cooing.

Leonard shrugged and stood up. He walked toward the silo.

"Wait here," Livonia said.

A few minutes later, a small shape emerged from the door to the silo. Robin shook beneath the blanket around her shoulders. From beneath the blanket, one heavily scuffed sneaker protruded. Livonia leaned down and whispered something in her ear, and the child walked to John and Dave.

"Grandmother says I should tell you what I know," she said.

"Good," Dave said. "Let's start with the gun that killed your father. Do you know where it is?"

Robin nodded.

"At the beach where they found him," she said.

"How did it get there?" John asked.

Robin looked to Livonia. The old woman shook her head slowly up and down.

"I can't remember," Robin said.

"Did you put it there?" Dave asked.

The child shrank back into her blanket, as though she would disappear if she could. She pulled the blanket up to cover her face. As she did, she lifted it above her feet. Dave again saw the scuffed sneaker, which had once been white. It had Velcro fasteners, one of which was loose and flapping. Of more interest to Dave, however, was her other foot. It was bare.

"I don't know," she said again.

CHAPTER TEN

THE clatter of the Toyota diesel helped keep Kelly awake. "It's very dependable," the clerk had said. The name tag on his red vest indicated he was Maurice and that he tried harder. "And it gets great mileage."

Now, Kelly stared ahead at the line of cars awaiting customer inspections, and then flipped on the dome light so she could see her face in the rearview mirror. Her reflection showed eyes watery and red from the strain of fourteen hours on the road, punctuated by stops at every rest area on the Thruway from Ardsley, just north of the city, to Clarence, south and west of the customs station at Niagara Falls, where she now waited her turn to pass into Canada.

She glanced down at her clipboard where she'd listed the fourteen stops she had checked. She knew that Allie's friend Grace's hypoglycemia would have necessitated frequent pauses for food, at intervals of no more than two or three hours apart. The rest stops were between thirty and forty miles apart, meaning that it was probable that Grace and Allie would have hit about every third one. She had considered gambling on this probability, by guessing which stops were most likely, but she had decided that she best be methodical. The notes on the clipboard now confirmed the wisdom of that choice because several stops had been closed for renovations. And even at those where she had been able to make inquiries, she had gathered very little solid information.

Kelly now intended to find somebody to talk to, somebody she could show Allie's picture to, somebody who would confirm the vague recollections of one cashier and one waitress at two of the Thruway rest areas. The fact that Grace was black and Allie white prompted recollections, a sad reminder of racial consciousness for which, at the moment, Kelly was profoundly grateful.

However, she was not at all sure of the accuracy of these reports. True, two people at opposite ends of the state, one in Plattekill, near Poughkeepsie, and another in Seneca, south of Rochester and about 100 miles east of where she now sat rubbing the road dust out of her eyes, thought they had seen the two girls. Each had studied the photograph of Allie and each nodded sagely. But these two witnesses disagreed on important particulars. The cashier in Plattekill, a plump woman in her early twenties, was sure that Allie's hair was in a long pony tail, secured by a large red, plastic clip, just like it appeared in the photograph. However, Allie had permed her hair at the beginning of the summer, affecting the heavily moussed and artificially disheveled look that Kelly abhorred. In any case, Allie would never wear a pony tail. The counter waitress in Seneca, a middle-aged woman whose eyes spoke of some ongoing strain in her personal life, had the hair right, but was certain Allie was the taller of the two, though in fact it was Grace who was almost six-feet tall. The waitress was insistent, saying that Allie looked like the basketball player Grace should have been. She remembered nothing about Grace except her color.

Kelly realized that she had almost been dozing, and that a considerable space had opened up between her and the car in front of her. She watched as the driver of that car spoke to the customs officer, and then she pulled up. The customs official was a lean man with silvery hair and a bored expression. He walked to the front of her car, circled it, and then came to her window. An amused smile now played on his lips.

"Never seen one of these before," he said.

"Pardon?"

"Toyota diesel. I heard the clatter and thought your engine was missing real bad. But she's a diesel. Says so right there on the back of your car."

Kelly forced herself to form a friendly smile while she struggled to find a response. A simple "yes" seemed inadequate.

"It gets good mileage," she murmured after an awkward moment. "You must see thousands of cars."

"That's the point. That's all I see all day is cars."

"You must see people, too, driving the cars."

He looked at her as though he had her figured as slightly deranged.

"Most of the time, right, there are drivers. Look, lady, if you're looking for your husband, or a runaway child, try the police. Now let's do the questions. Where are you from?"

"Michigan, I mean Brooklyn."

"You and your car live in Brooklyn?" he said. His expression turned kindly.

"Yes. What I mean to say was that I'm returning to my summer home in northern Michigan. I left Brooklyn this morning. I live in Brooklyn." She paused and then smiled. "With my husband and my car."

"That's nice," he said.

"And I am passing through Canada, without stopping. I am not carrying any firearms or explosives, or alcoholic beverages, or untaxed cigarettes, or other contraband materials. Nor am I a terrorist. My trunk is not filled with fertilizer to build a bomb. I am not plotting any subversive activities while I travel the QEW." She paused and forced an accommodating smile. "But I am looking for somebody."

"Your husband?"

"No , he's in Michigan. At our summer house."

"With his car?"

"Yes."

"That's nice."

The officer's face now wore a fixed grin, as if talking to an obstreperous child whose presence had become insufferable.

"Driver's license, please," he said. "And registration.'

Kelly found the documents, but placed Allie's photo on top of them.

"Look, officer," Kelly said, "I've been on the road all day, talking to a couple of dozen people. I'm tired, and I'm anxious. About my daughter." Instead of looking at the photograph, the officer stared at the car behind her.

The officer slid the picture behind the other papers, checked the photo of Kelly on the license against her, walked around the car noting the match of the license plate number, and then handed the papers back to Kelly with the picture still hidden.

"Move on lady. Stop at the next town, and talk to the police." He waved his arm. "Just move on."

She took the picture into her hand, leaned out of her window and extended her arm so that the photograph was in front of his face.

"Look at it, will you please?"

He took her wrist and pushed her hand back, but he glanced at the photograph.

"She would have been traveling with a black girl, a very tall black girl, who probably gave you some lip."

He stared hard at her.

"She related to you? Somehow?"

"My daughter's best friend."

His arm continued waving as though it were moving on its own volition. But she saw his brows furrow.

"Maybe," he said. "Maybe I did see a couple of kids like that yesterday, or the day before." He pointed toward the one-story building that stood to the side of the check points. "Wait for me over there."

She pulled off to the side, and then watched as the officer leaned over the car that had been behind her and questioned the driver. He straightened up and came striding toward her. For a moment, she was sure he was going to arrest her, although she could not figure out why except perhaps the incoherence born of too much anxiety and too many hours on the road. He nodded at her as he passed, and she felt reassured. For want of anything better to look at, as she waited, she studied the sign announcing the availability of currency exchange inside the building. The officer emerged several minutes later with another officer, who went on to the check post.

"I had to convince my friend Tom, there, to fill in for me while I spoke with you, and anyway this is all highly irregular." He looked toward the line of cars waiting to be processed at his post. "Tom wasn't too happy about it, but I reminded him that he owed me one."

"I appreciate that," Kelly said. She opened her door and eased herself out of the car. The road seemed to quiver beneath her feet, and she wasn't sure if she was feeling traffic vibration or muscle fatigue. She leaned against the front fender, half hoping that the officer would invite her inside for a cup of coffee.

"I've only got a couple of minutes," he said, as though reading her thoughts. "Sorry. But Tom doesn't owe me that much."

Kelly stretched, raising herself onto her toes, and then settled her feet flat onto the ground. The road still seemed to shake.

"You said you might have seen my daughter."

"Might is the operative word," he replied. "I'm not sure whether it was last night, or the night before. I only work nights. This hot little car pulls up, a Miata convertible, red. It's a small car, a two seater, and this really tall black girl is behind the wheel. She got out to talk to me." He raised his hand above his head. "She was a good two or three inches taller than me. And she was wearing this turban around her head, so she looked even taller. I remember her pretty clear."

Kelly fought to control herself.

"And that's all?"

"Not exactly. There was another girl in the car. I think she was white, but I wouldn't swear to it."

"The black girl's name would have been Grace."

The officer scowled, and then looked at the line of cars waiting to be passed into Canada.

"Lady. Give me a break. I only noticed this kid because of the way she looked and because she got out of the car. Hardly anybody does that. Everybody knows to wait until we come over."

"But you remember the make of the car," Kelly said.

"A hobby of mine. To provide a little interest. Not all of them. But I try to take note if there's anything interesting. Sometimes the car, sometimes the driver, most of the time nothing."

"Is there anything else you can tell me?"

"One thing. The black girl asked for directions to Woodstock. I asked her if she meant where that concert was, and she smiled and said she had missed that one, but she wanted to go to the town in Canada. I told her how to go, and they drove off."

"Thanks," Kelly replied. "And don't bother. I know the way."

"Sure. On the way to that summer house. Where your husband is waiting for you." His voice was now tinged with sarcasm. "That is nice," he said, and he strolled back toward his post.

A thought hit Kelly from someplace deep in her subconscious. Later, as she drove on to Woodstock, she asked herself why she still carried the picture at all.

"Officer," she called to his retreating back. "One more thing, please. It's very important."

He shrugged in a weary gesture that indicated he had decided to humor her in order to get rid of her. He made his way back to her car. She held out the picture of Michael. It was fifteen years old, but he hadn't changed that much, a few more lines on his handsome face, and his blond hair now mostly gray.

The officer took the photograph, walked around the car and held it in front of the headlight. She tried to study his face, but could not see it well as he stooped over. Yet there was something in the time he took to look at the picture, or perhaps the fixed little smile on his face as he handed it back to her, that told her not to fully credit what he next said.

"Your husband?" he asked.

"Was," she said curtly.

"Are you looking for him, too?"

She hesitated for just a second.

"No," she replied. "I only want to find my daughter."

"Never saw him, that I can remember," he said.

Woodstock, of course, that would be just like Grace, a thought bred of her irreverent sense of humor, leavened no doubt by a little pot or hashish, nothing stronger, Kelly was fairly sure, else she would have forbade Allie her friendship with the quixotic Grace, an academically gifted iconoclast, a year Allie's senior. Grace often lamented having been born too late for the sixties, and equally frequently expressed her intent to bring some of the wild spirit, the paradox of unfettered altruism and self realization of that decade, into the new millennium. Still, Kelly, on the whole, liked Grace, sometimes wished Allie shared some of her friend's fire, but she also worried about Grace's darker nature, her willingness to push the edges too hard and too recklessly.

These thoughts encouraged Kelly to drive straight on to Woodstock. Kelly was quite sure that Grace had every intention of at least driving through the place, if for no other reason than to be able to say that she had done so, perhaps to declare that she had revisited the love generation by finding it in a place whose only connection with that time was its name, as though space and time could somehow be collapsed and distorted. That would be just the kind of metaphysical joke that Grace would enjoy. And Allie would go along with it, Allie the pragmatist, who needed Grace to drive her to Michigan and therefore would humor her friend's eccentricities.

In spite of Kelly's intention to continue driving, an hour after leaving the customs station she found that the road was shifting in front of her, and then she noticed that the car seemed to be drifting from lane to lane despite her best efforts to keep it centered. She pulled off in Hamilton, Ontario and found a diner within a mile of the exit. She remembered the motel fronting on Lake Erie where she and Dave had spent the night on their way to Michigan just last week, and although she did not feel like enjoying the view any more now than she had then, she was strongly tempted to take a room there and resume her search the first thing in the morning. She argued with herself as she ate a pasta salad, smothered in some indeterminate dressing. She wasn't really tasting the food, but she recognized that she was feeling stronger and that the grumbling in her stomach that she had willfully ignored all day was now disappearing. Nonetheless, as she pushed her plate away, noticing disinterestedly that she had finished the salad, she tried to decide between the claims of her body, which sought a soft bed and lakeside motel room, and her nerves, which demanded that she push on immediately.

Her nerves won.

It was ten o'clock when she exited the highway and drove toward Woodstock. As she approached the town, it became apparent that almost everything was closed. On her right, a quarter of a mile or so ahead she saw the lights of a shopping center. The rest of the town was shrouded in darkness.

When she pulled into the shopping center, she saw that two stores were still illuminated. The first was a coffee and donut shop, where several cars were parked and shadowy figures seemed to be congregating. The second offered a large plate-glass front, screened by curtains hung behind the window. A sign announced that the establishment was a billiards parlor, and judging by the light showing around the edges of the curtain, it was still open.

She found a parking spot near the donut shop. She could now see that the shadowy figures in front of the donut shop were teenagers, mostly male. There was a group of four or five, and another of two or three. A haze of tobacco smoke hung above their heads. She sensed their eyes follow her movements from her car into the shop. Pausing right before the door, she looked directly at a youth who was leaning against the building. She noted the diamond stud in his left ear, shaved sides of his head topped with a blond tuft, the cigarette in his hand and the thick gold chain around his bare neck. She sought his eyes to determine the degree of menace she might find there, and saw that his blue eyes were not particularly hostile, but not indifferent either. Rather they seemed bemused as they roamed down her body, and she felt those eyes as if they were hands. She waited for him to finish his survey, not giving him the satisfaction of a response, and when he saw that he was not going to get one, he flicked his cigarette towards her feet and then turned to say something to a companion who was largely hidden by the shadows at the corner of the building. She ground the butt into the asphalt.

As she walked through the doorway, she heard a snicker coming from outside and turned to see the young man's companion bent over in amusement. She walked to the counter attended by a girl of about sixteen who looked irritable and bored. The girl's eyes shifted back and forth from the two young men outside to Kelly.

"Can I help you?" she asked after a couple of moments in a tone of voice that indicated she clearly did not wish to do so.

Kelly considered buying a donut and stared at the racks behind the girl. Most were empty, and the few donuts still available looked as though they had been sitting there for at least a day. Flies buzzed around them, occasionally landing on the sugar covered ones.

Kelly pointed at a plain donut, sitting by itself on a far rack, untroubled by flies. The girl followed her arm, shrugged, and pulled a napkin out of a box on the counter. She held the napkin like pincers and pulled the plain donut from its shelf.

"Will there be anything else?" she asked, again in a voice that argued against wanting to bestir herself.

"Yes," Kelly said, and fumbled in her pocket for the photograph of Allie.

"Coffee is fifty cents," the girl said, "and the donut is eighty-five cents." She waited for Kelly to respond. "Did you want some coffee?" Her voice had dropped any pretense of courtesy and was now ugly.

"Yes, please, the coffee and perhaps some information."

The girl turned to the coffee urn and filled a Styrofoam cup. She entered the prices on the cash register, and placed the coffee on the counter next to the donut. She glanced back at the register.

"That will be a dollar forty, with tax."

Kelly handed her a ten dollar bill, and the girl's expression turned even more darkly sour. She began doing the conversion from American into Canadian currency on the register.

"Don't bother," Kelly said. "What I really want to know is if you have seen this girl." She placed Allie's photograph on the counter.

The girl shoved the bill into her pocket.

"No," she said. "I haven't seen anybody."

"But you haven't looked at the photograph. How can you be so sure?"

The girl forced a crooked grin on a face that seemed unused to smiling.

"Because I only started working here tonight, and I figure anybody you might be looking for would have been here before that. But thanks for the tip, anyway."

"Who would have been working here, then, the last couple of nights, or days for that matter?"

"The girl I replaced. She got fired for getting too familiar with the customers. Like those guys outside, you know what I mean?"

"Yes," Kelly said. "I know exactly what you mean."

The blond young man seemed to have been waiting for her. He leaned his body into the doorway as she left the shop so that she could not pass by without brushing against his chest. She stared hard at him, and he offered a smile in return.

"Excuse me," she said.

"Why? Have you done something, or do you want to do something?"

"I want to get by."

"Sure," he said, but he didn't move.

The exhaustion of the day settled over her, and she felt a little dizzy. She took a deep breath, and thrust her arm out to shield her body as she stepped through the door. He leaned in a little more and pushed back against her forearm, which now rested on his chest. She could see four or five of his friends watching the confrontation. He smelled of cigarette smoke and stale perspiration.

"You haven't said the secret password," he said, and she saw that his front teeth were uneven and stained from nicotine.

"How about, get the hell out of my way?"

He smiled broadly.

"Sorry, that's not it."

"Then how about this?" She pulled her arm back and then banged her elbow as hard as she could into his sternum. He doubled over, trying to catch his breath, and she made her way past him. She took a step toward her car, but now his friends formed a semicircle in front of her.

"That wasn't very nice," one said. She recognized the slender figure of the boy who had been in the shadows at the corner of the building when she arrived.

"That's okay, Frank." The blond youth had recovered his wind, and his voice, coming from the doorway, was conciliatory. "Maybe we haven't been going at this the right way."

She turned to face him.

"Just what is it that we are doing the wrong way?" She looked past him into the store and saw that the girl was leaning over the top of the counter, a small smile playing in the corner of her lips. He followed her eyes.

"I heard what you were asking MaryAnn. She wasn't being very helpful. But maybe I can."

"Do you know something?" she demanded.

"I know many things. I know that I like older women, tough ones like you."

"About my daughter." She started fumbling for the picture.

"You don't need that," he said. "She was here, with her friend, a long, cool, dark fox. Right?"

She wanted to scream yes, but instead realized she had to be cautious.

"Like you say you overheard my conversation with MaryAnn. How do I know you saw her?"

"You don't, but what have you got to lose?"

"My time and my patience."

He motioned his friends to step back, and then leaned toward her.

"You want information, and I want you." His eyes traveled up and down her body, and then he grabbed her elbows. "But no more of that stuff. I can play rough, too."

"You remind me of the dog who was always chasing the car."

He frowned for a moment, and then his eyes brightened.

"Don't worry. I know what to do with what I catch."

Her eyes roamed the nearly deserted parking lot and settled on the billiards parlor.

"I'll shoot you for it," she said. "Winner take all."

"Pool?"

"Right. Unless you're afraid you might lose, to an older woman at that."

For a moment his eyes said that he was perhaps in over his head, but with a quick glance at his friends, he nodded.

"You're on. One game of straight pool. No warmups. You win, and I'll tell you where you might find your daughter. I win, and you and I go for a ride to this nice private spot I know." He smirked. "You win either way. By the way, my name is Al."

"Well, Al," she said, "let's see what you've got."

It didn't take her very long. She watched him take his first shot after she broke, and she could see that he was good, but not nearly good enough. All she had to do was find the energy for the concentration and the steady hand she would need. She let the game stay even, making the obvious shots, as she played the stripes, and missing the more difficult ones as though they were beyond her reach. He played to his friends who ringed the table at a discreet distance. He sank an easy carom into the corner, and he had only one solid ball left to make. It was in an awkward, but not impossible position against the far rail. He would have to clip it on the right side, just so. He leaned far over the table, and sighted.

"Go ahead, do it." The voice belonged to Frank. Al straightened up and glared at him.

"Sorry," Frank murmured.

Al leaned over the table again.

"Bow wow," Kelly said. He didn't seem to hear, but when he hit the cue ball she could see that he had missed the shot. The cue ball hit too flush and drove the solid ball against the back rail. It came to rest in the middle of the table after thudding against the opposite back rail and then a side rail.

"That wasn't very nice," he said.

She shrugged. "I didn't promise nice. I promised to whip your ass in this game." She walked around the table to sight her next shot, but he stood in her path. He stepped back, but not away, so as she hunched over the table, she could feel his thighs against her legs, and then his hands on her hips. She let them remain there, and even shifted her weight so that she increased the contact with his legs. She had him now, and she wasn't going to let him distract her.

She aimed, stroked, and the cue ball sent her next-to-the-last striped ball into the side pocket. As the ball disappeared, she pushed back against him. He dropped his hands from her hips, and let her move freely.

"One more," she said, "and you're mine."

He studied the table.

"You'll never make it," he said.

"You're right," she said. "I don't have to." Her last ball was resting an inch from the end rail. Next to it on one side was the eight ball. She couldn't send her ball in that direction because she might drive the eight ball into the pocket. The way to the other pocket on the same rail was clear, but Al's ball in the middle of the table blocked that shot. She calculated several exotic shots, but decided instead on a different strategy.

She sighted the eight ball, stroked the cue ball with just enough English to send the eight spinning off the back, off a side and then to a stop three inches in front of Al's ball. The cue ball, meanwhile, remained close to where the eight ball had been. If Al wanted to hit his ball, he would have to hit the eight, with a good chance of sending it into a pocket.

He let his cue stick drop to the table.

"I know when I've been suckered," he said. "But I'm too much of a gentleman to complain."

He picked up his cue stick, stroked the cue ball gently against the eight. He wanted to keep the cue ball near the eight, but it spun softly to the side, leaving her a relatively easy shot for her last ball. She made the shot, and then almost without pause dropped the eight ball.

"Time to pay up sucker," she said.

"Like I said," Al shrugged. "I'm a gentleman with a taste for classy women."

"Skip the flattery, and give the information," she said.

Al's friends trudged out of the billiard parlor into the darkness, and he watched them go.

"Up the road about fifteen miles, toward Brantford. There's a motel."

"Tell me where. Exactly."

He did, and as he spoke the directions, Kelly saw his eyes seeking those of his friends, but one by one they started to turn away. On an impulse, after he had finished telling her where the motel was, she grabbed his head, one hand over each ear, and pulled his mouth toward her. She turned her head as though she were going to seek his lips, but stopped just short. She held the position for several long seconds. He was too shocked to react. Then she pushed his head away.

"A little show for your friends. You can tell them what you want."

A smirk started to form on his lips, but she pushed his mouth shut with the heel of her hand.

"But if I find out you touched my daughter, I'll rip your face off, layer by layer."

She did not wait for him to reply.

The sign for the Sundowner's Motel showed a neon red sun sliding into neon blue water. Kelly drove slowly by the parked cars, stopping by a red Miata.

"Son of a bitch," she muttered.

Staring into the darkness, she looked for a Camry. There were other cars, but she could not see them clearly. She drove to a stop in front of the office. The door was locked, and there was a bell next to it. A notice tacked next to the bell stated that after midnight a clerk could be summoned by pressing the bell button. She leaned heavily against the button while she peered through the thick glass of the door. Behind the glass was a heavy steel security mesh, but she could just make out a small room with a couple of worn upholstered chairs to one side, an empty display rack to the other, and a desk in the rear. A ceiling fan turned lazily above the desk, and beneath it hung an exposed light bulb, which cast a dim yellowish light over the desk. Smoke from a cigarette sitting in a large ashtray on the desk swirled into the yellow cone of light, carried by the eddies stirred by the fan.

A head was resting on crossed arms atop the desk, and then a hand reached for the cigarette. She jabbed the bell button, and the head rose from the desk, beneath a small cloud of tobacco smoke, and attached itself to a neck, shoulders, and finally a torso. The whole slumped toward her, reached the door, and then swung its arm to its left, beckoning her to move in that direction. Looking to her right she saw that there was a window, barely discernible in the shadows next to the door. She nodded and stepped toward the window. A light went on and illuminated the head of an elderly man. He had a few wisps of gray hair, and his voice came to her through a small speaker next to the window. His breath labored, and his voice was hoarse. There was a security mesh in front of the window, with a small space beneath it, through which money or a key could be passed. The old man's eyes seemed to be studying her. They were alert and apprehensive.

"We've been robbed," the voice said, and then paused to wheeze, "quite regularly. So the boss had all this installed. It's not very welcoming, but it seems to have cut down the robberies." He looked past her into the darkness.

"I'm alone."

"I see. Will you be expecting anybody? That might be a problem with this new system. I only have one key for each room."

"I'm not expecting anybody. I'm looking for someone." A knowing expression wrinkled the old man's eyes. "It's not what you think," she said. "It's my daughter and her friend. I saw her car outside."

"Lots of people come and go at a place like this. You can see that. Some of them drive the same car as others."

"A black girl, driving a red Miata with New York plates."

"I'm color blind, and I don't usually see the cars. I just take the money and hand out the key."

She reached into her purse.

"I can't help your vision. But maybe I can jog your memory." She slid a fifty dollar bill through the slot.

"Room only costs thirty-five. That's thirty-five, Canadian," he replied.

She pushed another fifty through the slot.

"I seem to remember a few folks checking in who might be who you're looking for."

"A few?"

He folded the bills together.

"Well, first there was this black girl, and another girl with her, younger I think, but I didn't get a real good look. I remember the black girl, though, because she asked me if I knew where I could get some peanuts."

"Then?" Kelly fought the quaver in her voice.

"A man." He began to turn away from the window. "Room 231. Can't say who's in it now. They've been kind of coming and going."

"All in the same room?"

He lit a fresh cigarette and took a deep drag, which resulted in a hacking cough.

"Yes," he said.

She reached into her purse, pulled out the picture of Michael and held it against the window. He blinked and then shrugged.

"I told you my eyes aren't that good, and I didn't get much of a look at him."

She pushed the picture back into her purse. It caught on the zipper, and she shoved it until it ripped itself free.

"I'll need a key," she said.

"Told you there's only one.."

"Make another. Room 231. You know how, don't you?" She reached into her purse.

"That won't be necessary. You've paid enough to tell me that you're serious." His fingers appeared and then reappeared holding a key. He punched in some numbers, swiped the key and slid it toward her. "Just drop it through there." He pointed to a slot beneath the window. The light went off behind the window.

She took the key, and then walked toward the two-story building behind the office. She found a door at the corner of the building, but it was locked. The key opened it, and she walked into a dimly lit stairwell. When she reached the top of the stairs, she paused. She was several stages beyond exhaustion, and she didn't know how she would deal with what she might find. The man could be anybody. Perhaps he was Al, though she would call him a boy. If Allie and Grace had found time to meet Al, though, they could have encountered somebody else, an even seedier character. She dismissed these possibilities. In her heart, she knew that the man was Michael, that he had beaten her in the race.

She noticed that she could see the parking lot through a dust encrusted window in the corridor. She peered down, and stared at a sedan parked some distance from the Miata. It might be the Camry. She was about to continue toward the room, when the Miata's lights flashed on. It backed wildly out of its parking spot and lurched forward as though its driver were drunk and could not find the right gears. Then it smoothed out and disappeared into the night. She squeezed the key in the palm of her hand, and hurried down the corridor.

Number 231 was the next to the last room on the right hand side. No light emanated from beneath the door, nor could she hear a sound from inside. She swiped the key and pushed the door open. A light came on inside the room. She blinked for a moment and then stared hard at Michael's startled face. He was sitting up in the bed. There was another shape beneath the blanket next to him. The shape stirred, and then an arm reached for Michael as though to draw him back down into the bed. She could not stifle the relief she felt. Her mind raced. The Miata pulling out of the parking lot. Grace behind the wheel. Angry and upset. That is why she jerked the clutch. If Grace was leaving in the Miata. Then, my God, then the other shape underneath the blanket must be Allie, the incarnation of her worst nightmare, the one that until this very moment she had refused to acknowledge.

The arm that had snaked out from beneath the blankets and found Michael's chest was black.

Grace sat up in the bed, holding the sheet in front of her breasts, and stared at her, and then back at Michael.

"Hello, Mrs. Abrams," Grace said. "You wouldn't have some food with you in your purse would you? Something with low carbohydrates and high protein?"

CHAPTER ELEVEN

ELEANOR Simpson was standing on the porch when John and Dave drove up. She was a tall, angular woman, whose plain face, unadorned by cosmetics except for a hint of lipstick, tried unsuccessfully to relax into a smile. Thirty years of frowning at sixth-graders had stiffened her facial muscles into a permanent scowl. Dave half expected her to be flourishing a pointer or a yardstick. Instead, she held his cordless phone. Extending the phone in front of her, she started to step toward him, but she was stopped by the gyrating bulk of Hooper whose rear end shook in a spastic rhythm. Eleanor glanced down at the dog, and nudged it with her knee. Hooper looked up at her and wagged his tail harder, unable to decide which human deserved his attention. She worked her way around the animal, and then hopped off the porch with an agility that belied her gray hair, and trotted toward them.

"Mr. Abrams," she began, "that dog of yours, I mean I couldn't stay in the house with him."

"I know," Dave replied, "he has digestive problems."

She glanced at the phone in her hand, as though suddenly aware that she was holding it. "Your wife just called. I told her you should be back soon, but she said she couldn't wait. She said since she was on the road and might be in what she called a cell phone black hole when you tried to call her, well, she wanted me to take a message for you."

"Did she find Allie?"

"If you'll wait just a minute, I'll tell you everything she said. I have it all written down." Her face reddened into a very mild blush, and then reverted to its usual scowl. Dave felt himself silently encouraging her to succeed in maintaining a warmer expression. "When I was just a young woman, I used to teach shorthand in a business school. Who would have thought it, but I still remember how to do it. So I took down everything she said."

"Yes?" Dave said.

"Oh, it's on the porch. I hope you don't mind, but I had to go rummaging about your desk to find something to write on. I don't make a habit of that, you understand."

"Of course."

It seemed important for Eleanor to nail down this point.

"I didn't even put on the light," she continued. "That made it a bit harder. But fortunately, I found one of your legal pads right on top of your desk, near the phone, and a pencil, too, though the point wasn't too sharp."

"I think," John tried, "that Dave would like to know if Kelly found Allie."

Eleanor tightened her scowl so that her forehead wrinkled, and her jaw quivered.

"Why, of course not. Do you think if she had, I would be babbling on about that dog, and a pad and pencil. If you'll just be patient a moment, while I retrieve the paper, I'll tell you what she did say." She turned on her heel and trotted back to the porch. Hooper threw himself at her, and she backed him off with a knee to the dog's chest. Dave and John followed her onto the porch and waited while she peered at the yellow sheet of paper. Dave snapped his fingers and pointed to the ground. Hooper lay down, and then Dave opened the screen door, reached in and flicked on the porch light.

"Thank you," Eleanor said. "I couldn't find that switch before."

Dave looked at the shorthand symbols on the page. They meant nothing to him, but he could see that there were only a few lines, and his heart sank. Somehow he knew that in this case, brevity was going to mean bad news.

Eleanor squinted at her notes.

"I left my reading glasses home. I came here right away when John called. Now let's see. She was calling from Woodstock, in Canada, that is."

"I know the place," Dave said. He had instructed his brain to frame only the most civil comments, although what he wanted to do was lift Eleanor off her feet and shake her until the information she contained spilled out, like so many coins from a piggy bank.

"Well, yes," she said. "Kelly mentioned that you would know the place. She did find Michael, she said, and he was with another young woman." Eleanor looked up. "I edited that part a bit. Actually she said something a bit more colorful."

"Did she say that the young woman's name was Grace?"

Eleanor glanced down at her notes.

"In my editing, I don't think I put the young woman's name. It didn't seem right, for the situation, you know, being in a motel room with a middle aged man, and all, but I do believe that's the name she said. Apparently, they, that is Michael and Grace, were in bed together. Allie was not there. Here's the important part. Kelly said that Allie had taken Grace's car, and that she continued on herself, and she, that is Kelly, was going right after her, after she took care of Michael." Eleanor looked up. "I don't know what she meant by that, and I didn't ask. Anyway, she said she would call again some time tomorrow." Eleanor glanced at her watch. "I guess that means, since it's after midnight, some time later today."

"Was there anything else?" Dave asked.

"No, that's it," Eleanor replied.

"Thank you very much," Dave said. "You've been a tremendous help."

Eleanor tore off the note pad.

"I can transcribe this, and give you a copy."

"That won't be necessary. Thanks anyway."

John walked Eleanor to her car, a late '80s Oldsmobile that gleamed in the moonlight. When he returned, he shrugged his shoulders.

"She's really a sweetheart. She was trying so hard to do this job right, that I guess she got a bit carried away."

"A tad," Dave said.

"She'll be back, first thing in the morning, if you want her to. I expect you have things you want to track down. And so do I."

"I had hoped to speak to Frankie, then maybe the sheriff, and..."

"You want me to see what I can to do to locate Charlie's truck."

"Right," Dave said. "It wasn't at his place when Kelly and I went out there and found Frankie. It's got to be somewhere, and where it is might begin to tell us how he got to the beach after Frankie supposedly shot him."

"And while I'm at it, I'll see if my friend Livonia can tell us what happened to Robin's other shoe, right?"

"That would be a very good thing to know," Dave said, "but I wasn't sure it was the kind of thing you could ask Livonia."

"Let's just say we go back a long time. I couldn't tell you before that she would help us find Robin because I didn't know that she would. I never know what she is going to do. Fascinating woman."

Dave found himself smiling.

"Yes," John said. "I've thought about it. But at my age, never mind hers?"

"Why not?"

"That's what I've asked myself a hundred times."

The bruises on Frankie's face had settled into a deep, mottled purple. Her right eye was swollen shut, and the left was just open a slit. Both cheeks were swollen as though they were squirrel's pouches filled with acorns, and her cracked lower lip extended well beyond her teeth. She shuffled, in obvious discomfit, as she was guided into the interrogation room by the matron, who held her elbow and half pushed her into the chair across the table from Dave.

The matron was a short, stout woman, with a warm, good natured face. She smiled at Dave. "I'll be just outside the door," she said. "Just knock when you're ready." She glanced at Frankie.

"I don't know if she'll talk to you. I couldn't get a word out of her, and I usually can."

Dave waited until the matron shut the door, and then he reached across the table to take Frankie's hand, which she had balled into a fist. She did not respond to his touch.

"How are you doing?" Dave asked. "Has a doctor been by to check you?"

Frankie's eyes stared straight ahead, through Dave.

"Do you need a pain killer?" he asked, but again she did not seem to hear the question.

After a moment, she turned her eyes to his hand.

"Robin," she said.

"She's all right," he replied. "Livonia Walkingstick is looking after her."

She pulled her hand free and moved it slowly to her mouth.

"She is okay?" Her voice wavered between a whisper and a sob.

"Yes," Dave said. "She was hiding in that old stone silo. Do you know the place?"

Her face softened for a moment, as though in recollection.

"My brother Leonard and me used to hide out in there when we were kids." The memory seemed to evaporate in the heat of her anger, and she brought her hand down hard toward the table, as though she were about to slap it, but then let her palm fall softly to the surface.

"Bring my daughter here," she said. "I must talk to her."

"I'll try," Dave said. "That might not be so easy to arrange. The sheriff is going to want to talk to her, and I'm not sure if Livonia will cooperate, or if Robin will, for that matter. She was very scared, when I saw her."

Frankie's expression stiffened again into a mask of indifference.

"I need to talk to you about what happened that night, when you think you shot Charlie."

The mask lifted and was replaced by a nasty smile.

"I did shoot the bastard."

"Then how did he get to the beach?"

"Bring Robin here," she said, and the mask returned to her face.

"Robin says she knows where the gun that shot your husband is," Dave said. "Do you think she does?"

"She doesn't know what she's talking about. She was confused. Maybe she saw it on the floor of the living room."

"She said it was on the beach."

"I shot Charlie. I passed out. I don't know what happened to the damned gun." She leaned toward Dave, her eyes narrowed.

"Maybe you picked it up," Dave said.

"No. Just bring Robin here."

The matron opened the door and Dave had the impression that she had been standing there with her ear pressed against the keyhole.

"Would you see that the doctor looks in on my client? She might need something for her pain."

The matron nodded. "Or to settle her down. I've already called the doctor."

"Good. I'll be back later to see how's she doing."

Dave found Sheriff Herman Briggs, "Buddy" to his friends, at the bait shop in the newly refurbished marina in the harbor off the bay. The sheriff was a large man, with a square face accentuated by close-cropped hair. He was talking to Tom Snyder, a failed farmer, now self-proclaimed fishing guru, who ran the shop. Snyder was in his sixties, and he wore a scruffy mustache, turned down toward his pointed chin. His gray hair, pulled back into a ponytail, was held by a dirty piece of blue ribbon. The walls of his small shop were adorned with photographs of beaming fishermen holding their catches of lake trout, salmon, and walleyes. Besides the photographs, there were charts of the waters of both bays, and these were marked with red circles here and there. Tom was standing in front of a chart, pointing to one of these circles.

"Right here," he said, with a nod to Dave, inviting him to savor the information, "just off the point, at the drop-off. I tell you George

Murphy was pulling them bass in as quick as he could get his line back in the water. You go out there, and you'll see them jumping. Just sit on the deep side, and cast in toward the shore. George was using crawlers but you'll do even better with wigglers. If you want some, Buddy, I got some fresh in the back."

Sheriff Briggs turned to Dave.

"Do you fish, Mr. Abrams?"

"Used to do a little. Saltwater, though, in Sheepshead Bay, flounder and fluke, mostly."

"The kind that just sit on the bottom, until you bonk them on the head with your sinker, right?"

"Something like that."

"Well," the sheriff grinned, "maybe you'll let me take you out one morning and introduce you to lake fishing. You might find it more interesting, though it isn't as good as it used to be."

"Will you be wanting those wigglers?" Snyder asked.

"Maybe on the weekend. I don't think I'm going to have much chance before then, not if I'm any judge of the look in Mr. Abrams's eyes, which says he hasn't come here to talk fishing. Am I right, Mr. Abrams?"

Dave had been measuring Briggs' tone, watching it dance between amicability and derision.

"You're right, sheriff," he replied. "Although you could say I am on a fishing expedition."

"Understood. Maybe you'd care to walk with me to my boat. It's being refueled down by the dock."

Once outside, Briggs took a few steps and then paused to look back at the bait shop.

"I thought we'd better discuss business outside. Tom loves to talk, but he has trouble distinguishing between fish stories and real stories, if you take my meaning."

"I appreciate your discretion, sheriff."

"I'll tell you what, Mr. Abrams. You want to talk to me, and I'm supposed to be out on the water." He started walking toward the dock where a marina attendant was removing the fuel pump nozzle from the boat's fuel tank. The attendant handed a receipt to the sheriff. He scrawled his name and handed it back. He stepped on board the boat.

"Coming, Mr. Abrams?"

"I guess so." He glanced at his watch. "I just left my client, after a less than satisfactory interview, and I want to check some other things."

Briggs smiled.

"No problem. I'll have you back in an hour." He untied the bow line. "Hop aboard."

"Let me show you something," Briggs shouted above the roar of the patrol boat's powerful engine, which the sheriff had been running at almost full throttle since they left the dock. While Dave sat with growing impatience, alternately glancing at the compass and his watch, they ran north northeast across the bay for half an hour. Briggs now cut back on the throttle and pointed to a beach. "When I was a young man, I used to spend a lot of time on that beach. Drinking with people like Charlie."

The breeze was light, and the water almost calm. The boat turned slowly into the wind.

"That beach we're looking at," the sheriff said, "is outside of Omena, just north of Peshawbestown."

Dave glanced at the strip of sand, and then back over the blue waters.

"Geography is always interesting," Dave said, "but I need to talk with you about having Robin Asebou visit her mother."

Briggs nodded his large head slowly, apparent sympathy in his eyes.

"I'd like to help you out. I didn't know you had the girl."

"I don't have her. But I do know where she is."

"Got you," Briggs replied. "Like I said, I know these people. Years ago, you'd almost have thought I had become one of them. We'd go to the bar in Omena, and when they closed we'd take our bottles of cheap booze in brown paper bags, and we'd come to this beach here, and some hours later we'd fall asleep, and then we'd wake up in the morning and stagger into town waiting for the bar to open up again."

"And then," Dave prompted, "something happened. Maybe you were drafted."

"No, that wasn't it. If my number had come up at that time, I probably would have been fool enough to head for Canada. What happened, is one morning I woke up on the beach at dawn, and looked at my drinking companions, knowing that when they staggered to their feet they would head back to town and wait for the bars to open. The next night would be the same, and the next morning, and I understood that they truly had nothing to live for, but I did."

"A girl?"

"No. That wouldn't have been enough. I found the bottle far more attractive in those days than any woman could have been."

Briggs' eyes seemed to have turned inward, and they beamed, as though in the recollection of pleasure well beyond sex or even alcohol, and Dave understood.

"You found God, then," he said, "in the morning sun, on this beach."

Briggs seemed almost not to hear him, but he nodded, a barely discernible movement of his head. "But what about your old friends, like Charlie Williams?"

Briggs blinked his eyes, and looked at Dave, almost surprised that he was still there.

"I ignore them as best I can. All of them. The alcoholics will die young, refusing the hand of the Lord that could lift them up, and the others have reverted to their pagan ways, and have built themselves a new temple."

"The casino?"

"Right."

Dave felt himself being drawn into an argument he did not want to have.

"When can Robin see her mother?"

Brigg's face, which had been wearing an almost beatific smile, turned fierce.

"A whore, married to a drug-dealing pimp. You might as well hear the truth from me. That's what she is and he was. It's a blessing that he's dead, and she's going to jail for a long time."

Dave stood up, as though he could walk away.

"It's a long swim, home, counselor," Briggs smiled. "Sit down, and we'll see if we can work out an arrangement."

Dave eased back into his seat, and then he took two or three deep breaths.

"I'll disregard your characterization of my client. Just set up a visit. It's very important to Frankie. I'm not going to get a coherent statement from her until she's sure her daughter is safe."

Briggs pressed his large thumb against a couple of hairs on his chin his razor had missed.

"I'd like to be cooperative, but the child may be a material witness. I think I'd like to talk with her first."

"That might be a problem," Dave said.

"Work on it counselor. I can get a subpoena, if I have to." He reached over to turn the key to start the engine, but then he looked back at Dave. "Oh, there's one more thing you probably should know. Charlie Williams, besides those other shining qualities I listed before, also seems to have been involved in this mess at the casino. Something about laundering money that was being processed by a Smurf, who happened to be one of the tribal leaders."

"As you said," Dave replied, "Charlie's dead, and a good thing. You think that for your reasons, and perhaps I'm just as happy he won't have the chance to beat up his wife."

"Why, of course," the sheriff replied, his voice rich with hollow camaraderie. He reached into his pocket. "Oh, I almost forgot." He pulled out a piece of paper and handed it to Dave. It was the top of a store receipt, bearing the name, "Runners Shop" with a web site and an 800 number. On the line below was part of an address, just a string of the top half of numbers and letters. "That mean anything to you?" Briggs asked.

Dave started.

"Well," Briggs insisted.

"National chain, isn't it ?" Dave said. "I believe there's one in Traverse City."

"Used to be, but it closed," Briggs replied. "We found this piece of paper in Charlie's pocket, you know the one that you saw was turned inside out, that and five hundred dollars in cash in his wallet. You have to wonder where a man like Charlie would get his hands on that kind of money." He grinned. "You don't think he was going to order some fancy running shoes, do you?"

"Not likely."

The sheriff turned the engine on. Then he threw the engine into gear, and the boat leaped forward past a green stretch of water that marked the dropoff and into the deep blue of the bay. Against the hum of the engines, and while he kept a pleasant look on his face, Dave debated the probability that Charlie Williams shopped in a defunct local outlet of a national chain, just coincidentally the same one that Michael worked for in the South Street Southport.

Coincidence? Not likely, he concluded.

As Dave drove back toward town, two other ideas were forming in his mind, each demanding attention. One would have to wait for an opportunity to talk with Kelly. The other, however, was one he could pursue. To do that, he would have to meet with Cathleen Preston.

She worked in the recently established Native language literacy program funded from casino profits and designed to prevent the Ojibwe language from disappearing. It was likely that Robin would have participated in the program.

Dave stopped at a gas station outside of Suttons Bay. While the attendant filled the Caddy, Dave dialed the tribal administration building. When he heard the tentative female voice answer the phone, he realized he was talking to the same young woman at the receptionist's desk. She seemed to remember him as well.

"Oh, Mr. Abrams," she said. "I'm sorry, but Mr. Leaping Frog is not in his office right now."

"That's unfortunate," he replied, "but I was calling to find out where Ms. Preston might be."

"Oh," the voice replied, and Dave detected a note of relief. "Let me see." He heard a shuffling of papers, and then the voice came back on the line. "You might just catch her in the tribal library. Do you know where that is?"

"Afraid not."

"Well, it's kind of hard to see from the road, but its just off the highway that passes by the administration building. You remember how you got here, don't you?"

He couldn't decide for a moment if she were being deferential or insulting, and then figured, remembering the relief in her voice when she heard that he was not looking for her boss, that she was attempting to provide the best service possible. Besides, she didn't look to be capable of insult.

"Yes," he said.

"Well, just north of here is the tribal fishing control building. It sits right on the water, so boats can pull up to its dock, and the library is in that building."

He returned to the car to find the attendant gazing at the Caddy's hood with the look of a safecracker examining a safe.

"Must have a hell of engine under there," the attendant said. He was at least sixty, and the lines branching out from his eyes spoke of modest life expectations that had not been met. "Not like these put-puts in them little cars they sell nowadays. Would you like me to check the oil?"

"331 cubic inch, overhead valve V8, 210 horsepower, big enough for the fifties, but I'm in a hurry."

The man's face fell, and Dave handed him a twenty for the fifteen dollars worth of gas.

"Keep the change," he said, and the man smiled.

Cathleen Preston turned out to be a round faced, young Indian woman in her twenties with long black hair in a braid reaching down her back. Her brown eyes shone with the intensity of one engaged in a mission. Her handshake was firm, and her smile warm.

"I'm representing Frankie Asebou," he said.

"Robin, that poor child. What she must be going through, her father dead, and her mother accused of the murder."

"I'm pretty sure Frankie didn't do it," Dave said. "Can you tell me anything that might help me?"

She looked puzzled.

"About Robin?"

"Yes."

She put her forefinger to her chin. "Let me think," she said. "I run the literacy program, as I'm sure you know. Growing up on the reservation we were only taught English. And that was true for my parents as well. If it weren't for Livonia and a few others like her, our language would have disappeared and with it..." She raised her hand as though it was unnecessary to complete the thought

"I understand," Dave said. "But we were talking about Robin," he said.

"She was a very apt student, although her attendance was spotty. She'd have to help her mother out at the store. That store was a wonderful opportunity for the family, and then she'd go off to listen to her grandmother's stories." She paused. "She was learning the language so well, we talked about her beginning to help me."

"Did you ever see any signs of abuse on Robin, any bruises, any behaviors that might point in that direction?" Dave asked.

Catherine shook her head firmly, but her eyes lost their sparkle.

"No, I can't say I did. Charlie seemed to have saved that kind of attention for Frankie. But now you mention it, I do remember something from two or three years ago. It struck me as odd at the time, but now I recall it. It was in June."

Dave sought the connection but found none.

"Around Father's Day," Catherine said. "We were wondering why white people thought it necessary to have a holiday to honor fathers. Or mothers for that matter. But the question did not come up on Mother's Day."

"Whatever the reason for the holiday," Dave replied, "I don't think those who thought it up had Charlie Williams in mind."

"No doubt," she replied and her eyes turned fierce. "Robin was always, how should I say it, too dutiful around him."

"But no bruises or anything more concrete?"

"I'm sorry. I can't help you with that. I can't say I ever saw anything like a bruise. But what does all of this have to do with proving Frankie innocent?"

"Just background," Dave replied. "You've been quite a help."

As Dave got back into the Caddy, his head ached from the conviction that was growing stronger in his mind.

CHAPTER TWELVE

KELLY pulled the door shut until she heard the catch click. The noise amplified in her mind like the iron bars of a dungeon keep rather than the cheap, hollow door of a motel room. She searched her pockets for the room key, suddenly convinced that she had dropped it inside and that she would not be able to re-enter the room.

When she felt the corner of the key digging into the palm of her right hand, she lifted the card out of her pocket. Holding the key inches from the slot, she hesitated and then dropped it into her pocket, staring at the white indentation in her flesh. She took a breath and again groped in her pocket for the key. She thought she would be able to handle anything she might discover in that room, but seeing Grace almost made her forget the violator, and she now understood that up until that moment she had never believed that Michael would have touched that babysitter. Having rationalized that fear, driving it deep into the recesses of her subconscious, where it festered and grew into a nameless dread, she had convinced herself that in keeping him away from private time with the girl, she was only being super cautious. How else could she have thought about the man whose bed she had shared and who had fathered the daughter she loved more than life? No, she had not truly believed that he was capable of abusing somebody else's child. But looking at him now, she saw a stranger much more than when his hands crashed against her face because then those same hands could be gentle upon her flesh, if only she could figure out how to tame them. Even a few moments before, when she saw him, bare chested and satisfied, her mind leaped back twenty years to when she loved the feel of him against her, his slim body, his blond hair and blue eyes, when she would wonder how she could have been so lucky as to have caught the handsomest young man in the neighborhood. Even through the bad times that followed, she had never quite forgotten the contours of his body, the tight mound of muscle on his shoulders, or the narrow hips of the athlete he had once been, or how she loved to wrap her legs around his waist. She knew that never exorcising those memories caused her now to pace in front of that door.

With a start, she remembered how the Miata had jerked its way through the parking lot, and she was sure now that Allie must have been driving it. She took a step back down the corridor, her hand mindlessly fumbling in her purse for her car keys, but then she stopped herself. She knew where Allie was going, and she would catch up to her soon enough. First, she had to steady herself and figure out how to deal with the man who was behind that door. She pulled the door key out of her pocket. She was about to insert it into the lock when the door knob turned. She stepped back, and in a moment the door swung open. Michael stood before her, now fully dressed in jeans and a pullover knit shirt. His feet were bare.

"It's not what you think," he said.

"Isn't it?"

He reached his hand out, as though to touch her arm, and she recoiled. He shrugged.

"It's probably no use," he said.

"No, it's not."

He shifted his eyes toward the room.

"I'm taking Grace with me," she said, "I'll buy her a bus ticket back home."

"You don't have to do that. She's okay with me."

"I don't think so, but we can ask her."

She started to sidle by him, but he held her wrist. She stared hard at him, searching his eyes for a sign of recognition, but his expression was blank. He let go of her, and she walked into the room.

Grace, now wearing baggy shorts that reached her knees and a sweatshirt bearing the logo of Notre Dame University, was sitting on the bed, her arms clasped around her chest. She was rocking slightly back and forth, and her eyes glistened.

"Grace," Michael said softly, and Kelly could feel his breath on the back of her neck. The girl glanced at him, shuddered, and started to rock more violently. He turned and walked out of the room. He closed the door behind him.

"I'm ready to go home," Grace said.

Kelly sat next to her on the bed and held her until the rocking stopped.

"I didn't know..." Grace began.

Kelly pulled her closer.

"I know you didn't. Don't try to talk about it now. Where are your things?"

Grace's eyes darted around the room.

"My suitcase, it was, no," she paused, "it's in the car."

"Your car?"

Grace nodded.

"I think Allie drove off in it," Kelly said.

A small smile formed on Grace's lips.

"She would. That girl is determined. She said she was going to get to you, if she had to walk the rest of the way. That was when she saw what was going on between me and..." The smile disappeared, and she brought her hand to her eyes. Kelly saw that she had long, delicate fingers.

"Later," Kelly said, "if you want, we'll talk about it later. You just wait here." She stood up. "I've got to finish my business with him." She walked to the door, but then she hesitated.

"Just tell me one thing," she said. "Did he force you?"

Grace shook her head.

"Did he hurt you?"

The girl shook her head again.

"No," she said. "But I wish he had."

Michael was leaning against the wall opposite the door when Kelly stepped into the corridor. He was smoking a cigarette, and he flicked an ash onto the floor, next to his bare feet.

"I'll need my shoes," he said. "I'll be on my way. You know, places to go, people to see. I'll leave the nymphet in your good hands, as you want." A smile she could only describe as evil played on his lips, and his tone was mocking. She found herself staring at the red tip of his cigarette. He brought it to his mouth for a deep drag, and then he exhaled, blowing the smoke upwards and in front of his face. He waited for it to clear.

"A distraction I picked up inside," he said.

Kelly turned her head toward the door.

"Apparently, you didn't learn much else."

"She's seventeen, of age. Something else I learned. To make these important distinctions."

"She's a child. And you know it," Kelly snapped, and then she caught herself. She was responding to him just the way she used to when they were married, arguing a point, and she would know she was right, and that he knew she was, but he would delight in the role of sophist, as if to mock the fact she was in school while he had dropped out, proving to her that he could play the academic game better than she, if he chose to. The same condescending arrogance was in his tone now, but it was darker, colored by his time in prison. What had been marital mocking was now something far blacker, something rooted in his soul that had been nourished and flowered in his cell. He had been studying her face as it registered these thoughts.

"Maybe you are beginning to understand," he said. His features softened. "At least you should now see that it was never your fault."

"It's far too late for that," she replied, though his words had penetrated her antipathy.

"You're right, much too late." He ground his cigarette out against the window ledge, and stared through the glass for a moment.

"Our daughter is down there, trying to maneuver that silly little car into a parking spot."

Kelly rushed by him and followed the direction of his glance. She saw Allie get out of the Miata, which was parked at a diagonal, immediately below her. She watched as Allie made her way to the door at the end of the wing. When she turned around to say something, she did not know what, to Michael, he was gone. A moment later, he returned with his shoes on, and a nylon airline bag slung over his shoulder.

"Allie is not yet sixteen," Kelly said. "Is that the only reason?" She felt the relief relax her back muscles. She knew that she had to give voice to that question, to his face, and no matter what his answer, she would sleep better for having asked.

"I know her birthday," he snapped. "And no, that was not the reason." And then he added, as though giving comfort was something he had unlearned in prison, "And Grace is far more interesting."

Kelly heard the footsteps coming down the corridor. Allie began to run toward her mother, but stopped when she saw Michael.

"He followed us, mom," she said. "He must have heard me talking on the phone with Grace."

"It doesn't matter, baby, just come to me now," Kelly said.

Michael strode toward Allie, who pressed herself against the wall. He came abreast of her and leaned toward her as though to give her a kiss on the cheek. The girl recoiled, and stared at Kelly as though for help. Then, she slid along the wall until she reached her mother. Michael shrugged and walked back toward them.

"This didn't work out so well, did it Allie?" he said. "We'll have to do better next time."

Kelly felt Allie press herself against her side, and she threw her arm around her.

"You must be kidding," Kelly said. "There will be no next time."

"Oh, but there will," Michael said, his eyes fixed on Allie. "You won't keep me from my daughter."

"You have no right to her," Kelly said.

"I have every right. And I will see her again. Soon. Don't you, or your lawyer husband, try to stand in my way."

He took a few steps down the corridor and turned back.

"I'll be in touch." He adjusted the bag on his shoulder and pushed through the door at the end of the corridor.

Kelly sat between the two girls on the motel bed. Its thin mattress and unsure springs sagged beneath her greater weight so that Allie and Grace leaned into her. They would have, anyway, even had she been perched atop a boulder on a mountain.

"He found me on My Space," Grace said. "Came on to me. Didn't hide the fact he was older. I found that…you know, flattering. It was only later he said who he was. By that time, I didn't care. I just didn't care."

Kelly did not try to find the words to soothe, for she recognized that each girl in her way was, for the moment, beyond succor. Grace's eyes, usually bright and challenging, misted beneath her tears. Allie had her eyes closed, and she wept against her mother's shoulder.

Kelly thought about reaching for the phone that sat on the night table just beyond Allie. She straightened her posture slightly to suggest that she might want to shift her position, but Allie lifted her head long enough to murmur something unintelligible, and Grace dug her fingers into Kelly's leg. Dave, Kelly concluded, would have to wait.

Kelly awoke with a dull throb in her neck and down her back. She realized that she was laboring for breath, and she attempted to sit up, but something had her pinned to the bed. She blinked her eyes open and saw that she was lying beneath the two girls, one on each side, their heads touching and resting on her rib cages beneath her breasts. Grace's long leg was thrown across her thighs, and Allie's arm was crammed behind her neck, forcing her head half off the mattress. She dislodged Grace's leg and managed to sit up. The girls rolled away from her, but neither woke up.

She checked her watch and saw that it was four o'clock. She got up, stretched, and walked to the window. She pulled down on the bottom of the plastic shade yellowed from nicotine. It felt as though there were an oily film on the plastic, and the shade would not turn on its roller. Lifting it aside, she stared out of the window, expecting perhaps to see Michael's car, thinking that he would not have left in the middle of the night, no matter where he had to go. But this window looked out of the opposite side of the building onto a field. She could not see much more than the flatness of the land, broken here and there by shadowy shapes that could have been low shrubs, tall weeds, or heaps of trash. Even though she could not see them now, she was sure the field was littered with beer cans.

She returned to the bed. Both girls were sleeping deeply, side by side. Grace's lean and muscled legs were dangling half off the bed and her elbows were tucked into her belly. Allie, softer and rounder, had curled her knees up to her chest. She stretched her legs and flipped onto her back. Her deep red hair splayed beneath her head and she threw her forearm over her eyes. Her blouse pulled up, and Kelly saw the pale flesh of her belly, and exposed navel. She pulled her daughter's blouse down.

The girls appeared as secure as though they were in their own rooms, rather than a ratty motel off a highway, halfway across Canada, one of them changed forever because of her adventurous spirit, the other, scarred from bearing witness to her father's seduction of her friend, and yet both, now, looking as if all they needed were teddy bears to complete the reversion to an innocent childhood that would not survive the light of the sun. Kelly felt a chill in the air, and she took the edge of the thin blanket that lay beneath the girls and rolled it over them. Grace moved closer to Allie as she felt the blanket cover her, and she grabbed the edge to clutch it to her chin. Kelly watched with a tender expression on her face until she turned her glance to the sheet that now lay exposed next to Grace. She turned her eyes away from the small, rusty spot of dried blood, and then she stared at it hard, and her fists tightened in an anger she would not soon forget.

Grace and Allie sat huddled in the back of the Toyota while Kelly walked toward the office. As she neared, she saw that the old man was standing in front of the door. He was shorter than she had imagined, a figure bent like a gnome, wearing plaid pants held up by suspenders over a stained white shirt. He puffed on a cigarette with one hand, and held a cane with the other. He lifted his eyes to the sun and stretched.

"Morning," he said. "Did you sleep well?"

The question was so wildly inappropriate that for a moment Kelly entertained the notion that this strange little man was some kind of colleague, or co-conspirator of Michael's. But she could not convince herself that he was that evil, and so she merely shrugged.

"You know these motel beds," she said. "I always wake up with a backache."

"Can't say as I do," he said. He started a cackle that immediately degenerated into a hacking coughing fit. He leaned heavily on his cane, and then turned to spit a blob of phlegm that seemed to have been rooted someplace deep inside of him. He yanked a soiled handkerchief out of his pocket and wiped his lips before facing her again.

"I always sleep in my own bed in my own house," he continued. "Maybe working in a place like this for so long has taken away my appetite for traveling."

"You didn't happen to see the man leave, the one who was in this room?" She handed him the room key.

He glanced at it.

"That's the master I gave you last night. It don't have a room number on it."

"But you know which one I'm talking about, and the man who paid for it."

He shook his head slowly.

"No. But I did hear a car leaving here about three or four. That would have been a little after the other car came back." He pointed toward the Miata, still sitting at an angle at the end of the parking area. "But then I'm sure you know about that one, both of them, I figure, so I don't know why you're troubling me about any of it."

His voice began to rise in indignation but he again found himself doubled up in a cough. "Day man'll be here shortly," he said after the fit subsided, "and I'll be on my way home."

"To your own bed," Kelly said.

"Nope. I'll stop off for some breakfast first, at this donut shop up the road, and then head for home."

"That wouldn't be in Woodstock, next to a pool hall, would it?" she asked.

She thought she saw a flicker of a grin on his lips, but he could have been holding back another cough.

"Funny thing," he said. "I've been going there for years, and I never did look to see what was next door."

A rusted-out late seventies Dodge Diplomat pulled up to the office, and a man stepped out. He, too, looked ancient, and he was also quite short. He waved at them and walked into the office.

"That's my relief, so I'll just give him back this master key and be on my way."

"Is he...?" she began.

"People say we look like brothers," the night clerk chuckled, and then he made his way in an uneven gait, probing the ground before he put his cane down as though he were searching for something, toward the office. A moment later he emerged and got into his own car, a well maintained Honda Civic. She glanced at the Miata, and then she trotted over to his car. He was staring intently at the ignition key, as though he were about to recite an incantation. She knocked on the window, and he turned his head toward her. A cigarette dangled from the corner of his mouth. He rolled down the window, and held the cigarette toward her. She stepped back, and he knocked the ash off. Digging into her purse, she pulled out her wallet where she found a fifty dollar bill.

"I want you to keep an eye on that Miata until I figure out how to get it back to New York."

His bony fingers snatched the bill from her hand.

"I'm going home now," he said. "But I'll give the day man a call. He don't have much to do during the day, you know, so he can watch it for you." He ground out his cigarette into the small, overflowing ashtray, and took another from his pack. He was smoking unfiltered Camels. He lit the cigarette with a match, and then he handed the matches to Kelly. "The name of the motel and the telephone number," he said, "so you can keep in touch. I come on at midnight."

She glanced at the matchbook cover, which showed the name, Sundowner Motel, above a yellow sun sliding into blue water, just like the neon sign. Beneath the water was the telephone number, and a statement announcing the availability of special commercial and day rates.

She pulled a pen out of her purse and turned the matchbook cover over to its blank side.

"What's your name?" she asked, her pen poised over the cover.

He exhaled a pungent cloud of smoke.

"Just call after midnight, any night but Sunday. There won't be anybody else to answer the phone but me." He folded the bill and slipped it into the breast pocket of his shirt. "Thank you," he said. "It's been a profitable night."

She watched the Civic's slow progress out of the parking lot and onto the highway, and then she returned to her own car. Allie and Grace were now sitting, fully awake, at opposite sides of the back seat, as though they were no longer comfortable with each other. Kelly got into the car.

"I'm going to get us some breakfast," she said. "Then I'll find a bus station for Grace, and after that, Allie and I will drive on to Michigan."

"My car?" Grace said, her voice almost sullen.

"I've made temporary arrangements. I want to get you home."

"Are you going to talk to my parents?"

"Maybe later. I think you should have the first shot at that."

Grace seemed to relax.

"I'll think of something," she said, "like the car broke down." Her face broke into her usual smart ass grin.

Kelly marveled, for a moment, at the girl's resilience. Allie, she figured, might need much more time.

"We'll get you plenty to eat on the way," Kelly said to Grace. "So you can keep yourself out of trouble until you get home."

CHAPTER THIRTEEN

T was seven a.m., and Dave had been sitting at the dining room table left by the Wilsons for over an hour, after a restless night of intermittent sleep, lying on his side with his nose four or five inches from the telephone on the night table next. Staring at it would not make it ring, but feeling the empty space next to him as a tangible and disconcerting presence, he could not remove his gaze from the phone. He now knew its every feature, well enough to draw it if he had the skill, its beige cover spotted with white paint from the time years ago when it sat in his apartment on Sackett Street in the Carroll Gardens section of Brooklyn, its rotary dial, also spotted with paint and still bearing a sticker with his old number, when he was working all day and going to law school at night, too poor to buy a more contemporary phone. Kelly grew fond of it when she visited in those days, so they kept it after they married even though increasingly it looked like it would be more appropriately housed in a museum than on a night table next to a bed. He stared at its extra long cord twisted in byzantine coils, and its handset resting in the receiver's cradle so the cord was drawn across the face of the dial, just the way Kelly preferred.

At sun up, he lifted himself out of the bed, made a pot of coffee, checked to see that the cordless phone on the kitchen wall was working, and sat down at this old table. In front of him on the deep grained wood of the table top lay the stack of papers from Heilman, delivered by messenger the previous evening. Dave studied the coroner's report, then closed his eyes and called up the image of the body on the beach, Charlie's beefy hand clawing at his neck, which ran with dried blood, the uneven stain on his shirt like a rusty ink blot test in the form of a bloated spider with long, hairy legs.

Dave took a deep swallow of his coffee, and a moment later, heard John's car pull up the driveway. He got up and took a step toward the door when the phone rang. It was Kelly.

"You say Allie's alright," John said. "That's the most important thing, isn't it?"

"Of course," Dave replied. "She said she's okay, certainly physically fine, but disoriented."

John started to respond, but then just nodded, as though he realized the futility of empty words of comfort. Instead, he asked, "And the other kid?"

"Kelly put her on a bus in Woodstock. She said something about having made some arrangements for her car. She and Allie are going to drive straight through, and should be here some time tonight."

"Is that such a good idea?" John asked, "I mean with what Allie's been through?"

"Kelly offered to stop off at Greenfield Village for a day or two, something she's been wanting to do with Allie for a long time, but Allie said no, she wanted to come straight up here, to see you."

John's lined old face rarely exhibited surprise, but it did now as his eyebrows lifted.

"Me?"

"Well, not you exactly. She said she wanted to come up here to look for your fingers, like you and she used to do when she was a kid."

"I'll be damned," John said.

"There's one more thing. About Michael. Kelly said she's pretty sure he's heading in this direction because he made it clear he wants to see Allie again."

John began to shake his head in disbelief as Dave continued.

"I know you think Kelly is not clear-headed about Michael, but there is something else." He pulled the torn piece of paper out of his pocket and slid it to John. "I found this at Peterson Park the night Charlie was killed."

"Found it, where? On the body?"

"No," Dave replied, "that's the good news and the bad. If it were on the body, you know as well as I that I should turn it over to Briggs or Heilman, but it was a good distance away."

"Far enough to ease your sense of ethics and also stretch its relevance."

"Exactly. It was snagged on a branch along the line I believe Charlie took when he fell through that fence. His jacket pocket was turned out, and his hand appeared to be grasping for something that wasn't there."

"Pardon me," John said, "but that sounds like a description of the straw you're after."

"I thought so, too, until Briggs showed me a piece of paper that could be the top section of this one. If it is, it connects Michael to Charlie, because the name on that paper is the store where Michael supposedly works."

"Somewhere between possible and implausible," John grunted.

"Yes, but I am more than a little curious, and concerned that he might be coming this way, whether to stay near Allie, or for some other business."

"Prison," John said slowly, "sometimes does strange things to a man. I guess this Michael is not the one I knew from years ago."

"No, it doesn't seem so. But just what he is, is not very clear."

Dave slid the list of prosecution witnesses across the table. John laid the paper in front of him, then moved it several inches so his eyes could focus.

"Your old friend isn't wasting much time," John said.

"Heilman wants another confession," Dave replied, "this time one that will hold up in court, and then a guilty plea. Nothing much. He sent over the list long before he had to, to convince us to make his life simple. He has more pressing matters on his desk, he says, than the murder of one Indian by another. And judging from my talk with the sheriff, Mr. Heilman is going to get more than enough help from Briggs." He pushed the medical report toward John. "And the coroner is helping by smoothing out some rough edges." Dave put his finger on a place in the report. "Here," he said.

"Fluid in the lungs," John read. "Likely from pneumonia or congestive heart failure."

"Heilman's going to argue," Dave said, "that Mr. Williams was shot by his wife, twice, the second fatally, and she was too drunk to realize what she had done, so drunk that she permitted him to lie dying on the floor until she sobered up, at which point she somehow hoisted him into the truck and dumped him off the cliff at the beach."

John's eyes had remained on the report while Dave spoke, and now he looked up.

"So, according to the coroner, Charlie was dead when he went over the cliff," John said.

"Right," Dave affirmed.

"And you have another idea," John said, "about that water."

"Yes," Dave replied. "His body was at water's edge. His face was just about in the water. And you didn't see anything in that report, did you, about a cedar needle underneath Charlie's fingernails?"

"No," John replied. "But that would be easy to overlook, especially," he frowned, "if you did not want to look too hard."

"We mentioned that to Heilman on the night of the shooting, and he said that the lab boys would check it out. There was something there. We all saw it."

"Cedar is fairly common hereabouts."

"There was a cedar tree with a branch ripped off where Charlie fell."

"Branches often come off, for all kinds of reasons," John replied in a quiet voice, and then he shook his head. "I don't think you've got anything there."

"Maybe not," Dave conceded, "but if he was alive on the beach…"

"While Frankie was lying drunk back in their house," John finished the thought. "But you will need more. Heilman will say

Charlie had that needle under his fingernail from some other place. He can concede that Charlie's body broke the fence, but he will say he was dead when Frankie dumped him off. Time of death on the report is too approximate to help you or Heilman. He'll probably speculate that she got some help transporting the body from some other Indian."

"Do you see any candidates for that job on the witness list?"

"Sure," John said slowly, "at least half a dozen. And one who's not on the list, our friend Leonard." He stood up. "I guess I can start seeing what these folks might have to say." He started to slide the list back to Dave.

"Take it," Dave said. And in any case..."

"You'll be waiting for Kelly and Allie."

"Yes, but I just can't sit here all day, like I did last night, staring at the door instead of the phone. I'll find something more productive to do."

"You might want to go and talk with Livonia. I saw her this morning, on my way in, setting up her stand, and she indicated she might have something to tell us."

"Will she tell it to me?"

John walked to the door.

"Well, you won't know unless you go out there and ask her."

Livonia was sitting behind her stand, her broad brimmed straw hat pulled well down over her eyes so that only her chin, with its mole, was visible. Dave cleared his throat once or twice, but the hat did not move.

"Livonia," he said in a loud voice that seemed to startle the quiet of the morning. The woman's head tilted back until her eyes appeared.

"At first, I thought you were having respiratory problems," she said, "and I thought the polite thing to do was wait until you were through coughing, or whatever it was you were doing." She pushed the hat away from her eyes and blinked in the sunlight. "I've lived a long time among you folks, and I still don't understand your manners."

"John said you might have something to tell us about what happened to Charlie Williams."

"Yes," she replied, "but I'm not sure what to do. You see, there's one dead Indian, and another that says she shot the fool, and then there's the girl. We hear all the talk about town, how that born-again sheriff is saying that the whole thing is the devil's work, the devil alcohol, that is. I tell you ever since that man crawled out of a bottle he's been impossible. But we know how he, and everybody else like him, meaning just about everybody but us, sees things."

"One drunken Indian killing another. That's how the prosecutor described the case to me."

Livonia wiped a bead or perspiration off her forehead and then resettled her hat.

"So, why should I talk to you? My question is who am I supposed to be helping?"

"Frankie won't talk to me until she sees her daughter."

Livonia fixed her eyes on Dave in a steady squint that pulled the skin next to her eyes into long wrinkles.

"How is Frankie?"

"Not too good. Physically, she'll heal. But her mind is not clear."

Livonia nodded.

"It has been clouded for a long time." She leaned over the counter toward Dave. "What will happen to the girl if I let you bring her to see her mother?"

"I think she'll have to talk with the sheriff, or the prosecutor. I don't think I can work it any other way."

"And if she doesn't talk to Frankie?"

"I'm going to have serious problems building a defense, which is going to be tough enough to do anyway."

"Tell me this. Why are you trying so hard to defend someone you do not know, in a situation where anybody with sense can see that you're going to take a beating. And don't go and quote the Constitution to me."

"It's personal."

Livonia nodded.

"So you see something in Frankie you have seen before."

"Frankie and Robin. In Brooklyn Frankie's name was Bonita. I never did learn the name of her daughter."

"Then I'll see what I can do. The child is still spooked. Her father's spirit is troubling her."

"Fine." Dave picked up one of the fossil stones and held it to his ear. "It's not talking to me this morning. John said you might have something to tell us."

She shook her head sadly.

"I guess I have to trust you to do the right thing." Livonia said, "So, listen. 'Ke ne bou haw yea pe mos say.' That's what this man told me."

"What man?"

"'Ke ne bou haw yea pe mos say,'" she repeated. "He only talks Ojibwe when he's drunk. What he says means, 'He died and he walks.' The man who told me that is Billy Lockwood. He was talking about Charlie, and John knows where to find him."

"But I..." Dave began.

"That's all I can tell you, and it may be too much. Ask John."

Billy Lockwood was sober when Dave spoke to him later that morning. Billy lived on the edge of the tribal land, off a two-track dirt road that wound between towering maples and fir. The road brushed Billy's house, a trailer perched on cement blocks, and then ran into the side of a cherry orchard a couple of hundred yards past the house.

Dave pulled into the dirt driveway that led in a gentle loop to the trailer. He stopped the Caddy behind a Chevy Caprice wagon, which had a two by four bolted on to replace the rear bumper, and red plastic tape over the tail lights. Billy sat in an aluminum chair on a porch fashioned out of two layers of the same blocks that supported the trailer. The chair occupied almost all the space. Next to the chair was a six-pack. Moisture beaded the bottle tops. Billy started to reach for a beer, but straightened up.

"John O'Brien told me how to find your place," Dave said extending his hand. "I am Dave Abrams, an attorney defending Frankie Abesou."

Billy shook his grizzled head, then stroked the gray stubble on his chin. When he opened his mouth to speak, saliva bubbled in the gap where his lower front teeth should have been.

"John," he said, "sure I know him." He held out his right hand with his middle fingers folded into his palm, and waggled his thumb and pinky. "Everyone knows that man. But nobody knows you, Mr. Abrams."

"John gave me directions, but Livonia Walkingstick was the one who told me you might have something to tell me."

"Might," Billy repeated, but he did not offer to continue.

"Ke-ne-bou-haw-yea-pe-mos-say," Dave said slowly.

Billy squinted at Dave, tilting his head backwards slightly, and shielding his eyes from the sun overhead.

"That's crazy," Billy said. "Who said that? He is dead and he walks."

"You did. You said it at the Harbor Bar, over in Omena."

"I talk English. Why would I be talking Ojibwe? And saying crazy things, like I was talking about zombies or something?"

"You talk Ojibwe when you're drunk," Dave said.

"I never know what the hell I'm saying when I'm drunk."

Dave shrugged.

"OK. We've played our game." Dave reached into his pocket and pulled out his wallet. He found his card and handed it to Billy. "If you want to talk to me, you can give me a call, at the number on the back of the card."

Billy stared at the card.

"Don't have a phone," he said. "So I might as well see if I can help you now." He rubbed his forehead as though to jog his memory. "I might have seen something at the Harbor Bar. When I parked my truck, I saw him in my headlights. She-gos-se. The weasel. He was a fat one, you know, weasels are usually pretty sleek, but this one was sitting up on its hind legs, with its belly dragging on the ground. He had long white fangs, looked like they were dripping blood, and he was holding a rabbit in his front paws, with another one on the ground. That's what I saw."

"I want to hear about Charlie Williams."

Billy picked up a bottle and twisted the top off. The sun seemed to have gotten stronger, and he held the bottle to his forehead. Then he brought it to his lips and took a deep swallow.

"You don't understand," he said. "That's what I'm trying to tell you. She-gos-se. Charlie Williams. Later, after I been drinking a while, I saw him, just for a second, on a stool, at the end of the bar. When I left to go home, there was still one rabbit on the ground, the one he didn't eat." He opened his mouth to expel a deep and satisfying belch. He took out a handkerchief, wiped the top of the bottle, and held it out to Dave.

"No thank you," Dave said, glancing at his watch. "I just had breakfast a little while ago. 'She-gos-se.' Is that the best you can do for me?"

Billy sat still for a moment, the bottle still extended, and then he nodded his head.

"But if I think of something, I'll be sure to give you a call." He tucked the card into his shirt pocket.

"You don't have a phone."

"There's one at the Harbor Bar."

"But I don't understand much Ojibwe."

"I know," Billy replied, "but I think you're learning." He took another swallow.

Robin was sitting behind Livonia's stand. The girl's eyes followed Dave as he walked toward her. When he was within a step or two of the stand, she shrank against Livonia's side.

"Here she is," Livonia said. "I told her that she should talk to you, that you would be able to bring her to her mother, but I don't know if she will talk." Livonia stood up. "I've got some things to get out of my car," she said, "over there. It'll take me a little while." She turned and headed toward an old station wagon, so coated in dust that it was difficult to determine the color, which might have been a deep green or blue. Robin started to get up, as though to follow Livonia, but then she sat down again. Dave noticed that her eyes had regained some of the confidence they had when he first saw her at the pow wow.

"Grandmother says I should talk to you, but I don't think I have anything to tell you."

"I'd like to try a couple of questions, Robin."

"Grandmother also said that you would take me to see my mother."

"I want to do that, and I will. I need you to try to answer a couple of questions first."

Robin's face darkened.

"Is this some kind of deal? I talk to you, and then you take me to my mother?"

"No," Dave said. "I'm going to take you anyway. But I don't think I can stop you from being questioned by the prosecutor. It'll be better if I talk to you before he does."

"I don't trust him," she said slowly. "And I don't know much about you."

"A common opinion today."

Robin, though, seemed not to be listening. Instead, she fixed her gaze on him as though trying to read his soul.

"Either you are a meddlesome fool. Which is what I first thought when you gave my mother your business card. Or you are a well-intentioned fool. Which is what Grandmother thinks."

"A fool in any case, though," Dave said.

"I will speak to you. A little. It's not a good idea to give any kind of fool too much to think about. He might become confused."

"I'll do my best to keep a clear head. Let's try a simple question of fact first. When I saw you the day you came out of the silo, you were missing one sneaker. Do you know what happened to it?"

"It came off my foot."

Dave felt his irritation begin to rise, but he also knew that Robin was far too important to permit him to lose whatever little trust he might be able to generate. He took a deep breath, and looked at Livonia's car. The tailgate was down, and the old woman was bent over as though looking for something. He turned back to Robin.

"Do you know where the sneaker fell off?"

She shrugged.

"It happened the night, that night. I don't know where."

He studied her face, and listened to her tone, as she spoke, seeking any sign of fabrication. She appeared to be telling the truth.

"Let's try a different approach. Tell me what you remember from that night."

"Do I have to?"

"Yes, because I have to hear what you have to say. And because Mr. Heilman is going to ask you the same question."

"I was in my bedroom. Mommy and Daddy were fighting, like they usually did, especially when they both had been drinking. I heard things, and I put a pillow over my head, so I wouldn't hear them anymore."

"What kinds of things?"

"Loud voices. Glass breaking. Grunting noises. Like pigs in a pen. Then a loud noise, like an explosion."

"A shot?"

She nodded, and this time Dave detected something a little less than sincere.

"I guess so," she said. "I'm not familiar with the sound of gunshots. And then I pulled the pillow closer around my ears until I couldn't hear anything more."

"And then? Did you come out of your room after a while?"

"No. I stayed where I was. It is always better that way. Then I climbed out of the window."

"Didn't you want to see what happened?"

"Of course. But I was afraid. After a while, I looked in through the living room window. I saw my mother lying on the floor. And..." she paused. "My father, was on the floor, too."

"Did you see a gun?"

"No. I didn't know that there was a gun. I thought they both must have fallen asleep. It wouldn't have been the first time. So I did what I always do, when the weather is not too bad. I took a long walk."

"To the beach?"

"Yes. I have a place there that I always go to."

"And then?"

"I must have fallen asleep. And when I woke up, I saw my father. Down by the water. I went to him, and called to him, but he did not move." She took a long, studied breath. "I said I would talk to you a little, and I have spoken much. I am afraid that you are getting confused, as I thought you would."

Dave wanted to say that her story was confusing, that it contained gaps wide enough to drive a truck through, but he figured that he would have to wait for another opportunity.

"So let's finish it up. You woke up, found your father dead, and then the police came."

"And took me to that hospital. But I didn't stay."

"Yes," Dave replied. "I know all about that. One last question. Do you have any idea what happened to your father's truck?"

Robin looked over toward Livonia, who, as though on cue, stood up and slammed the tail gate shut. It did not stay, so she slammed it again, with greater force. It clanged and remained closed. Livonia started walking towards them.

"No," Robin said, answering Dave's question.

"Was it in the driveway by your house that night? Do you remember seeing it when you climbed out of the window?"

"No, that is, I don't remember. It should have been there. He always drove it places."

"Nobody seems able to find it."

She shrugged again.

"Maybe it was stolen," she said. "In the confusion."

Livonia sat down next to Robin, and the girl collapsed against the old woman's side.

"O-ko-mes-se-maw," she said, "I have answered his questions, the best way I could. Can I see my mother now?"

Livonia looked at Dave, her eyes sending silent recriminations.

"I'll arrange it with the prosecutor as soon as I can," Dave said. "Maybe I can set something up for tomorrow."

"Do it," Livonia said. She pulled the girl closer to her, and began to stroke her hair, with long, gentle motions.

Dave waited, unwilling to interrupt their communion, but he had one more question to ask, this one for Livonia. She seemed to sense his eyes on her, and she lifted her hand to him to indicate that he should wait. A moment later, she whispered something in Robin's ear. The child nodded, got up, and walked to the old station wagon.

"I appreciate that," Dave said. "I just wanted to know if you could tell me what Billy meant when he answered my question about seeing Charlie in the bar that night. He said he saw a weasel, eating a rabbit."

Livonia moved her head slowly up and down.

"He was telling you what he saw, but what you do not understand is that he was telling you he saw Charlie."

"Well, which is it?" Dave asked. "A weasel or Charlie?"

"Both," Livonia replied.

Hooper heard the clatter of Kelly's diesel first. Dave was again sitting at the dining room table, going over his notes. He had summarized the main points of Robin's story, and circled the ones, such as how she could not explain her father's presence at the beach, that were most troubling. In fact, he had been for the past several minutes guiding his pencil over the circles he had already drawn so that they were now thick and black, and in several places the paper had torn beneath the insistent pressure of the pencil's point.

The dog had been sleeping under the table and he now clambered to his feet, pushing Dave's legs out of the way as he did. His tail wagging, he began a troubled trot to the front door. His feet slipped on the bare floor so that his front legs splayed apart and he almost collapsed onto his chest. He gathered himself and lurched to the front door in a motion not unlike a small boat cresting high waves.

Dave now heard the engine, and he started to stand up. He sat back down again, though, and let the relief he felt wash over him like a warm breeze on a late winter afternoon. As he stood up, he heard first one, and then another, car door slam.

Kelly walked in, her arm draped around Allie's shoulder, and the three of them fell into a clumsy embrace. Hooper thrust his massive head into the tangle of legs, and for a moment it seemed they would lose their balance. Allie broke free and kneeled next to Hooper. She circled his thick neck with her arm.

"Yes, you ugly beast. I even missed you," she said. Then she looked up at Kelly and then Dave. Her mouth was fixed in a smile, but tears welled in her eyes. Dave threw his arms around her, and she rested her head on his chest.

"We need some sleep," Kelly said.

"Have you eaten?" Dave asked.

Kelly shook her head.

"It doesn't matter," she said. "We're home. And we'll talk in the morning."

Dave glanced past her to the Toyota, and saw that the car's lights were still on.

"That's fine," he said. He framed her face with his fingers. Her skin felt damp.

"I've been a little anxious the past few days," she said. "And then a couple of hours ago, I got really tired and we had this close encounter with a semi on the interstate. Allie volunteered to drive us the rest of the way." She forced her lips into a weary smile. "But I had seen her drive, and it was dark."

"I could have, Mom," Allie said, and for the moment her voice had the insulted tone of a teenager who feels she is not being permitted to grow up, but then her expression changed so that her face bore the look of a terror she could just manage to control.

After Kelly and Allie were settled, Dave returned to the dining room table with a pot of freshly brewed coffee. Allie had asked, shyly, if she could lie down with her mother, just for a little while. Kelly had not waited for the affirmative answer Dave was about to offer, but instead led her daughter to the small bedroom next to hers and Dave's. She kept the door of that room shut tight while Allie was visiting Michael, although she had not been able to pass it by without a catch in her breath. She opened the door, now, and led Allie into her room.

"She left Pooh Bear in the car," Kelly said. "I bought her a new one in town." Dave retrieved the stuffed animal from the Toyota, turning off its lights at the same time. He saw the fresh crease on the front fender, running just to the beginning of the rear door, and he shuddered with the realization that the brush with the truck Kelly mentioned had been within a few inches of a fatal collision. When he returned, Kelly and Allie were already asleep, and he placed the toy on the pillow next to the girl.

CHAPTER FOURTEEN

WELL after midnight, Dave lay in bed and listened for the sound of breathing on the other side of the wall that separated him from Kelly and Allie. His head lolled onto his chest, but his eyes remained open. Then he heard feet padding outside the door, and a moment later he felt Kelly's breath as she leaned over him, and then her lips on his forehead.

"I thought you would be asleep," she said.

"I tried, but I guess I was waiting for you."

"I think Allie will be okay, at least, until the morning. And I am glad that you were waiting." She reached her hand to the dream catcher, hanging above the bed. "I think I'm going to need this tonight, but it would be better if it were the giant, economy size."

She was still wearing the hooded sweatshirt she had traveled in through the unexpectedly chilly evening, and she now sat on the bed and lifted it over her head. She reached down and pulled off her sneakers. Then, she turned back the blanket and lay down next to Dave. She rolled onto her side to face him and bunched the pillow to rest her head.

"Michael, that man..." she began.

"You don't have to, now, I mean, if you don't want to."

"I don't. But I have to tell you that I think he's heading this way. He might even be here already."

"I'm not surprised," Dave replied.

She lifted her head off the pillow, and then she cupped his chin with her hand, squeezing her fingers gently against the sides of his jaw.

"Why not?"

"Because a piece of a receipt from the Runners Shop was found in the pocket of Charlie Williams."

She let her hand drop, and in the darkness of the room, he could see her head shake from side to side.

"I see," she said after a few moments, in a strained voice. "There seems to be no end to his surprises. Could it match the one you found?"

"It might. Do you have any idea?" he asked, and then he sensed her stiffen.

"No, why should I?" She was silent, and when she spoke again her tone softened. "I'm sorry. But I can see him only one way now, the way he was when he got out of that bed, and then after it was all over, you know, he tried to hug Allie, and she shrank from him. It's just, thank God, I got there in time. All I could think while I was driving was what was I going to do if I didn't find her, she's my only child, and I thought I had lost her."

"She's sleeping right in the next room." He knew as soon as he said these words that they sounded as hollow as water against the sides of an empty drum.

"Of course she is," Kelly replied. "The question is, how much of her did I bring back with me?"

John arrived as Kelly and Dave sat staring red-eyed at each other across the small table in the kitchen, neither one having the energy after a sleepless night to attempt to fix breakfast. John looked at them without offering a greeting, and then pulled the frying pan off the wall and placed it on the stove. He set a pot of coffee brewing, cracked some eggs into a bowl, added a dash of milk and salt, and then scrambled them.

"Hope you like your eggs this way," he said. "I'm a man of limited culinary skills, and you're getting the best of them right now."

"Any way will be just fine," Dave said.

Kelly stood up.

"You really didn't have to," she said.

"Have to has nothing to do with it. You two look like you've had a time of it. How's Allie?"

"Still sleeping," Kelly replied. "We spent the night checking on her. And as peaceful as she looked, I kept wondering what kind of dreams she was having."

John turned to her, spatula poised.

"There's no use trying to think like that," he said.

"That's what Dave kept saying to me. And then he'd get up and look in on her himself."

John served the eggs and coffee, setting a place for himself and Allie

"Do you mind if we talk some Frankie Asebou business?" John asked. "It might help, and anyway it's got to be attended to."

"Sure," Kelly said. "You start filling in Dave on whatever you have to tell him. I'll just go up to Allie's room for a second."

John placed his hand on her shoulder, as though to restrain her, but she pushed against it with her head turned toward the stairs. He took his hand from her shoulder and pressed it against her cheek.

"You go on, then, and see if she's awake. I hear she's been asking after me, or at least my fingers, and I'll want to see her as soon as she's ready." He watched as she ascended the stairs, and then he faced Dave. "I've made some progress, and the news is not entirely good." He reached into his shirt pocket and handed Dave the list of witnesses.

"I haven't had time to speak with any of these people, of course, but I know most of them. I've annotated their names. The pattern is very clear."

Dave studied the notes in John's surprisingly small and neat handwriting.

"Prostitutes and pimps," he said. "Any guesses on the others, that you didn't recognize?"

"They appear to be johns. With maybe a small-time dealer mixed in, for variety."

"And to provide a motive for Frankie's prostitution. All of this goes to her character, to show that she is capable of having the mindset, the *mens rea*, to commit murder."

"Who don't, under the right circumstances?" John snorted.

"So Heilman will assassinate her character, perhaps admit a degree of spousal abuse to provide motivation." Dave took a swallow of his coffee. "He probably figures he needs more to get a lock on this case. The physical evidence is unclear, even with the coroner's very friendly report. And he has problems. Like no murder weapon, the transport of the body from the scene of the shooting. A confession obtained under duress, which he probably won't be able to use."

"Maybe that's why he and Briggs are so anxious to get their hands on Robin."

"To testify against her mother, as an eyewitness. That would certainly give him what he needs, drive Frankie to another, admissible confession." He felt a pain begin behind his eyes, and he rubbed his forehead.

"There's more, isn't there?" John prodded. "Something about the child. I wouldn't be surprised."

"Yes," Dave said slowly, and the pain eased hearing John give voice to the thought he did not want to accept. "She told me her story, marginally coherent, with big spaces, some of which can be explained away. But I think she knows where the gun that shot Charlie is."

"Because she used it?"

"Maybe. I'd hate to think so. I'd rather try to get Frankie off, even though she might have been playing us all this time, might have known what her daughter did and has been protecting her." He stood up and walked to the coffee pot before he realized his cup was still half full. "It's a hell of place to be," he said. "Who do I choose, the mother or the daughter?"

"Neither," John said as he got to his feet, "until we know more. I've got a lead on that damned truck. I've got to go see a man, who knows a man, who might be able to tell me where it is. I'll be back later."

Kelly, her face drawn, entered the kitchen. She took her seat at the table and lifted a fork full of eggs to her mouth.

"They must be cold," John said. "I could whip up some more in two minutes."

Kelly shook her head.

"They're fine. Allie's still sleeping. I just wanted to sit with her for a while."

"Maybe the next time, Allie will want to take that walk with me that she was talking about."

Kelly's face relaxed into a small smile.

"I'm sure she'll want to see you. I'll tell her that you were asking for her."

John had been gone for a few minutes when Kelly brought her coffee cup down hard on the table.

"If he shows up here, I'll kill him. I want you to know that, and to understand that I am perfectly serious. You didn't see him like I did, or hear how he told me that he was going to spend time with Allie again, or see the look in Grace's eyes when I put her on that bus." Her eyes were bright with fury. "And I have been thinking about why he might be coming here, other than Allie, and all I can tell you is that he seemed to have gotten himself quite an education while he was in prison. But please don't ask me about him again. Just tell me if you see him." She stood up.

"If you're going to check on Allie, I'll go with you."

They walked up the stairs in silence but together.

Dave sat in the Caddy in the parking lot behind the county courthouse as he waited for Livonia to show up with Robin. He tuned the radio to the local public broadcasting station and settled back behind the wheel. The elegant and mournful melody of Bach's Air in G floated out of the speakers, and he reached for a cigarette in his pocket, as he used to do before he quit three years before. The gesture, though, remained and he performed it as a kind of ritual farewell to the habit he still regretted breaking. He patted the flat surface of his shirt pocket. A moment later, he heard the loud pops of exhaust gases finding an exit through a spacious hole in a muffler. He turned toward the noise and saw Livonia's station wagon come to a stop next to him. If anything, Livonia's car appeared to be even dustier than the last time he saw it.

At first, he could not see anybody in the car but Livonia. Robin's head, though, lifted from beneath Livonia's cradling arm, and the girl offered a shy smile.

"She's trying to be brave," Livonia said when they were standing between the two cars. "She's a good, strong child, but she is very afraid. If she did not want to see her mother so much, I would not have been able to bring her. As it is, I had to do a lot of talking to get her into the car."

"I'll make it as easy as possible. The prosecutor wants her cooperation so he probably won't push too hard."

"Humph!" The sound exploded from Livonia's mouth. "The child's cooperation to hang her mother."

"But he's also an impatient man," Dave continued. "If he starts to force the issue, I'll pull Robin out of there."

"I want to go in with her," Livonia said.

"I don't think you can, nor do I think it is a good idea. Robin has to be able to tell her story on her own. If this thing goes to trial, you won't be able to sit up there on the witness stand with her."

"It's, all right, O-ko-mes-se-maw," Robin said, her voice soft and broken by a tremor. "I can't tell more than I know, right?"

"That's right, child," Livonia said. "That is all you can, or should, do."

Heilman rose from behind his desk to greet Dave and Robin as they entered his office. He extended his hand, but Dave's eyes stayed fixed on the court stenographer sitting with her machine next to Heilman's desk.

"What is this?" he asked.

Heilman kept his hand out for a moment, and then dropped it.

"Just for the record, Mr. Abrams. You understand, don't you?"

Dave placed his hand on Robin's shoulder. She was standing stiff, her back muscles tensed.

"No," Dave replied. "I do not understand. You are withholding a very ordinary, one might even say human, privilege to this child, that she be permitted to see her mother. I reluctantly agreed to an informal chat with you so that you would let her make that visit." He glanced at the stenographer whose fingers played over the keyboard.

"That'll be enough. For now," the prosecutor said to the stenographer, who began to stand. "I said, for now." He motioned for the reporter to sit down again. The young woman looked confused and uncomfortable, but took her seat, her hands held stiffly at her sides as though unaccustomed to that position when the keyboard was so close to her.

"Off the record, and with me present throughout," Dave insisted.

Heilman shrugged.

"Of course," he said and nodded to the stenographer. With a sigh that shook her thin shoulders, the reporter folded up her machine, and left the office.

"Any other ground rules, Mr. Abrams?" Heilman asked.

"Go ahead. I'll tell you if I have a problem."

"I'm sure you will." Heilman motioned to a chair in front of his desk. "Do you want to sit down, Robin?"

"No," she replied. "I do not feel tired, and I do not think this conversation should take very long."

Heilman's face showed bemused interest.

"All I want to know," he said, "is what you saw or heard on the night your father was shot."

"I have already told all that to Mr. Abrams. Don't you two guys talk to each other?"

"When we talk," Heilman replied, "there tends to be a lot of static."

"I noticed that," Robin replied. "You should learn how to talk more clearly."

"Well, then, tell him what you told me," Dave urged.

"I was hiding in my bedroom," Robin began. "I heard my mother and father fighting. They often did, especially when one or the other one had been drinking. I heard loud noises, glass breaking, something like an explosion. Mr. Abrams asked me if I heard gunshots, and I told him I am not familiar with that sound. It could have been, but it could have been something else. I got scared and climbed out of my window. I looked into the living room from another window, and I saw both my mother and my father on the floor. I thought they were asleep. They would often fall asleep at times like those. Then I took a long walk to the beach, where I always go when I am upset or scared. The sound of the water against the beach, and the stones, from the shell of Makinak, the Great Turtle, make me feel more comfortable." She paused as Heilman's face registered confusion. "That is a story Grandmother tells me."

"Thank you," Heilman said.

"That is all I have to say," Robin said. "I fell asleep on the beach, and when I woke up, men took me to the hospital."

"You were sitting next to your father's body," Heilman said, pushing a little.

"No," Robin replied. "I was near it, not next to it, and I did not know it was there until I woke up."

"You have no idea..." Heilman started.

"No. I do not."

"That will have to be all for now," Dave said.

The phone rang, and Heilman picked it up. Dave watched the prosecutor's face brighten as he muttered a series of increasingly enthusiastic affirmatives into the mouthpiece. Then he hung up the phone. "Abrams, I told you when we first talked about this case that I had other fish to fry. That's what that call was about. The biggest fish, one Leaping Frog, is ready for the pan, so let's get our business settled. You know what I want, and I'm prepared to be reasonable about a plea." He gestured toward the door of his office. "You can head over to the prison. I'll call ahead and tell them you are coming. Frankie should be waiting for you when you get there. See if you can talk some sense into her."

The same cheerful matron led Dave and Robin to the jail visitor's room.

"You should have seen her eyes light up when I came to get her to tell her that her daughter was coming to see her. You wouldn't have believed it was the same person." She placed her hand on the doorknob. "You know the routine, Mr. Abrams. I'll be waiting outside until you're done. She won't be any trouble today. I'm sure of that."

"But today," he said, "I'll wait with you. I think this should be private, don't you?"

The matron beamed.

"Why, of course. I just thought, you know, that you might want to hear what they have to say to each other."

"No, I don't think so," Dave said.

The matron leaned toward Dave so that he could hear her lowered voice.

"I think it'll do her a world of good to talk to her daughter."

"I hope so," Dave said. He pushed the door open and watched as Robin walked, without haste, toward her mother, who was waiting on one knee, arms opened and stretched outward to receive her daughter in an embrace. Dave closed the door.

Dave felt a nudge on his shoulder and turned to see the matron.

"It's time. I was told no more than half an hour." She shrugged. "I'm sorry. I understand. I have a daughter myself."

"Five more minutes," Dave said.

"Can't do it," she replied. "I have to feed that daughter." She knocked on the door, and a moment later Robin emerged, her face tense.

"Thank you, Mr. Abrams," she said. "It was good to be able to talk to my mother." She seemed close to tears. Dave took her arm, and she permitted herself to be drawn to him. "It is very difficult," she said.

"I have to talk with your mother for a minute. Can you find your way back to Livonia."

"Don't worry, Mr. Abrams. I'll take her down," the matron said. "And then I'll be back for you. Mr. Heilman didn't leave any orders about you seeing Mrs. Asebou."

"I have the right..." Dave began.

"Don't tell me about it, and don't take too long. I'll walk slow on my way back." She opened the door, and then guided Robin down the hall.

He expected to find Frankie more relaxed, but she held her body stiffly at the table.

"Frankie, we're not doing too well in this matter. I didn't want to intrude into your time with Robin, and we may be interrupted in a few minutes. I need a couple of answers."

"You have my confession."

"Do you want to go to jail for a long time for something you didn't do?"

"If I don't, who will? My daughter?" Her face hardened even more. "I may be inside here, but I can see what is going on. Robin told me how you questioned her, and the prosecutor. Maybe you're both doing your job, but she's only a child. My child."

"I don't think Robin killed her father," Dave declared. Afterward, he would not be able to decide why he made that assertion. He could have been trying to loosen Frankie's tongue. Or perhaps he wanted to believe it to be true. Frankie's expression softened for a moment, but then turned skeptical.

"Look, Mr. Abrams. I never asked for your help. Never asked for you to be my attorney. It just happened. I guess I think you're on my side. So I'm going to tell you one more time. My confession is what I remember. I shot at the fat bastard. I saw him stagger and fall. I passed out. I don't know anything more than that. You saw how I was later. If I didn't kill him, I don't know who did."

Dave did remember how she looked, how the dried blood ran down her thighs, and how her breasts bore the bruises of Charlie's rough fingers, and her face the marks from his fists.

"Maybe you just want to think that you killed him," he said.

A smiled played on the corner of her lips.

"That's the first thing you have said to me that shows me you might understand." The smile disappeared. "If you do, you'll know that my daughter is all that means anything to me."

"She all but told me that I couldn't do much more than plea bargain for her," Dave said. He, Kelly, and Allie were sitting on the porch after dinner. Kelly glanced first at Allie, and then at Dave.

"I'm sorry," he said.

"We can discuss that case, later," Kelly said.

Allie flushed.

"You mean after I'm in bed. I'm not a child, you know, and I'm not so fragile as you seem to think I am."

"I thought," Kelly said, "that we could find something more pleasant to talk about, like how calm the bay is tonight. I thought later maybe we could pull our chairs out on the lawn and look for the meteor shower. There's supposed to be one tonight, starting at about ten o'clock."

"I thought that was supposed to be tomorrow night," Allie replied, her voice sullen. "I guess I'll go inside to listen to the news on TV. We wouldn't want to miss that shower." She stalked through the door and into the house.

"You might as well tell me what you meant now, about Robin," Kelly said. "I just don't know how to draw the lines for Allie. She doesn't realize what a shock she's just experienced."

"I know. If you want to go in with her, we can talk about this some other time."

Her face wrinkled in irritation.

"Didn't you hear what I just said? I'll leave her alone, for now. Talk to me about Robin."

"It's simple. Her story is too clean. She tells it straight, each time the same way. And her manner is so controlled. She had Heilman backing off, with that quiet, insistent voice of hers. But it's all too neat. And there are gaps. Heilman saw them. I know that."

Kelly glanced over her shoulder and into the small front room of the house where Allie sat watching television.

"Such as?"

"The biggest one is, how the hell did she get to the beach? It's a longer walk than she lets on, though not impossible. And once there, how could she not take note of her father's arrival, even if she were asleep? He must have made a loud noise when he came crashing down from that cliff, even if she could have slept through the gunshots, which I doubt."

"Maybe she arrived after he was dumped."

"She would have seen him, lying there like a beached whale."

"Unless she didn't want to see what she saw. That's possible. And now doesn't remember any more than she's saying. That could be, too."

"I suppose. But there are other things, the missing gun, the missing truck, her missing sneaker. Somehow she knows where all those things are. I'm sure of it."

"She could be protecting her mother. Or think she is."

"Or it might go the other way around."

Kelly stood up and walked to the door. "If so, I'd do the same. I think I'll sit with Allie for a while." Dave nodded, and she walked into the house. A second later she was at the door. "I think you might want to see what's on the news right now," she told Dave.

Heilman looked as though he wanted to gloat, but managed to restrain the self-congratulatory smile that pushed against his cheeks and his lips. Standing next to him on one side was Sheriff Briggs, and on the other, looking distinctly uncomfortable as though unable to decide whether he should join in the congratulations or regret the stain on his people, was Deputy Crow. Heilman announced that he would be presenting a case concerning money laundering at the Ojibwe Casino to a grand jury in the morning, and that he was confident that months of painstaking investigation by a team composed of members from both his office and the sheriff's department would soon see their work fully vindicated. A reporter asked the prosecutor if it were true that evidence of the infiltration by organized crime of the casino operation had been uncovered.

"No, I can't confirm that," Heilman said.

"Can you deny it, then?" the reporter asked.

"No comment, and thank you," Heilman said, and strode away from the bank of microphones.

"Beautiful," Dave said. "Particularly that last part. I'll bet he doesn't have anything on that organized crime angle, but he let it seem as though he did, and only professional ethics stopped him from saying anything more."

"Well," Kelly offered, "at least you know why your little murder case is a distraction for him."

Allie shifted uncomfortably on the sofa, her face contracted in thought.

"I want to help. With Frankie's case," she said. "And I think I know how. I can get Robin to talk to me. At least, I could try. She probably doesn't know who to trust now. I know what that is all about. Maybe she'll open up to me."

"Don't even think about it," Kelly said.

"I won't," Allie replied. "I'll just do it. Right, Dave?"

Dave could not restrain the smile, but he said, "You get that straight with your mother, and then we'll see."

"We'll talk about it in the morning," Kelly said.

"Like we always do, right?" Allie replied.

"It's good to see you getting back to your old, difficult self," Dave said.

They had been in bed for a couple of hours when the phone rang. Dave clicked on the lamp, and picked up the phone.

"Mr. Abrams," a female voice said.

"Yes?"

"I don't know if you remember me. I work at the tribal administration building. You gave me your card for Mr. Leaping Frog."

Dave sat up. Kelly rolled toward him and opened her eyes.

"Yes, I do remember, Ms...."

"Bonnier."

"What can I do for you? It's very late."

"I know. I'm sorry. But I didn't know who else to call. We're in trouble, big trouble, and he seems to have given up."

"He, meaning your boss?"

In the background, Dave heard a loud knocking, followed by Ms. Bonnier's voice, mumbling as though she had her hand over the phone, and then a click.

"That wasn't Michael, was it?" Kelly asked.

"No, the woman from the administration building. Said 'they' were in trouble. Then something happened, maybe a knocking on the door, and she hung up."

"Where was she?"

"Don't know," Dave replied. He turned off the lamp. "We can try to get some sleep. Somehow I think we'll know where she was and why she was calling before very long."

CHAPTER FIFTEEN

DAVE was right. Within an hour, the phone rang again. "Abrams, I've got to talk to you." Heilman's voice was tense with anger.

"Are you mad?" Dave said. "It's three thirty. Call me in the morning."

"Now," the prosecutor said, "unless you want to find your name on the top of the list of suspects in a double murder."

Dave shook his head before responding.

"I might be half asleep, but I think you just said something absurd."

"Never mind. Somebody called in an anonymous tip. Which we responded to. And now we've got two bodies in a room at the Resort Hotel. Mr. Leaping Frog, and his companion, Judy Bonnier. One with her throat slit, the other with a knife sticking out of his chest. There was some damn porno movie on the television. And the last phone call recorded from this room was dialed to your number, the same one that's on the back of your business card, the same one I just dialed. So get your ass down here."

Deputy Crow was waiting outside of the front entrance to the hotel. As Dave stopped the Caddy, Crow strode over to the car and opened the driver's door.

"Mr. Heilman is waiting for you upstairs in the room."

Dave started to take the key out of the ignition, but Crow leaned in and grasped his hand.

"Don't worry about your car," Crow said.

"I always do," Dave replied. "A habit from living so long in places where you can't trust your neighbor."

"It'll be taken care of." Crow put his fingers to his mouth and whistled. A young man in a hotel uniform appeared. Dave got out of the Caddy, and the young man drove it away. Crow led Dave into the lobby. The elegant furnishing, all glittering glass and metal, was still brightly lit though it was now after four a.m. The deputy steered him to an elevator and punched number 12.

"This floor has the luxury suites. All of them with balconies and a view of the bay," Crow said.

The elevator slid to a silent stop, and the doors opened with just a whisper. Crow pointed to a room directly across from the elevator. He needn't have bothered, since the door was open and a technician from the coroner's office was gesturing to somebody in the room. All of the other doors on the corridor, save one, were shut. The one was open a crack, and Dave could just see the startled eyes of a woman, her face framed in her wildly disordered white hair, staring at him. He nodded at her, and she closed the door.

"She peeked in before we could stop her," Crow said. "She probably won't sleep again for some time."

The technician who had been standing in the doorway now backed out holding one end of a gurney. He pulled, walking backwards while another technicain pushed from the other end. Dave stepped aside so that the gurney could be wheeled onto the elevator. The body was covered with a drab gray blanket.

"Can I?" he asked Crow. The deputy nodded, and Dave lifted one corner of the blanket. His eyes first focused on the purplish skin along the long slash on her throat. Dried blood ran in a narrowing stream from the wound down between her breasts and gathered in her navel.

"Must have just nicked an artery," Crow said. "She probably bled to death. Recognize her?" the deputy asked, trying to sound casual, but not quite succeeding in eliminating the trace of eager curiosity from his voice. "This is Judy Bonnier, Leaping Frog's girlfriend."

"Yes, we've met," Dave said.

The technician pushing the gurney looked at the deputy.

"We'd like to move this one out of here," he said. "There's another one waiting for us, you know."

"Go right ahead, Conroy," Heilman said from across the hall. "And Abrams, if you don't mind, come right on in."

As Dave stepped toward the prosecutor, he again saw the door across the corridor open. A face, framed in white hair stared back at him from the open door, but then it disappeared and the door shut again, this time with an audible slam.

Inside the room Sheriff Briggs was kneeling down next to the other body. Leaping Frog was lying on his back. He was naked, and the handle of a knife protruded from his chest. His legs and arms had begun to lift off of the floor. A chair and a table a few feet away were overturned. A large screen television set, housed in a wall unit, was still on, but the screen was blank. The time on a DVD player flashed 12:00 a.m.

"Mr. Abrams, meet Mr. Leaping Frog. Or have you met before?"

"He was out when I called on him," Dave replied.

It seemed to Dave that Leaping Frog had been a handsome man in his late thirties or early forties. Now, his face was ashen, his eyes open, but the eyeballs rolled back behind the lids. Dried blood had splattered his flesh from neck to belly and gathered in a ragged pool six inches across around the blade that had pierced his heart.

"Been dead two to four hours," he said.

"Do you New York lawyers double as coroners?" Briggs asked.

Dave pointed to the legs.

"Rigor is starting," Dave replied. He stared hard at Briggs. "You pick up things along the way, if you pay attention."

The technicians returned with their gurney. They looked at the sheriff, and he nodded. They hoisted Leaping Frog onto the gurney, and then covered him with a blanket. The sheriff rose awkwardly to his feet.

"What we got here, Mr. Abrams, is one damned circus." Briggs walked over to the player and pushed a button. The screen filled with the naked bodies of two women and one man entwined on a bed in a knot of arms, legs, and torsos so that it was impossible to determine which body parts belonged to which person. All of them were moaning. He studied the screen for a few seconds and then turned the player off. "Jesus," he muttered under his breath, and shook his head slowly from side to side. "You wouldn't think human bodies could bend like that. Looks like it must hurt. Maybe that's why they sound like sick pigs in heat." He turned toward the bed. "Over there, was a young Indian woman with her throat slit." He reached into his pocket and withdrew a plastic evidence bag containing a business card. "This was in her hand. Her boyfriend was on the floor, as you saw him, and although I don't know when he died, I'm willing to bet that when we pull that knife out of his chest, it'll be a shiv, maybe with a six or eight inch blade, the kind favored by punks who don't like loud noises. We have overturned furniture with no blood on it, although there should have been some from one of these two."

Dave glanced around the room.

"You forgot to mention the champagne."

Briggs heaved his large body toward a cocktail table in front of the television, where a bottle of champagne sat, still beading in its ice bucket.

"It's full." He pointed to the two elegant, tall stemmed glasses. "They are dry. The desk clerk remembers taking an order for room service, about midnight."

"On the face of it," Heilman said, "it looks like Mr. Leaping Frog and his girlfriend were interrupted during one of their occasional trysts. Maybe they had seen the evening news, and knew their run was over. First they get angry and throw some furniture around, and then they change their minds and order the champagne. Somebody comes in and ends the party for reasons we do not yet know. That's a puzzle, as is the phone call, and your business card."

"I have talked to the woman," Dave replied. "Three times. Once at the tribal administration building when I was looking for her boss, and gave her my card, and once by phone a couple of days ago, only because she answers Leaping Frog's phone."

"Why him?" Heilman asked.

"It's not important. Just something to do with developing my defense of Frankie."

Briggs held up two thick fingers.

"That's two," he said. "By any chance did you speak with Ms. Bonnier tonight? Somebody from this room called your number. We've had this line traced since we've been aware that Leaping Frog regularly used this room for his private time with his mistress. So suppose you tell us about it."

"That was the third. She did call some time around one. Said 'they' were in trouble. Then there was noise in the background, and a click."

"That's all?" Heilman asked.

"All she wrote," Dave replied.

"I don't suppose you have any idea what she wanted," Briggs said with an encouraging nod.

"I can only guess. Like you said, probably had something to do with the fact that she and her boss had seen Mr. Heilman's announcement on television. She had my card, didn't know who else to call. But, of course, your guess is as good as mine."

"You had not said you would represent her, right?" Heilman asked.

"Of course not," Dave answered.

"Just being sure. Could be," the prosecutor continued, "you are getting a reputation hereabouts as the attorney for lost causes."

"There are worse things to be known for," Dave said. "And now, if you will excuse me, I have a breakfast appointment that I don't want to be late for."

Heilman waved his hand toward the door as though he were dismissing a recalcitrant student.

Deputy Crow was sprawled on a sofa in the lobby as Dave strode out of the elevator. The deputy's eyes snapped open as the elevator door shut.

"I'll get your car for you, Mr. Abrams," Crow said.

Dave looked toward the desk and saw the clerk turning the pages of a newspaper. The paper was upside down.

"I'll take care of it, deputy," Dave said.

Crow stifled a yawn. "Fine with me. The sheriff said I could go home once you left, and it's been a long day."

Dave strolled to the front desk, and out of the corner of his eye he saw Crow push his way through the revolving door. The desk clerk put down the newspaper.

"Anything interesting in the paper?" Dave asked.

The clerk glanced down and his face reddened. He was a young man with a thin face marked by acne scars.

"Not much," he said.

"About that champagne, ordered from room service," Dave began.

"I already told the sheriff." He glanced down at a notebook. "Ordered at 11:55. I remember that, because I had to jump on it. Room service isn't offered past midnight. Except in emergencies, like if somebody needs a prescription, or something."

"Some folks might think champagne constituted an emergency."

The clerk grinned.

"Yes sir. But we don't," he said.

"You wouldn't know who delivered the order."

He nodded.

"I called it into the bar, and then sent Kyle to pick it up."

"Did you see Kyle get the bottle?"

"No. He was about to finish his shift, but he was happy enough to take this order."

"Mr. Leaping Frog was a good tipper, I imagine."

"Yessir. He was." The young man's face darkened. "It is too bad about him, and," he hesitated, "about him and his friend."

"Do you know where I can find this Kyle?"

"Sure. He's my kid brother."

Dave heard the revolving door start to move. He pulled out his wallet and wrapped a twenty dollar bill around one of his business cards.

"Have him give me a call, will you? Local number on the back."

Crow was at his side. The clerk looked at the card and stuffed it and the bill into his pocket.

"Any problems?" Crow asked. "Your car is outside. I had the doorman call it up for you."

"No problem. I was just discussing current events with this fine young man. He told me he was thinking of going to law school, so we chatted about that."

"Is that so, Ralph? I thought you wanted to go into the hotel business."

"These kids," Dave said, "they change their minds a thousand times. You know how it is."

"No," Crow said, "I always knew where I was going. And right now it's home."

It was dawn as Dave drove up to his house. As he got out of the car, he turned to look at the sun rising over the waters of the bay. Usually, the gilding of the blue water brightened his spirit, but today the bright colors irritated his tired eyes and did nothing to improve his disposition.

Inside, John sat at the table. Hooper rested his head on John's thigh, as John scratched the dog behind his ears. Hooper turned toward the door as Dave entered, but did not get up.

"Fickle animal," John said. "Loyal to whoever is scratching his ears at the moment."

Dave saw that the coffee pot was half full, and he poured himself a cup. He glanced toward the stairs that led upstairs.

"Nobody answered when I knocked, so I figured I'd just wait," John said. "I didn't want to disturb you if you were sleeping in. I just fixed myself some coffee."

"We've had quite a night," Dave replied. He sat down and spooned sugar into his coffee. "I've just come back from the Resort Hotel."

"I'm not surprised, " John said.

"You heard?"

"I still have my CB set so I can pick up the sheriff's radio. What I heard is that Leaping Frog and a young woman were found dead in a hotel room."

"Yes, and she called here, probably right before she died. Heilman asked me about the call. They've had that line bugged."

"I can't make much sense out of all this yet," John said. "The reason why I came here this morning is that I have a good lead on that truck. I thought you might want to come along with me to check it out."

"Fine. I'll just go and check in on Kelly and Allie."

John stood and stretched and then walked across the kitchen to the stove to fill his coffee cup.

"No hurry," he said. "From what I understand, it's not going anyplace. As for Michael, I know a fellow..."

"You seem to know a lot of fellows," Dave said.

"Well, you live long enough and that's what happens, but this one might help us out, about Michael. This fellow is a corrections officer. He's worked in a lot of places. I'll give him a call, first thing, after we check out this truck."

Kelly and Allie were asleep with their arms thrown around each other, their heads on the pillow, their hair, thick and red, forming one disheveled mass against the white of the pillow case. Kelly had her arm across her daughter's body in a gesture at once careless and profoundly protective. Their intimacy struck him. He remembered how on a cold rainy night years ago, he looked in on his son and felt the warmth of the room against the sheets of cold water pounding the window pane, and how he had sat down on the edge of the bed to watch the gentle rise and fall of his son's breathing in his untroubled sleep, and then how he had leaned over to kiss his cheek.

A movement in the room brought him back, and he saw Kelly disengaging herself from the tangled bedclothes. Allie stirred and stretched as Kelly got out of bed. Kelly waited until she was sure that Allie was not waking, and then she padded to Dave.

"Looking in at you and Allie just now," he said, "for some reason, I thought of Jonathan."

"Maybe…" she began.

"Yeah, maybe." His tone came out more harshly than he expected. "I'm sorry. It's just I don't like to give myself false expectations."

"I understand," she said in a voice just above a whisper. Then after a pause during which she held his eyes, she continued in an everyday tone. "I thought I heard John talking to you."

"You did. I'm going with him to check out Charlie's truck," Dave said. "Maybe we'll find something."

Kelly turned to stare at her daughter, who was now tossing fitfully.

"She has a demon to exorcize, and I'm going to help her do it."

"Demons," Dave said under his breath, "can be damned stubborn."

CHAPTER SIXTEEN

KELLY invited the water to wash over her skin. Then, she lathered herself with soap. She ran the soap around her eyes, her nose, her mouth, and then down her body. Usually the touch of her fingers on her breasts caused her a mild arousal, a pleasant stiffening of her nipples, but at this moment she felt only as though her breasts, like the rest of her flesh, had been anesthetized by a thin but stubborn layer of analgesic dirt. She turned the water on to a hotter temperature, and the soap lathered more fully. Again she scrubbed her flesh, and then waited for the hot water to run out. When it did, she forced herself to stand beneath the icy stream, even as her flesh rebelled and she started to shiver uncontrollably. The water washed the soap off the front of her body, and she shifted her position so that it could splash off her back.

Above the steady roar of the water, she heard a knock at the door.

"Mom, are you alright? You've been in there for almost an hour."

Turning the water off, she stepped out of the shower. She still felt Michael's presence clinging to her as though it were a second skin, this one flayed from a dead serpent.

"I'm fine," she called through the door to Allie.

Allie entered the bathroom, wearing one of Dave's T-shirts as a nightgown. She had a towel wrapped around her hair. Kelly studied her daughter, her unblemished skin, her thin arms and lean legs. She drew Allie to her, held her for a moment, and then stepped back.

"What's that all about?" Allie asked.

"Just good morning," Kelly replied. "You'll have to wait a few minutes to get some hot water for your shower. I think I used it up."

"No wonder. You look like you've been submerged in a pool for days. Are you sure you're all right?"

For a moment, Kelly read the concern in Allie's voice as a precursor to the long process at the end of which the child takes responsibility for the parent, but the feeling passed as quickly as it had come. She was not ready just yet for a senior citizen home.

"Thanks," she said, adding a touch of irony to her voice. "I'm fine."

"Good. Because when I come out I want to talk to you about last night. About my father, and about trying to talk to Robin. Have you thought about that?"

"Yes," Kelly replied. "And I think that maybe it would be worth a try."

Allie smiled.

"I knew you'd come around," she said. "I'm going downstairs for a cup of coffee while I wait to take my shower. Would you like to join me?"

Kelly recognized that Allie was trying her adult mode, and she did not want to disappoint her.

"Sure," she replied. "I'll be down in a minute."

She waited for Allie to go downstairs with an impatience disproportionate to the short delay. But ever since she had stepped out of the shower, she had been hearing car engines on the road, and she was sure one had stopped at the foot of the driveway and was waiting. She steeled herself to look out of her bedroom window. She peered through the window, down the driveway and to the road. There was nothing there. She heard the roar of an engine, and she waited, but no car appeared. She opened the window, which had been shut against the cool night air, and strained to listen. She heard and saw nothing, yet she knew he was out there, and not very far away.

Rolling his cigar between his fingers, John then took a deep drag. His eyes sparkled.

"You haven't looked this happy in years," Dave said.

"Never mind that," John replied, attempting without success to harden his voice. "Just keep your eye out for that turn. It isn't marked, but it's coming up soon. It'll be a two track on your right, about a quarter of mile after this orchard we're going by right now."

Dave glanced out of the side window at the lines of cherry trees, still burdened with fruit.

"Ferguson's place," John muttered. "Looks like he gave it up this season. He used to be a good farmer. But I've been watching him lose interest, not pruning the trees like he did, not mowing the weeds, or spraying, says it costs him more than he's getting paid. His place will be on the market before long, if it's not already."

The orchard ended and gave way to a hill covered in pines, spruce and maples, each elbowing the other for a place in the sun. At the crest, John nudged Dave's arm with his elbow.

"There, just up ahead, you see it? Where the road levels?"

"I do," Dave replied, and he pressed his foot lightly on the brake pedal. The Caddy slowed, and Dave steered it onto the two track.

"Better pull off to the side," John said. "We'll walk the rest of the way. You never know, she might be waiting for us, with a shotgun on her lap. She doesn't like company, unless she's invited them."

They started walking up the road, their feet raising a cloud of dust behind them.

"If she's waiting, she'll know we're coming," Dave said.

"That's the point," John replied. "To give her notice. That way she won't take as much offense."

They rounded a bend in the road, and John held Dave's arm. Ahead of them, they could see a small tent, perhaps large enough to sleep two. It was sitting off the ground on a plywood platform supported by cinder blocks on each corner. John pointed beyond the tent where a pickup truck was parked.

"I see it," Dave said.

A wisp of smoke curled above a Coleman stove, on the ground next to a straight-backed wooden chair. John stepped off the road and into a densely wooded thicket. Dave followed.

"Don't know quite what to make of it," John said. "She must be around here somewhere. Let's see if we can get a closer look at that truck."

They kept to the woods, circling behind the tent, stopping every few steps, but they could detect no movement. They reached the truck.

"Are you sure it's Charlie's?" Dave asked. The truck looked like dozens of others he had seen, a Ford, its original dark blue color now gray beneath a thick coat of dust, the metal blotched with rust along the bottom of its body. John pointed to the back window, which was patterned like a spider's web, a hole radiating cracks.

"That tells me it's his. That's a bullet hole, from a time he was drunk once and thought somebody was trying to steal his truck. Turned out there was a 'coon in the back scratching at an old blanket."

Dave hopped onto the bed of the truck.

"Like this one?" he asked, picking up a stained and torn blanket that seemed once to have had a design woven into it, but now looked more like a discolored rag. John was about to answer, when something fell out of the folds of the blanket. Dave stared down at the small object for a moment, and then took it into his hand. He held it out so John could see it.

"Well, I'll be damned," John said.

Dave studied the inside of the sneaker.

"Size seven. Do you think if we played the Prince, Robin might turn out to be our Cinderella?"

A blast exploded into the air. They turned to see a woman holding a pump action shotgun pointed toward the sky. She jerked the handle on the cartridge tube back and forth expelling the spent shell, then lowered the weapon so it pointed directly at them.

"Good morning, Patsy," John said, lifting his hand to his head as though he would tip his hat, if he were wearing one.

Patsy nodded, but she continued to level the shotgun at them.

190

"Better get down," John said.

Dave shoved the sneaker into his pants and hopped off of the back of the truck. He and John walked toward the tent. Patsy followed their progress with the shotgun barrel and then joined them. She broke the shotgun, placed it on the ground, and sat down on the chair in front of the tent.

"A girl can't even take a minute to relieve herself without folks showing up," she said. Her voice was soft, with a touch of a lisp, and she was smiling as she leaned over and cracked two eggs into the skillet on the stove. A few strips of bacon sizzled in the same pan. She straightened up and brushed back a couple of strands of her abundant black hair from her forehead. Her hair fell to her shoulders and looked as though it had not seen a brush or comb in several days. She was wearing a thin print dress that could not comfortably contain her ample figure. She had bright green eyes to go with her black hair. Her face had once been pretty, but now was bloated and blotched from hard times. Still, it was not hard to imagine that some years earlier, Patsy had been a very attractive woman.

"Well, John aren't you going to introduce me to your friend? And what's he got in his pants that he don't want me to see?"

"I'm Dave Abrams. I'm representing Frankie Asebou."

Patsy moved her head to indicate she already understood the connection.

"And this," Dave said, "is a child's sneaker. I just found it in that truck. I was wondering how it got there."

"Haven't any idea," Patsy replied. "But I don't take kindly to folks nosing around my property."

"We noticed," John said. "You can blame me. I told him I didn't think you would mind, seeing as how it's not your truck anyway."

"Then what's it doing sitting on my land?"

"That's exactly what we were going to ask you, Patsy," John replied. "That's Charlie's truck. You know it, as well as I do."

"It was, but it ain't now. It's mine."

"Did he give it to you, then?" John asked.

"In a manner of speaking."

"Was that before or after he got himself shot, over at Peterson Beach?"

"I've done business with all kinds of men, in all kinds of conditions," Patsy smiled, "but I don't ever recall doing anything with a dead man."

"Was it a gift, then?" Dave asked.

"Let's say it was more like an inheritance." She leaned over and lifted first the eggs, and then the bacon, onto a plate that was next to the stove.

"You'll have to excuse me," she said. "It's my breakfast time, and I only have one plate."

"We need to know how that truck came to be here," John said.

She glanced down at the shotgun.

"Come on, now, Patsy. You know you're going to talk to us sooner or later, here, or maybe in court, so why don't you just tell us now. Go ahead, eat your breakfast. We don't mind if you talk with your mouth full."

Patsy shifted her eyes back and forth between her shotgun and the fork in her hand. She stabbed a piece of the fried eggs and brought it to her mouth. She chewed and then licked her lips, slowly.

"OK, John. I knew somebody would be poking around here looking for that truck. I'm just as glad it was you."

"Were you with Charlie the night he was killed?" John asked.

Patsy brought another piece of egg to her mouth and nodded.

"Before," she said. "Let's get that clear right away. I don't know how he got killed. But I can tell you this, if I had done it, I would have blown his face off with this." She pointed at her shotgun. "I wouldn't have used no handgun, not for an oversized pig like Charlie."

"You said you were with him that night," Dave said. "Could it have been at the Harbor Bar, in Omena?" He paused, and then decided to go for it. "We have a witness who places Charlie, and a woman whose description fits you, there that night."

"Hell of a witness," Patsy muttered, her air of bravado turning to recalcitrant defiance, "who sees things that ain't there."

Dave glanced at John whose wrinkled face now formed itself into a cordial smile.

"Patsy," he said in a soothing voice, "don't be difficult. You know all we have to do is call the sheriff and have you taken in for questioning. He'll send out his technicians, and they'll find your fingerprints all over that truck. He'll ask you about Robin's sneaker, and he'll probably find some evidence that that truck was at Peterson Beach, and he won't be as gentle about it as we are. Besides, who do you want to help? Us, or Sheriff Briggs?"

Patsy turned her bright green eyes to John.

"I could tell you stories about that one, from years ago, before he got religion. I knew him then." The last words carried the full measure of her scorn.

"Then talk to us," John encouraged.

She looked down at her plate, shrugged, and placed it on the ground.

"I was with him that night. He came into the Harbor Bar, already plastered. He was laughing and boasting how his poor fool of a woman was passed out back at their place thinking she had killed him. He was showing people this big lump on his head where she had cracked him with a bottle before she shot him, or thought she did. He said it was the funniest damned thing that ever happened. Then he pointed to this scratch on his neck, and then that huge belly of his, and laughed and laughed, saying how drunk she must have been, he was standing not five feet from her, and all she could do was nick him. He was flashing money around and buying people drinks. So he bought me one, and then another." Her face was now hard. "We went off in the truck to the beach, after the bar closed. We were both pretty well lit. I think we fell asleep for a while. Then we talked about going down to the beach, but neither of us thought we could manage those stairs, so we climbed into the back of the truck. I started to smooth out that blanket, wondering if I'd be able to bear his weight on me, but I had plans for that money in his pocket. I figured he owed me from times before, which I don't want to go into right now. How the hell was I to know that the kid was hiding under the blanket?"

"And then?" John's voice was just audible.

She shrugged.

"The kid jumped over the side of the truck, and Charlie went after her, staggering like the drunken bear he was. He swiped at her as she went by. Maybe he knocked her sneaker off. I don't know. I was just trying to keep out of the way. And then I drove his truck here."

"That's all you know?" John asked. "Think hard."

"I don't want to get that kid in trouble. She's had enough with that man for a father."

"We're trying to help her, and her mother," Dave encouraged.

She scowled.

"Then you know the deck is already stacked against you and them, and I don't want to add another card to the pile. Oh, Christ. You want to know. That kid had a gun in her hand as she took off. That's what Charlie was trying to grab."

"Is that it, then?" John's voice was as soft as a whispered amen in church.

"Yes," she said. "That's it. Last time I saw him he was trying to catch up to the kid. I didn't wait around. Now, if you'll excuse me, I'll finish my breakfast. I like to eat alone."

"Do you know where to find her?" Allie asked.

Kelly shook her head. She was finishing a note to Dave, telling him that Heilman had called, and that she and Allie were going to try to talk to Robin.

"We'll think of something," Kelly said. "Maybe we'll start with Livonia."

"We could wait," Allie said, "until Dave gets back."

Kelly shook her head.

"Your father is out there somewhere. I don't want to be sitting here waiting for him to show up, jumping out of my skin every time the phone rings. We'll try the gift shop, or maybe the administration building."

"If that doesn't work, we could head into town, to the jail," Allie said.

"To talk to Frankie? I don't think that's possible."

Allie shook her head and explained "To wait outside. I think I heard Dave say that Robin could visit her mother every day now. If you were in jail, I'd be there waiting for visiting hours."

Kelly found herself smiling.

"You can be such a comfort sometimes," she said.

Both the gift shop and the tribal administration building were closed. Somebody had taped a handwritten note on the administration building door, "Closed Because of a Staffing Problem."

"Is that meant to be a joke?" Allie asked.

"I hope so," Kelly replied. She tried the door, and found it locked. She looked out at the parking lot and saw a pickup truck. "It looks like somebody might be here. Let's just take a walk around. Maybe we'll find another way in."

They circled the building, trying a locked door on the side. When they arrived at the rear, they discovered another door, but it too was locked. Kelly shook it hard, and then knocked her fist against it. There was no answer.

Across from the door was a dumpster, and beyond it a field filled with two-foot-high weeds.

"We're out of locked doors," Allie said. She glanced at her watch. "And we don't want to be late for Robin's visiting time."

"Right," Kelly said, but still she did not move. She turned back to the door just in time to see the handle move. A moment later it opened and out walked the one eyed custodian.

"It's you again," he said. "I was hoping your husband might come snooping around. I have something for him, but I didn't know how to get it to him. So I figured I'd just come out here, and see if he showed up. Put that sign up to keep other folks away."

"I guess it pays to be nosy," Kelly said, "and persistent. What have you got?

He gestured toward the dumpster.

"Trash?" Kelly asked.

"Underneath," he said. "They don't pick up the trash for another two days. I was here first thing when I heard the news last night, looking for a safe place. I thought about stashing it in my cleaning cart, but I needed something better than that, so I figured the dumpster would be good for a couple of days."

"What is the 'it'?"

The man didn't answer but broke into a trot to catch up to Allie who was headed toward the dumpster. He passed her, and when he reached the dumpster he threw back its lid and vaulted into it. He disappeared, but then he stood up holding a grease stained fast food bag. He hopped back out.

"It's in here," he said, holding the trash. "I took extra precautions." He pointed to the Burger King logo. "The others in there are from McDonalds. I checked. This way I'd know which it is." He handed the container to Kelly. It smelled of stale meat. A fly buzzed the bag and landed.

"Open it up," he said, his voice impatient.

Kelly lifted the bag, and the flies buzzed angrily. She swatted it with her hand, but it landed inside the bag next to the remains of a hamburger. Next to the hamburger, in a plastic baggie, was a small notebook.

"That's it," the man said. "I took it from Leaping Frog's office this morning, early, in case the sheriff came."

"The sheriff had a late night," Kelly said.

The man grinned crookedly.

"I guess he did. But I didn't want Briggs to have this. Figured your husband would know what to do with it."

She opened up the notebook and flipped through the pages. There were numbers and initials on each page.

"You'll figure it out, after a while," the custodian said. "It'll tell you lots of interesting things, like why Charlie Williams used to go to the bus terminal so often, when he never went nowhere."

Before Kelly could ask the questions she was forming, he closed the lid of the dumpster with a clang and trotted back to the building. She reopened the lid to toss in the bag and put the notebook in her purse.

"Let's get over to the jail," she said.

Dave dropped John off at his farm and drove home. His mind was sorting through Patsy's story, and so he at first did not understand why the farmhouse doorknob didn't turn. He stood there with his hand still twisting the knob, picturing Robin hopping over the side of the pickup truck, a gun in her hand, her huge father staggering after her. That part made some sense. She could have picked up the gun from the floor some time after Frankie shot at, and missed, Charlie. Why she was in the truck, or what happened after she hopped out of it, remained unclear. He could just imagine her holding the gun in her small hand as her father bore down on her, but his mind did not want to accept the image of her pulling the trigger. Still, it could have happened that way.

He opened the door with his key. He stepped inside and found Kelly's note on the dining room table. Hooper ambled in and lay down at his feet. He gave the dog a cursory pat on the head while he read the note. Placing it flat on the table, he tried to convince himself that he was comfortable with Kelly and Allie wandering about while Michael was undoubtedly not far away. He lost the argument with himself and reached for the phone to call John, but it rang before he could dial. The agitated voice on the other end sounded familiar, but he could not immediately place it.

"Mr. Abrams," the voice said, "this is Ralph LeBraun. Remember me? The desk clerk last night, you gave me your card. It's about my brother. We need to talk to you."

"I'm a little tied up right now."

"I'm just trying to do the right thing, Mr. Abrams. You see my brother never did deliver that bottle of champagne, like he told the sheriff. He got scared, so he didn't say what really happened. And now he's talking about getting on a bus."

"Tell me where I can meet you. I'll be there as soon as I can."

"He's afraid to stay here. He wants to meet you in a public place. There's a hamburger joint called Big Beef, as you come into town from the east."

"I'll find it."

"We'll wait for you there."

Dave pushed the button on the phone, and then dialed John.

"I've got a problem," he said. "Kelly and Allie are out looking for Robin, and I've got to talk with the desk clerk's brother who appears to have something to tell me if I can get to him before he hops a bus."

"And you'd like me to see if I can catch up with Kelly and Allie?"

"Yes."

"You didn't really have to ask. I was going to do it anyway after my friend filled me in on Michael's time in prison."

"Bad?"

"Worse than bad. I'll find them, and then I'll get them home."

Kelly and Allie arrived at the jail at ten-thirty, and found a parking place at the rear of the building. As she nosed the Toyota into the spot, her eyes scanned the lot. There were only a handful of vehicles, and none of them looked like Livonia's old station wagon or Michael's Camry. She remembered thinking that the car looked like one that would be owned by a respectable and prosperous businessman, and she recalled, too, the irrational hope that Michael was just that, although she knew his salary as a shoe store salesman could not support such a vehicle.

They had been waiting only a few minutes when Livonia's wagon pulled in next to them. The old woman looked through her window at Kelly, her face betraying no surprise, and she waved a greeting. Allie smiled, but Robin turned away. Livonia's door swung open with the sound of metal grating on metal. She got out slowly, and walked to the Toyota. Kelly began to push her door open, but Livonia gestured for her to remain in her car.

"We'll talk to you when we come back out," Livonia said. "Their time is too precious to waste any of it now."

Her tone was flat, as though she were stating a simple proposition of fact. Kelly smiled and nodded. Allie leaned out of her window and started to call to Robin who was walking toward the entrance of the prison, but Kelly touched her shoulder.

"Let's just wait. If we push this, we'll lose it."

Allie's face registered her impatience and she sank back against her seat.

"We're only trying to help," she muttered.

Allie slumped against the backrest and lowered her head to her chest. She closed her eyes, and did not hear the footsteps approaching until they were right outside her door. Then she snapped her eyes open in time to see his face inches from her own. Kelly had been a second quicker, and her arm thrust itself past her to reach the window button. The man's hand reached into the car, and Allie threw herself away from him and onto the seat. She buried her face against the worn upholstery, which smelled sweet from a piece of chocolate that had become wedged at the rear of the cushion a long time ago. She heard the driver-side door swing open, footsteps, and then her mother's voice in tones angrier than she had ever heard her use.

"Just get the hell out of here. This is a prison, you know, guards and cops all over the place. Maybe they can find space for you inside. Are you mad?"

His answer came soft as a whisper between lovers.

"But of course I am. Don't you know that yet?"

He smiled, an evil and arrogant smile, but then his face contorted in pain, and he pressed his palms against his forehead as though to squeeze the pain out. He stood like that for a moment, and then his facial muscles relaxed. He reached into his pocket and pulled out a bottle of aspirin. He popped four or five into his mouth and swallowed hard. His face again wore a wicked grin.

"Can the theatrics," Kelly said. "You haven't answered me."

"You ask too much of me," he said, his voice still intimate. "You always did." He held out the bottle. "Just aspirin. I've been having headaches. Maybe the climate doesn't agree with me."

"Or the company. You should listen to your body when it's telling you something."

"But that's just the thing. I always do." He replaced the bottle into his pocket. "You asked several questions. I will only answer one. I came here, because I am lonely for my daughter." He turned toward a car that was approaching. "I need years of her company to make up for all the time I missed."

Allie raised herself from the seat.

"How could you think that I..." she began, but he had his eyes on the approaching car. He trotted away in the opposite direction, toward his Camry, which was parked at the other end of the lot. As he was about to get into it, he lifted his open palm and blew a kiss.

The other car, an old Plymouth, drove toward Kelly and Allie. John leaned out of the window.

"I saw enough of what happened," he said. "Tell me the rest when we get home."

Big Beef had seen better days, unable to compete with the more modern fast food places. Dave remembered Kelly telling him that it used to be a drive-in, with waitresses carrying orders on trays that hooked onto open car windows. Now, the paint on its walls and ceilings was a fading off white, the linoleum was cracked, and the windows were covered with cigarette smoke residue. A ceiling fan struggled against the thick, hot air, and perspiring waitresses brought food to the customers sitting at Formica tables. At one of these, in the rear of the restaurant, between the door to the rest rooms and an ancient jukebox, positioned with their backs to the wall and their eyes staring at the entrance, were Ralph and his brother Kyle. As Dave approached, Kyle got up and walked into the rest room. Ralph gestured for Dave to sit down.

"He's really spooked," Ralph said. "And I don't blame him. Problem is, I don't know how to help him."

"What about your parents..." Dave began.

"Dead," Ralph replied without emotion, "a long time ago. I've kind of raised him."

A middle-aged waitress with a friendly smile dropped a couple of stained menus on the table.

"This place has a certain, unique atmosphere," Dave said.

"Believe it or not, the burgers are good. And cheap."

The door to the rest room swung open and Kyle took his seat next to Ralph. He was sweating profusely, more than could be explained by the warmth in the restaurant. He drained his glass of water and wiped his forehead with the back of his hand.

"Go ahead, Kyle," Ralph encouraged, "tell Mr. Abrams what you told me this morning."

"I didn't mean to lie to the sheriff," Kyle said. "I didn't know what else to do."

"Just tell it to me straight, now," Dave said.

Kyle took a sip from his brother's water glass, and then breathed hard enough to shake his thin shoulders. In contrast to his brother's cratered face, his was smooth, and it did not look as though he had yet begun to shave.

"Well, all right. I guess that's why we're here." He seemed to relax a little. "It's not for the food, no matter what my brother says about it."

The waitress ambled over again.

"I'll just have coffee, black," Dave said.

"Two cokes," Ralph said. "It's a little early for lunch."

The waitress scribbled on her pad, "No problem," she said.

"Well," Kyle began, "you know about the order of champagne for that room. It came right at the end of my shift, but I wanted to take it because I could get a good tip. Leaping Frog always seemed to have a lot of cash on him. So I picked up the champagne and I took it up to the floor. But when I got off the elevator, this guy stopped me in the hall."

"What did he look like?" Dave asked.

Kyle hesitated as though trying to remember, although Dave read the effort as false.

"Kind of ordinary," he said after a while. He spoke the words a little too fast.

"Try harder," Dave said.

Kyle closed his eyes. When he opened them, they held an expression of certitude.

"He had a scar." He ran his hand over his own cheek. "Just like this."

"Tell me what happened."

"Like I said, he stopped me. He said he was a friend of the party who ordered the champagne and he wanted to play a joke on them. He gave me a hundred dollar bill to let him deliver the order. I took the money and went home."

Dave stood up and took out his wallet. He placed a fifty dollar bill on the table.

"You can have a meal, or two, on me, if you decide you're hungry." He leaned across the table and grasped Kyle's shoulder. "Don't worry. You did the right thing telling me. I'll square it with the sheriff."

"What about the guy. I think he killed those people."

Dave looked at the boy.

"If he did, he's probably miles away from here. But I'll talk to the sheriff about sending out a deputy to keep an eye on you." He turned to Ralph. "A word?" Ralph got up and Dave steered him a few feet away. "I don't know if your brother is in immediate danger. I saw the bodies. The killer knew what he was doing, and so I'm puzzled why Kyle is still alive to tell us about him. Nonetheless, however you do it, keep him around until the deputy arrives. I'm going to need him later."

Ralph shook his head slowly from side to side.

"I can probably stop him from leaving, but he'll never agree to testify."

"I don't think he'll have to. The worst thing he'll have to do is maybe come in and give another statement."

"I don't know about that, either."

"Just do the best you can. And thanks."

The waitress returned and eased her heavy body between Dave and an empty table.

"I think my friends are ready to order now," he said.

As he left the restaurant, he tried to figure out why Leonard Asebou would have killed Leaping Frog and Judy Bonnier.

Then it occurred to him that there was somebody who might have an answer.

Her white hair was neatly coiffed today, but her nervous eyes were behind thick glasses as they looked past Dave at the yellow tape across the door to Leaping Frog's suite.

"Hasn't the sheriff spoken to you?" Dave asked.

"I was too upset that night. They said they'd get back to me, but they haven't yet. When they do, I could tell them about the two men I saw."

"Two?" Dave asked.

"Sure that Indian. He came first. Then the one with gray hair, and the big cross on his chest, he came second. When I heard all that noise, furniture being thrown around, that's when I called the police. They wanted to know who I was, but I just hung up and locked my door." As she spoke, her eyes shifted from Dave to the door of the room across the hall. She stepped back into her room.

"I think that's all I can remember," she said, and she began to shut her door.

"Just one more question, please," Dave said. "Do you wear your glasses all the time?"

"Only when I really want to see," she said, and pulled the door closed.

CHAPTER ⁻SEVENTEEN

KELLY and Allie were sitting in the Toyota when Dave drove up to their house. Their faces were a study in contrast: Allie's drained of all color, and her mother's dark with determination. John leaned against the car, attempting to look casual, but his revolver was clearly visible in his waistband. Allie did not respond to Dave's greeting, but Kelly did.

"Michael attacked her," Kelly said, her voice as hard as her expression.

"In the parking lot, outside the jail," John added. "I saw the end of it and got them home, but I can't get them inside, so here they sit."

Kelly glanced at Allie.

"She hasn't calmed down enough yet. She says she feels his hand on her shoulder."

For a moment a look of annoyance flashed on Allie's face.

"Mom. Don't talk about me like I wasn't here," she said. But the moment passed, and the color again drained from her face.

She lowered her head to her mother's breast and shook with sobs then pulled back and forced a smile. "I'll be all right," she said. "Why don't you tell Dave what happened, and in a little bit I'll go with you into the house. I just want to sit here for a while longer."

Dave started to open the door for Kelly, but she waved him away. She pushed the door hard and it swung on its hinges to its full extension, and then she twisted herself out of the car. She grabbed the side of the door as though she were going to slam it shut, but then she looked at Allie and closed it gently.

"That son-of-a-bitch," she muttered. "I was hoping when I heard your car drive up that it was him. John has his gun. And I would have used it on him. I wouldn't let John do it."

Dave tried to embrace her, but she pulled away.

"Just the same," he said, "I'm glad it was me."

She fixed him with her angry blue eyes. He waited for a softening of her expression, but none came. Dave began to say that it wouldn't do any of them any good to shoot Michael, but he didn't believe it himself, and even if he did, her eyes told him that she was not in the mood, probably would never be, to hear such a platitude, particularly coming from him.

"Then, let's see if we can figure a way to put him away."

"Where he can get the help he needs?" she snapped. "I don't want him evaluated by some psychiatrist who is going to say he should be put in an institution." She took a step closer to him. "Have you forgotten Bonita Mercado? Do you want me or Allie to wind up like they did?" Her face relaxed just a little. "At least she had the satisfaction of blowing that fucker's head off."

"No," Dave replied quietly. "In fact, I think of Bonita a lot. And I want to do it much better this time."

"Good. But you'll excuse me if I concentrate on Allie for now. I'm going to take her into the house, and stay with her for as long as I have to. And I want John, or his gun, I don't care which, to be here."

Kelly and Allie were upstairs, and Dave was sitting at the dining room table when John opened the door and poked his head in.

"Car coming," he said. His hand was on his revolver, but then he let it drop to his side. "It's Sheriff Briggs."

Dave reached the porch just as the sheriff did.

"How are you, Buddy?" John said.

Briggs nodded a greeting at John and then turned to Dave.

"Mr. Abrams. I'll get to the point immediately. You remember that piece of paper we were both discussing on my boat?"

"Yes," Dave replied.

""Well, you could have told me that the name of that store is where Michael Gallagher works, saved me some time, and the taxpayers some money on phone calls."

"I wasn't sure at the time," Dave said.

Briggs scratched his chin thoughtfully. "Well, I do appreciate that, so let me tell you what we now know. Got a call this morning from New York, the parents of a young lady, friend of your stepdaughter, that your wife's ex-husband had relations with, in Woodstock, Canada. They want to locate him, so they can bring some kind of civil suit. Seems they were told their daughter is at the age of consent. Makes you wonder how some people come to be parents, if they can't raise their kids any better."

"I wouldn't blame the girl overmuch," John bristled. "Michael Gallagher is a dangerous man. Just this morning he attacked my niece and her daughter. Right outside the prison."

"I'm sorry to hear that," Briggs said, "We can arrange protection for you, until this thing is over, which I trust, with your cooperation won't be too long from now."

John patted his revolver.

"That man will have to go through me before he gets near my blood."

"If you were anybody else, John, I'd take offense," Briggs said. "And even knowing you, the offer still stands. In fact I'll have Crow out here this afternoon."

Dave glanced at John, read the determination in his eyes, and said, "That'll be fine, sheriff. But talking about protection, we may need another man from your office. I have a lead, a very good lead, on the person who killed Leaping Frog and Judy Bonnier."

"I'm all ears, Mr. Abrams."

"I've got a witness," Dave said. "A very spooked witness. You'll have to trust me on that. I can't give him to you just yet. But the killer may be looking for him."

"Why not just bring him in? Protective custody."

"You could. But we might lose him. He's already got one foot out of here. If he even smells anyone coming his way, he'll be gone."

"Well," Briggs said. "I"ll see what I can do. But my department is already stretched pretty thin. I'll have to pull somebody in from vacation. Where's this witness at?"

"I'll have to set this thing up with his brother."

"Do. Now there is one thing you can help me with. I was hoping you might be able to suggest what connection there might be between Mr. Gallagher and Charlie Williams that would explain how that piece of paper wound up in Charlie's pocket."

"Well, sheriff, I don't know that I can establish that for you, but there does seem to be some sort of connection."

Briggs lowered his voice to a deferential tone. "I wonder if I might speak to your wife, about Mr. Gallagher. Maybe she can help us."

"No," Dave replied. "Not now. She's comforting her daughter. I'm sure you can understand that."

"Sure thing," Briggs said. "Well, I'll just radio in that protection order for Crow. He'll be out here shortly."

Dave watched the sheriff get in his car, talk into his radio, and then drive off.

"I'd like to think we're on the same side," he said.

"He does his job," John said. "But he's always got his eyes out for his own best interest, which not surprisingly coincides with the prosecutor's. Anyway, what I want to tell you is what I now know about Michael."

"Which is?"

"A very sad story," John replied, "but it has happened to better men than him. It seems that while in prison Michael made some new playmates. One of them was a friend of a friend of Mr. Charlie Williams. Michael was having some difficulty with the other inmates. That often happens with someone like him, you know, white collar criminal among harder sort. It can get pretty uncomfortable for a man like Michael, and this guy took him under his wing, so to speak. I don't know if he expected any special favors in return."

"And this guy was who?"

"Well, now that's where things get interesting. He was originally from up here. He got into trouble a couple of times, and then he moved on. Wound up out East and then in with Michael. A French Canadian named Edward Stanley. Folks around here just called him 'Big Ed,' for reasons that would be obvious if you saw him. When I knew him he was into pimping and a little bit of marijuana, small time stuff, but he was a nasty character. Oh, yes, and by the way. His best buddy here was Leonard Asebou. You remember him."

"Yes," he replied. "In fact, he seems to be popping up today. He's the one Kyle puts at the scene."

"Does he say Leonard killed Leaping Frog and his girlfriend?"

"No. Just that he was there. And he probably was. Because I had a chat with the woman across the hall. She's a bit difficult to follow. And her eyesight is questionable. But what I make of her story is that an Indian, could be Leonard, was there. But so was Michael. Her description of him, bad eyesight and all, is solid."

"Maybe this will help sort things out," Kelly said, as she walked onto the porch. She handed the little notebook to Dave. "I got it from that crazy, one-eyed custodian at the tribal administration building. He was hiding it in a Burger King bag in the dumpster behind the building. I don't know what's in it, but he seemed to think it was important." She crossed her arms in front of her chest and stared at Dave for a long moment and then walked back into the house.

"She'll be all right," John said. "I remember how tough she was as a kid."

"I don't think she's softened any," Dave said.

John held out his hand.

"If you don't mind, I'd like to take a look at that book."

Dave handed it to him, and he opened it. He stared hard at the first page, and then the second. He snapped the little book closed.

"Give me a little time. I think I can figure this thing out, " John said.

"Any ideas?"

"Well, yes. You see this looks like the little account books we'd sometimes come across down in Chicago. Some bad guys thought they were accountants, liked to keep very exact records, so they'd know if anybody was cheating them."

"Michael always liked numbers."

"Well, then, there you have it. Why don't you go in and see to Kelly, and I'll just sit out here on the porch, enjoy the view, watch for Crow, and study this book. You can send Hooper out for company, if you like."

John felt Hooper stir at his feet, and he lifted his eyes from the book. He peered down the long driveway, and then his hand sought the revolver in his belt. He got to his feet and opened the door.

"There's a car coming up the drive," he said.

Kelly and Dave looked at Allie, but neither moved. Then Kelly put her arm around the girl's shoulders, and directed her to the stairs.

"It's Livonia's wagon," John announced, and let his hand fall to his side. He opened the door and motioned for them to stay where they were. "Let me just see what she wants."

"I need to talk to her," Dave said.

"I know you do," John replied. "But it'll be better if you wait until I do."

Dave stood at the window, and watched as John walked to Livonia's car. The old woman and Robin got out of the car. Robin looked toward the window where Dave stood, and a moment later Allie joined Dave. Robin glanced at Livonia and then offered a brief, almost invisible smile. Allie waved, and this time Robin's smile lingered for a moment or two. In the meantime, John and Livonia had their heads together, apparently in animated conversation. Then Livonia motioned to Robin, and all three made their way toward the house.

"Let the children talk," Livonia said. "Alone."

"She can come up to my room," Allie said, and she took Robin's hand.

"I'd rather go back outside," Robin replied.

"I don't know if I like that idea," Kelly said.

Livonia closed her eyes for a moment, and when she opened them they were focused on Kelly.

"It is okay. I do not see him. He is waiting, and he is in great pain, like a wounded bear."

Kelly glanced at the window, then at John, and finally at Dave, who nodded.

"You're sure of this?" he asked.

Livonia nodded her head slowly but with purpose.

"Of course," she said. "We went to the beach so we could be sure of what we had to do before we came here, and we saw him, following us. He watched us at the beach, and he stayed there when we left to drive here. He did not follow us."

John opened the front door. "I'll just take a walk down the driveway."

"There is no need," Livonia said.

"I know," John said. "But you have your way of seeing, and I have mine."

John walked out of the door, and a moment later, Robin and Allie followed. He continued down the driveway, and they stood on the porch.

Allie studied John's retreating back until it disappeared around a curve in the driveway.

"We'll be okay out here," Allie said. "Uncle John will not let him by."

"He is old," Robin said.

"As is your grandmother, " Allie said.

Robin smiled and said, "Yes." Her expression turned serious. "But I have something I must tell you about my father."

Allie measured Robin's words. She did not want to appear too eager to pry.

"It is okay," Robin said. "O-ko-mes-se-maw knows what I am about to tell you, and she wants me to. She says it is the only way," she paused, and brought her arm in a sweeping arc, "to complete the circle. Do you see? It is important that you do."

"Yes, I think, no, I know I do. That man out there, who you saw, my father, has come back into my life, and he is no longer my father," Allie said.

"Then you have lost him while he lives, while I lost mine years ago, and then again just a short time ago."

Allie understood.

"Does your mother know?"

Robin bowed her head, and she seemed to be fighting tears.

"I have told her. I did so again today. She does not want to listen. She says she will go to jail, and I will live with O-ko-mes-se-maw. It will be better that way, she says. But I do not think so."

Allie sat down on the edge of the porch and beckoned for Robin to join her. Robin sat down beside her.

"We saw what your father did today, in the parking lot."

Allie shivered, and Robin put her arm around her.

"It must be terrible," Robin said. "And there must have been other times."

"Yes," Allie replied.

"You do not have to tell me anymore. I know that you will understand my story."

Livonia had remained standing inside with her back to the window.

"We will go to the beach, after they have talked," Livonia declared after minutes of tense silence.

"Afterwards," Dave said slowly, "I will want you to tell me what Robin has told you about the death of her father."

Livonia shook her head.

"She must do that herself," she said.

Dave studied the hard wrinkles on the old woman's face. It looked like the weathered stone on the ridge of a mountain that has endured the shifting winds of centuries without losing its essential character.

"I'll take the point," John said. He slid behind the wheel of his Plymouth and laid his revolver on the seat next to him. Dave held the Caddy door open, and Livonia, Allie, and Robin slid into the back seat. The sound of a car engine drifted up from the road, and they all stiffened. Kelly had her hand on the passenger door, and now she turned as though to shield Allie in the backseat. She saw John's hand slide along the seat toward the revolver. A moment later, a car appeared. It was Deputy Crow's cruiser. He got out with a glance at John, and he raised his hands.

"Things a little tense out here?" he said.

"We're heading to Peterson Beach," Dave replied. "It might be a good idea for you to follow along."

"No problem," Crow said. "The sheriff said I wasn't to let your wife and daughter out of my sight. I'll just radio in to tell him where we're going."

CHAPTER EIGHTEEN

THE day was dark and cloudy with a brisk breeze blowing gray clouds in front of the sun. Kelly shifted herself uncomfortably in the passenger seat. Dave thought she looked as though she couldn't get comfortable in her skin. He sought words of comfort that would not come. He leaned out of his window and signaled John to begin.

John's Plymouth lurched forward ahead of a cloud of black exhaust, and Dave put the Caddy into drive and eased it down the driveway. In his rear view mirror, he saw Crow's cruiser move in behind him.

"They will be waiting," Livonia said with a shudder, "at the beach, for Robin, and for Allie."

Dave caught the plural pronoun.

"I thought we were going after an 'it'," he said.

"The gun will draw them," Livonia said, "all of them."

Dave followed John into the parking lot at the beach. In the far corner of the lot, he saw a dark gray Camry. Kelly clutched his arm hard.

"I see it," he said. "I'll go tell Crow."

When he got to the cruiser, the deputy was on the radio. Dave pointed to the Camry.

"I just checked with Briggs," Crow said. "I can't see the license plate, but we have reason to believe that that car might belong to Mr. Gallagher."

"My wife says it does," Dave replied.

Crow got out of his cruiser and unsnapped his holster. "I'll just go take a closer look."

John, revolver in hand, was already walking toward the Camry, but Crow waved him away. John hesitated, and then retreated to the Caddy.

"He can handle it," Dave said to him.

"Not the point," John muttered.

"I know," Dave replied.

They watched Crow, his gun drawn approach the Camry and then call out words they could not hear. The deputy stood still for a moment, and then he circled the car, pausing at its rear to study the license plate. He waved to them, and headed back.

"Nobody in the car," he said. "I'll run the plate."

Kelly got out of the Caddy.

"You don't have to," she said. "It is his."

Crow's face showed irritation.

"That's not exactly a unique model," he said.

"But it is his," Livonia said from the back seat. "He and Charlie are both here."

Crow seemed as though he wanted to say something, but just looked at the women.

"I'll just check it out," he repeated, and walked to his cruiser.

Dave nodded and then he made his way to the edge of the parking lot, defined by the wooden railing that Charlie Williams fell through. It had not been repaired. Instead, a yellow warning notice was posted next to the broken railing. He peered down at the beach, and felt jostled as Kelly reached his side. Robin stood in front of the notice for a moment, and then turned her eyes to the beach below.

Livonia joined Robin.

"We will go down first," Livonia said. "Give us a couple of moments."

Crow trotted to the head of the stairs and appeared confused.

"Would somebody care to fill me in?" he asked. "The license plate checks. That's Gallagher's car." He gestured toward Livonia and Robin, now slowly descending the stairs. "But where are they going?"

"To recover a piece of evidence that might unlock the Charlie Williams case," Dave said. "I'd appreciate it, deputy, if you kept your distance and your eye out for Mr. Gallagher."

Crow shook his head.

"Patience," Dave said. "Mr. Gallagher is not interested in them, but he is after my wife's daughter. Remember, that's why you're here." Crow nodded his acquiescence, but then he pointed toward the water. A rowboat, with a huge outboard engine on its stern, bobbed uneasily on the gentle swells, thirty yards or so off shore. A man sat in the boat holding a fishing pole.

"I wonder what he expects to catch," Crow said.

Kelly's eyes, however, were fixed on a rough path that led down to the beach not far from the wooden stairs. The clouds had thickened, casting a gray gloom over the beach, but a shape was just visible, about a third of the way down, moving through the cedar trees that flanked the path.

"It's him," Kelly said. "I know it is."

Allie shrank against her mother, and Crow stared in the direction Kelly indicated.

"I see something there. I'll head him off at the bottom." The deputy started down the wooden stairs, taking them several at a time.

"I'll just go up to the top of that trail." John said, "and make sure he doesn't come back up."

"We might as well do what we came for," Dave said to Kelly, "unless you want to wait in the car with Allie."

"No," Allie said. "I have to go down there, with Robin."

Kelly hesitated, her eyes still looking for the moving shadow that now seemed to have disappeared.

"Maybe it wasn't him," she said. "We'll go down."

They found Livonia and Robin crouched at the back of the beach where the stony surface met the cliff. Livonia stood up and beckoned Allie to come. When she did, Livonia walked to Dave and Kelly.

"Let the children do this," she said.

Crow trotted back from a point where the trail came down to the beach.

"He didn't come down, and I don't see a sign of him."

The adults watched as Robin and Allie spoke in whispers for a moment. Then Robin nodded and Allie embraced her. A moment later, Robin reached down to where two fallen logs seemed to form a point aimed at a mound of fossil stones, just slightly elevated from those around it. She removed a layer or two of the stones, and pulled out a revolver. She held it by its handle as though she did not want to touch any more of it than she had to. Crow strode toward her, an evidence bag in his outstretched hand, and Robin stepped back.

"It is okay, ne-ne-tchaw-nes. Give it to him, my child."

Robin handed the gun to Crow, and the deputy turned to Dave.

"She says she shot her father with that weapon," Dave said.

Crow's face started into surprise.

"Are you sure?" Crow asked.

"Fairly," Dave replied. "When you run a ballistics test on it, we'll know."

A shot rang out, followed by a crashing sound coming from the path where the figure had disappeared. A moment later, the figure appeared on the beach. The sky was now an angry black, and lightning flashed moments before a clap of thunder. A shaft of light bounced off something on the figure's chest.

Michael broke into a run toward them. A second later, John, his revolver swinging in his good hand, emerged onto the beach. He paused to take a breath, and then he started a measured trot after Michael. As Michael got closer, they could see that his eyes were fixed on Allie. She threw herself against Kelly. Crow, his weapon drawn, stepped in front of them. Michael was now within twenty feet. Allie broke away from her mother and started to run toward the water, with Kelly and Dave on her heels. The man in the rowboat put down his fishing pole and stood up. He held a hunting rifle in his hands. Allie stumbled, and Kelly reached to steady her. They both fell. Michael glanced at the man in the boat and continued toward them. Kelly staggered to her feet and stepped in front of her daughter. Crow cut toward Michael from one side while John closed in behind him. Dave placed himself between Kelly and Michael, who was now within a few feet.

A sound rumbled like thunder, but it was a helicopter lowering above the beach. A spotlight came on from the belly of the helicopter, focused on Michael, who stood still, blinking in the light, which flashed off the crucifix on his chest. The man in the boat raised the rifle to his shoulder.

"Gallagher," the sheriff's voice floated down from the helicopter. It crackled and almost broke in the roar of wind and surf. "Gallagher, just stand where you are. Nobody needs to get hurt here."

Michael did not turn to the voice. Instead, he pointed his automatic pistol at Allie. Then, he waved it at the others.

"Back off," he demanded.

Nobody moved. Michael cocked the hammer. Its loud click seemed to fill the beach.

"Do it," he demanded. "I want my daughter."

Kelly pushed Allie back and stood in front of her.

In one quick motion, Michael had his arm around Kelly's neck and he spun her toward him, so that she stood like a shield in front of him.

He raised his pistol to her head. "Be still," he said. He reached to his neck with his free hand, and pulled off the crucifix. "This for my daughter," he said. "Here, deputy, take it. It's the best deal you're ever going to be offered." He glanced at the man in the boat. "Do it now, deputy."

Crow extended his hand, and Michael held the crucifix over it.

"Allie," Michael said, "come to me."

"Never," Allie said.

With an expression of great sadness on his face, Michael shook his head. Then he brought his hand to his eyes, and winced as though in pain. In that second, Kelly jerked his gun hand away from her head, and freed herself. The crucifix fell onto the stony surface of the beach. Kelly threw herself on Allie, and mother and daughter tumbled to the ground. Michael lowered his weapon, and reached for the crucifix. A shot rang out, and the fossil stones at Michael's feet shattered.

The shot came from the man in the water. The boat rocked on a wave as he pulled the trigger. The man sighted again, but the boat still pitched. Michael glanced at Kelly and Allie on the ground and then at the man in the boat.

"We're not through," Michael said to Kelly. He aimed several shots at the figure in the boat, but he was too far away.

The helicopter began to lower. The man in the boat lifted his rifle, and as the boat settled at the end of a roll, he pulled the trigger. Again the ground behind Michael exploded into fragments of rock. Michael raised his pistol and fired until he shattered the floodlight in the belly of the helicopter. The sky's blackness now shrouded the beach. Dave leaned over Kelly and Allie. Michael turned and ran toward the steps. John and Crow stumbled after Michael, but then John staggered from the impact of another shot from the man in the boat. He fell to the ground, clutching his left arm.

"Go on after him," John said to the deputy, and then he stared out at the boat. As if in response, the engine on the back of the rowboat roared into life, and the boat headed out into the bay. Crow resumed the chase, and Michael stopped long enough to get off a couple of shots at him, and then he was gone, up the steps to where his car was parked.

Livonia looked hard at the sky, which began to lighten as the storm clouds drifted away. She shifted her glance to the water where something was standing in the shallows.

Suddenly a strange, barking laugh broke the silence. All but Livonia started at Michael who was now standing at the top of the stairs, his head thrown back, his mouth open and his lips moving in a silent utterance that could have been a curse or a laugh.

Livonia pointed toward the water.

"Au-dje-djawk," she said, "the heron."

The shape now rose from the water's surface, its wings beating hard above its body, and then it soared into a graceful, swooping loop directly at them. It came down almost to their level, and then, just as it was upon them, it again worked its powerful wings, screeching its horrible laughing call. Rising above them, it completed a great circle that took it far out over the water.

Livonia lifted her wrinkled face to the sky and let the rain that was just beginning to fall cascade onto her face. She strained her head even further back, opened her mouth and captured the rain.

"Are you okay?" Dave asked John. The old man looked at the blood staining his shirt.

"Yes," he said. "It's nothing much."

Crow joined them.

"I couldn't catch him." He looked about on the ground. "The crucifix?" he asked.

Nobody responded.

"We'll have to find it later," he said.

"Don't you have to radio in?" John asked.

"Sure. But don't go anywhere without me," Crow replied.

As he walked away, John moved his foot, bent down and picked up the crucifix.

"I've got a feeling about this," John said.

Robin seemed to be stretching her spine to its fullest extension, and yet she looked too small for the chair in front of Heilman's desk. The stenographer's hands were poised over her keyboard, as they had been the last time. She looked at Heilman, who turned a questioning face toward Dave.

"Okay," Dave said. He pointed to the plastic envelope containing the revolver Robin had taken from beneath the stones at Peterson Beach. "Robin, tell us what happened that night."

"Everything I told you before was the truth," she said. "I just did not finish the story because I was afraid and because I had forgotten. Grandmother says I was wise not to remember."

"Try to remember now," Dave said, "and then I will talk to Mr. Heilman."

Robin straightened her shoulders, and took a breath. She looked like a child in school about to recite a memorized assignment.

"I went back into the house when my father and mother were sleeping on the floor, and I picked up the gun so that they could not hurt each other. Then I hid in my father's truck. I fell asleep, and the noise of the truck engine woke me up. It was already moving, and I could not jump out. I crawled under the blanket. The truck stopped outside of that bar, and my father went in. I did not know what to do, so I did nothing. That was a mistake."

The words poured from her in an even stream.

"It wasn't your fault," Dave said.

She turned her bright, hard eyes toward him.

"I should have walked home. But then he came out with that woman. They drove to the beach. I heard them laughing and rolling around and then she reached for the blanket. I jumped out of the truck. My father grabbed my foot and my shoe came off. I ran toward the stairs, but I tripped. He yelled at me to stop running, to give him the gun. He said he would beat me. I just stood there until he was right in front of me. Then he grabbed for me, or the gun, and I ducked aside. He went by me, half falling down. When he could stand he was in front of the fence. He was cursing me. He put his hand on his belt buckle, and I knew what that would mean if I let him catch me." She lowered her head for a moment, and when she raised it, her eyes glistened. "I just stared at his hands on his belt. Like so many times before, when he had come to me. But this time, I had the gun in my hands. I closed my eyes and pulled the trigger. I kept my eyes shut. I didn't hear anything for a little while. Then there was a loud pop like my father's truck always makes when it starts up. Then, there was the sound of something crashing." She brushed a tear away from her eye. "I saw him fall through that railing. He was holding his belly where I was aiming. I heard the truck pull away. I sat down for a long time, watching the truck. It was moving very slowly. I think it backfired again, and then it picked up speed. After a while, I looked over the railing, and I saw him. By the water. I buried the gun in my hiding place, but I did not go near him."

The stenographer's hands stopped with Robin's voice, and then the door opened. Livonia came in, and Robin threw herself into her arms. Mrs. Edwards led them into the outer office.

Heilman stared at their backs and then at the gun on his desk.

"I'll have to hold her," he said.

"She shot him while he was taking his belt off," Dave said.

"I heard," Heilman replied. "I'll have to think about whether I want to charge her, or turn her over to the juvenile court, or whatever."

"If you have to hold her, make it as easy as you can."

Heilman nodded, and he pressed the intercom button. "Mrs. Edwards, call the jail. Tell them the child is coming, and have them find a friendly matron to take care of her. And then, please send in Sheriff Briggs."

Briggs ambled in and closed the door behind him. Heilman pointed to the envelope bag on his desk.

"Sheriff, I want this weapon tested as soon as possible."

"Sure thing," Briggs replied, picking up the bag, "but even if the bullet matches, we don't know who pulled the trigger. I still think we got the right person in jail."

Heilman glanced at the stenographer.

"Maybe so, sheriff. We'll just check out the girl's story, starting with the gun. Meanwhile, any word on Mr. Gallagher's whereabouts, or the identity of the shooter in the boat?"

"No, and that crucifix seems to have disappeared."

Heilman turned to Dave.

"Any thoughts, counselor?"

"Somebody might have picked up the crucifix," Dave replied.

"I'm sure somebody did," the prosecutor said. "In any event, "it might just be time for you to bring in your witness, the one who places Leonard Asebou at the hotel. Maybe he was in the boat. Briggs tells me he doesn't have a man to babysit your witness."

"The kid is scared witless. With a little patience, I might be able to coax something out of him. Have you spoken to the old woman across the hall in the hotel? She puts Gallagher there, too."

"Just terrific. A scared kid and an incoherent senior citizen whose testimony might be compromised by her failing eyesight."

"Patience," Dave said. "Things are coming together."

"Patience," Heilman replied, "is a virtue I no longer seem to be able to exercise."

"Remember," Dave said, "that virtue is its own reward."

"Yes," Heilman smiled, "but virtue never had to run for re-election."

CHAPTER NINETEEN

DAVE found Kelly sitting with Allie on the porch. It was early evening, and the sky had cleared to a bright blue, with just a wisp of white cloud here and there. A cool breeze came in off the water and it smelled fresh. An empty bottle of Chardonnay sat on the table between their chairs. Each held a glass in her hand.

"We've been trying to calm down," Kelly said.

"We've come to bury my father, not to praise him," Allie said, her voice vibrating between a giggle and a sob.

Kelly downed the remaining wine in her glass, and wiped her mouth with the back of her hand.

"Did you take a really good look at his eyes?" Kelly asked. "He's not going to stop coming after Allie."

"Briggs is sending somebody out here," Dave replied.

"That wasn't my father," Allie said. "It couldn't have been."

Kelly pressed her hand against her daughter's cheek.

"Yes," she said, "it was."

Allie shrank from Kelly's touch, and then she seemed to suddenly remember something.

"Robin? What happened to her?"

"She gave a statement to Heilman," Dave said. "There really wasn't any other way. She's in custody."

Indignation flashed in Allie's eyes, and then faded as rapidly. She rose unsteadily to her feet. "In the morning," she said. "I'll have to see her."

"We'll talk about that, then," Kelly said.

"Nothing to talk about," Allie said, her words now slurred. "My father's gone mad, and my friend is in jail for killing her father. What's to talk about?" She steadied herself against the wall of the house, and then pulled open the door.

Kelly's eyes followed Allie, and then she picked up the bottle. "Sorry," she said, "we finished it."

"That's okay. There's some scotch inside, if I feel the need."

The next morning, Dave stood by the window staring at the police cruiser parked in the driveway. Kelly came to his side.

"Heilman told me his name was Phil Ormond," Dave said, motioning toward the deputy who was approaching the porch, "and that he was a lot better than he looks."

"I hope so," Kelly replied, "because he looks about twelve years old." She pulled his head to her for a kiss. "Go on ahead. Just get your butt back here as soon as you can. We'll be all right until then."

Mrs. Edwards lifted her head from the papers on her desk and began to smile a greeting at Dave, but then she saw John behind him, and her smile collapsed on her face.

Heilman waved them into his office.

"Is the coffee pot full, Mrs. Edwards?" he asked. "Sheriff Briggs should be joining us soon."

"I'll make a fresh one," Mrs. Edwards said. "I wasn't expecting so many visitors."

"Only two," Heilman said. "You know Mr. Abrams, and I don't have to introduce you to John, I'm sure."

"You certainly do not," she replied.

As Mrs. Edwards attended to the coffee pot, Dave took John's elbow.

"What was that all about?" he said. "She looks at you as though she were an ex-wife who isn't getting her alimony payments on time."

"Worse than that," John smiled. "Years ago I brought her husband home dead drunk. She's never forgiven me."

"Briggs is waiting for the ballistics report," Heilman said as he took his seat behind his desk. "He'll be over with it as soon as it's done."

John pulled the crucifix from his pocket.

"I believe you were looking for this," he said. "I absent-mindedly picked it up at the beach. Forgot all about it until I got home. You know how it is when you reach a certain age."

"Perhaps," Heilman said, "but I don't think you've reached it."

John held the crucifix toward the prosecutor. "I knew a priest, back in Chicago some time ago, and he had something just like this," John said. He pressed his thumb first on one point of the cross, then the other, and last the very top. "Now, let's see, what was the order? It's been a long time. You see this priest, well his brother got in trouble with a dealer, and there was this key that he, the priest, had to keep safe, a kind of insurance policy for his brother, and he had this crucifix." He pressed the top first, then the right arm and finally the left. The top of the crucifix slid down, revealing a shallow compartment. John turned the crucifix over, and gave it a gentle shake. A key fell out. "Yes, that was the right order," John said. "I had forgotten." He handed the opened crucifix to Heilman.

Dave reached into his pocket and took out the torn piece of paper he had recovered from Peterson Beach. He slid it to Heilman.

"My guess is that the key opens up locker 201 at the bus station."

"Naughty, naughty," Heilman said.

"It was just a scrap of paper until a second ago," Dave replied.

Mrs. Edwards stuck her head into the office.

"Coffee all around, gentlemen?" Heilman asked.

Dave and John nodded, and Mrs. Edwards forced a smile.

"I'll fix one for Sheriff Briggs, as well. He just called to say he'll be right over."

Briggs arrived before the coffee. He did not look happy, as he placed a folder on Heilman's desk.

"The ballistics report," he said. "It shows conclusively that the gun the girl hid on the beach did not fire the bullet that was pulled out of Charlie Williams. You know this is getting to be the darndest thing. The man's as big as a house, and his wife takes a shot at him, and his daughter, and nobody can hit him."

Dave did not listen after hearing the report. Instead, his mind created a series of images, revolving around a fixed center in which he saw Robin's small hand holding the gun that was far too big for it, the others on the edges of Robin listening to Livonia tell the story of the Turtle and the Snail, or in the shop bravely covering for her mother's defensive hostility, or handing him back his business card while Charlie's huge arm gestured from the window of the truck, all of these in a whirl, but the one in the center now dimmed, and he felt relief, tangible as a soft palm on the nape of his neck. Until that moment he had denied himself any hope that Robin might be spared the burden of having killed her father. A successful plea of self defense would not have erased the guilt that would have remained in her marrow.

"Well," he managed to say, "Sheriff, you've just made my day."

Heilman, though, looked like the child whose hand had been slapped away from the cookie jar. He picked up the folder, and scanned the report. He flipped it back onto his desk. It fell next to the torn piece of paper. Briggs' big hand reached for the paper.

"What have we here?" He studied the paper for a moment. "I do believe I know where the top half of this is."

"Abrams?" Heilman's voice was a half tone higher than usual.

"Like I said before," Dave replied. "It didn't mean anything until now."

"And you, of course, didn't have a clue, right?"

"Maybe a clue," Dave said. "We're talking about a connection to my wife's ex and her daughter's father. I had to be sure."

Mrs. Edwards re-entered carrying a tray loaded with coffee mugs that bore logos from different National Hockey League Teams. She placed the tray on the prosecutor's desk, and left, the smile still fixed artificially on her face. Heilman reached for the Boston Bruins mug.

"You are a man of many unanticipated interests," Dave said.

Heilman took a sip of his coffee.

"You didn't know I went to school out east."

"Well," John said. "It looks like we have almost all the pieces. Why don't we head over to the bus station, and on the way I'll tell you most of the rest."

Heilman did not try to cover his irritation.

"Meaning?"

John took the little notebook out of his pocket.

"Oh, it's all in here."

"Where'd that come from?" Heilman asked.

"You wouldn't believe me if I told you," John said.

"Try me. On the way." He pressed the intercom button. "Mrs. Edwards get hold of Deputy Crow and have him meet us at the bus station. Tell him to stand in front of locker 201 until we get there. Understand?"

Kelly and Allie had exhausted conversation. They sat grimly at the old dining room table, each trying to read, Kelly yesterday's newspaper, and Allie a paperback romance novel. They had discussed, briefly, Allie's insistent demand to visit Robin, but the cruiser on the driveway had ended that conversation. From time to time, one or the other of them would look up and through the window at the cruiser and the ridiculously young-looking deputy who stood between them and Michael, who they both fully anticipated to show up. Hooper lay beneath Allie's feet, and her hand sought the reassurance of his massive head. Grateful for the attention, if unaware of its motivation, he licked her palm with his rough tongue.

Kelly could not sit still, nor could she concentrate on the newspaper. She had tried several times to read through a guest editorial by a prominent local developer arguing for an easing of zoning restrictions. Ordinarily, such an opinion would incite her anger but today she could not frame her usual objections, and even found herself agreeing with the writer. She tossed the paper down and walked out the door to the cruiser.

Stephen Lewis

Deputy Ormond had his hands on the steering wheel, and his eyes fixed on the driveway. He turned to greet her, offering a gap toothed smile.

"All quiet, here, Mrs. Abrams."

Kelly felt the sun on her neck and cheek.

"It must be hot sitting in that car," she said.

"No problem," he replied.

"Would you like some fresh lemonade?"

"Don't bother. I'm fine. And frankly I'd be more comfortable with you in the house."

"It's no bother," she replied, "and if I sit still much longer, I will go mad."

"We can't have that," he grinned, "and so, yes, I'd like some."

Kelly had noted the page Allie was on when she got up to walk out to the cruiser. As she passed by now, she saw that although Allie's eyes remained steadfastly focused on the book, she hadn't turned the page.

She took elaborate care fixing the lemonade, selecting the ripest lemons she could find, then squeezing them into a pitcher, and adding just the right amount of water and sugar to create a taste that was neither too tart nor too sweet. She cracked open the ice tray and added half a dozen cubes to the pitcher. She took three glasses in the fingers of one hand, held the pitcher in the other, and walked back into the dining room. She placed the pitcher and glasses on the dining room table, hard enough to cause a loud clink. Allie did not look up from her book.

"The deputy would like some lemonade," she said. "Why don't you bring him a glass, and take one for yourself?"

Allie looked up as though awakening.

"Oh," she murmured, "sure." She forced a grim smile. "Is he cute?"

"Check him out for yourself," Kelly said, and poured the lemonade into the glasses. She watched through the window as Allie, followed by Hooper, carried the glasses to the door of the cruiser. The deputy opened the door and received his with elaborate courtesy. He was tall, and extremely thin, so that his service pistol

228

loomed large against his hip. He leaned over to pet Hooper, and then he drank his lemonade with his eyes still on the driveway. He and Allie chatted, and when her daughter smiled Kelly found a moment's respite, imagining for a moment that the deputy was a nice young man come to see Allie, and that Michael was no more than an unpleasant memory.

Dave, along with John and Heilman, found Crow pacing in front of the last locker on the right hand side. A few curious people stood a respectful distance away, and from time to time Crow would cast a meaningful glance in their direction and wave them further back. They would step back a few feet, and after a few moments begin to edge closer.

"What's in the locker?" a tanned, gray-haired man asked.

"That's what we're waiting to find out," Crow said.

The man's wife, whose pale complexion and rouged cheeks suggested that she did not share her husband's interest in outdoor activities, placed a foot tentatively forward.

"No need to get rude, officer," she said. "Life's boring enough for some of us, and anyway we do pay your salary with our taxes."

"Police business," Heilman said in an authoritative tone, and again the people shuffled a foot or two back, but craned their necks forward. He handed the key to the deputy.

"Open it up."

Crow fumbled a moment with the lock. Then he swung the door open. The onlookers moved in closer. A small boy of about five or six scurried next to the open door. Crow swept him up in his arms, and the child turned red-faced and howled. Crow walked him to his mother who stood with open arms. The child squirmed and worked himself free just as the deputy reached her. She was wearing a faded, flower print dress and worn sandals. A tattoo on her left shoulder was in the form of a rose.

Heilman reached into the locker, and using just the tips of his thumb and his forefinger, removed a semi-automatic pistol. Crow held out a plastic evidence bag, and Heilman dropped the gun into it. He then pulled out a slim briefcase made of fine, deep colored leather. Its clasps were secured by a combination lock, and it looked new.

"Michael's piggy bank," Dave said.

"That's all," the prosecutor said, standing with an audible grunt.

Crow slid a pen into the loop of the briefcase's handle and lifted it up. Heilman handed the bag containing the pistol to Briggs. "Try this one," he said. "Maybe we'll get lucky."

"Did you have any idea," Dave asked, "that Leaping Frog was working for somebody like Gallagher?"

"Yes, we did, but like I said on television, we had not been able to get anything solid about that connection. We figured Leaping Frog was working for some organization with a lot of dirty money in need of a wash, but we didn't have anything hard. What we did see is too much money coming in, and then going out to purchase more food and drink than was reasonable."

"But you were going to go after him anyway, weren't you?" Dave asked.

Heilman gave a weary nod.

"And you had a witness," Dave said, giving voice to his suspicion. "Not the best. But a witness nonetheless."

Heilman nodded again.

"Dead men can't testify to what they might know," he said. "We had been talking to Charlie. He was going to give us Leaping Frog. And then, we thought Leaping Frog might take us a step higher. If not, at least we would have cleaned up the local action."

"I had Charlie figured for a player with a weak memory," John said. "That's why he wrote that locker number down on a piece of paper that Michael was careless enough to give him. And now you've something on paper, but you still don't have anybody to testify to it. Leaping Frog must have thought his little account book, with all those bank accounts in code, would be his insurance policy. Lord knows what he expected to do. He felt the heat, and maybe he thought he could persuade Michael to give him traveling money."

"He underestimated Mr. Gallagher," Heilman said. "But we won't. And we'll get him. In the meantime, it may be time to call in your reluctant witness. Bring him in and we'll work something out for Robin and Frankie."

"You'd better find Mr. Gallagher soon," John said as Heilman slid into his car. "before that guy in the boat gets to him."

"We'll find him," Heilman said. "We'll find both of them."

CHAPTER TWENTY

A **TALL** wiry man was leaning against the cruiser, which was blocking the driveway. The sun was strong and directly overhead, and its rays bounced off the car's metal and formed an absurd halo around the man's head. Dave watched the man trot toward him, and for a moment, he was sure the man was Michael. He started to push his door open, but before he could, he was looking at the barrel of a service revolver and a beardless, red cheeked face that broke into a gap toothed smile.

"Mr. Abrams?" the deputy asked, but he kept the gun leveled.

"Yes." He reached for his wallet in his pocket, but the deputy's hand, amazingly strong, stopped his own. "I'll do that," he said, and he removed Dave's wallet from his pocket. The deputy studied Dave's photo license for a moment, and then handed him his wallet.

"Sorry about that," he said.

"Not at all. Just what you should have done. I wasn't so sure you weren't Mr. Gallagher."

Kelly was waiting on the porch.

"I've been going back and forth between pretending that there's no way Michael can get near us and believing that he would just materialize inside the house. Right now, I've got the doors locked," she said. "Allie is inside, with Hooper, probably staring at us out of her window." She wrapped her arms around Dave and pressed her body close. She was trembling.

Allie sat just inside the door, her arm around Hooper's thick neck. The dog wore a puzzled look as though he knew something was expected of him, but he was not sure what. Allie looked up at Dave.

"What's happening to Robin?"

"I'm working on it with Heilman," Dave said, "but he's a little preoccupied at the moment with your father."

"What's he got to do with it?" Allie demanded.

"Probably everything," Dave said.

Another police cruiser pulled up, and Crow got out. He waved to Deputy Ormond and walked up to the house. Dave opened the door as the deputy was about to knock. Crow held his balled fist in the air for a moment, and then let it drop to his side.

"I guess you folks are still a bit edgy. I'll be here tonight, so Phil can get some sleep. He'll be back in the morning."

Kelly pointed to the pitcher of lemonade on the dining room table.

"Would you like some?"

"Sure thing," Crow smiled. "It's been a hot one today."

Allie walked to the door.

"I'll just go say good-bye to Phil," she said. "Maybe he wants another glass, for the ride home."

"What's that all about?" Dave asked.

Kelly shrugged.

"Lemonade. I've been making it all afternoon, for want of something better to do. And Allie, once I got her started, has been taking it out to Deputy Ormond, that is Phil. About an hour ago, I heard a car engine on the road, and that's when I locked the door."

"I can walk out with her," Crow said.

"No," Kelly replied. "It'll be all right, and I don't want to terrorize her any more than she already is."

Dave watched through the window as Allie leaned over to talk to the deputy.

"I think the lemonade has more than served its purpose," he said.

Crow, too, had followed Allie with his eyes.

"I didn't want to say anything while she was here, so you can break it to her your own way, but that gun we took from the bus station locker is the one that killed Charlie Williams."

"So, now we have Mr. Gallagher for murder."

"Afraid not," Crow said. "His prints were not on that gun."

"Yes," Dave replied. "But he was the only one with a key to that locker. Given everything else, that should be enough."

Dave watched condensed drops of water roll down the side of the lemonade pitcher. He knew that Allie and Kelly were still awake, lying next to each other in the master bedroom, their eyes fixed on the ceiling and their ears attuned to every sound of the night, and that if there were a hundred deputies ringing the house in a human chain, they would not be able to sleep. He could not offer them security he did not feel, but perhaps he could take a step toward solving one problem. He reached for the phone and dialed. Ralph, the hotel clerk, answered on the first ring. Maybe he was jumpy, too.

"I need to speak to your brother," Dave said.

"I was going to call you, Mr. Abrams, but there's this big wedding party in the hotel tonight."

"What about?"

"That's just it. My brother. He told me he wasn't coming in, and that he had to talk to you. He was acting real strange. He had his suitcase packed. I tried to tell him it didn't make any sense to go, at least not until this whole thing was over. He just smiled at me, a kind of dreamy smile, like he was on something, but he doesn't do drugs, and he said he had plans. Just a minute."

Dave heard a slurred female voice.

"Where's the banquet room?" the voice asked. "I got a little lost coming back from the little girl's room."

The line went silent, and Dave surmised that Ralph had put his hand over the phone as though remembering a code of civility.

"Sorry about that," Ralph said.

"I need to talk to him," Dave said. "Where is he?"

"I don't know. He walked out of the house, and he took his suitcase. The important thing..."

"Which way did you say it was?" The female voice returned, perhaps a little more unsteady but now edged with irritation. This time Ralph ignored his manners.

"Just down that way. Turn right into the first corridor you come to. You can't miss it."

"You wanna bet?" she said. "I've missed it two times already."

"Well, three's a lucky number," Ralph said. "Mr. Abrams?"

"I'm still here," Dave said. One large bubble perched on the lip of the pitcher and then began its slow descent. "I've got nothing but time right at the moment."

"Before she comes back, oh Lord, here she comes again, I'll have to take her there, but look, he said he wanted to talk to you, in person, first thing in the morning. He's not interested in waiting for any deputy. He said if you didn't show, he'd catch the early bus at eight o'clock. I'll give you directions."

Dave reached for a pad.

"Go ahead," he said.

Dave poured himself a mug of coffee and carried it out to the car. As he slid behind the wheel, an arm waved to him from the police cruiser.

"Good morning, Mr. Abrams. You're up early."

"And so are you, Phil."

"I guess I'm used to it," the deputy replied, "and anyway I got my rest. Crow was happy enough to see me. Going some place special?"

"Yes," Dave replied, and started the engine. The sun was already up and felt warm on his head. He picked up a Dodgers baseball cap from the seat next to him and put it on. "I'll see you in a bit," he said to the deputy, and then he drove down the driveway.

Ralph's directions took him past the harbor in Omena, onto a side road and finally to a two track heading through woods toward an abandoned apple orchard. He was to travel exactly one mile and then stop. Kyle would be waiting. The two track was just wide enough to accommodate the Caddy, and it occasionally brushed against branches. Dave drove slowly with one eye on the odometer. When it recorded a mile he stopped, and saw that he was just short of the first row of orchard trees. Another track branched off to the right through the maples. He got out of the car and stared into the thick woods on both sides of the Caddy and then up the second track, but he saw no one. He settled his cap against his forehead and leaned against the fender.

"Over here," a voice called, and Dave followed the sound down the branch track to Kyle Ormond. He stood with a big grin on his face and his suitcase next to him on the ground.

Dave began walking toward Kyle, but sensed movement to his left. He whirled just in time to see the barrel of an automatic pointing at him, head high. Dave brought his left arm up hard against the wrist of the hand holding the gun. The gun hand flew up, but the weapon remained in the hand.

"Nice try, Dave," Michael said, "but sorry, no cigar." Michael lowered the weapon to point at Dave and racked back the slide. Kyle trotted over, suitcase in hand.

"Sorry about this, Mr. Abrams," he said. "But like I told you, I've got plans, and now I've got traveling money." He reached into his pocket and pulled out a wad of hundred-dollar bills.

"Shut up, fool," Michael said. "Go and make sure we're not disturbed." He pulled a revolver from his belt and handed it to Kyle. "Take this. I'm expecting company." The young man handled the gun as though it were alive, switching it from hand to hand before shoving it into his waistband, and then he walked down the trail.

Michael watched Kyle's back, and then moved his pistol a little closer to Dave's head. With his other hand, he swiped the baseball cap in one fast motion. "The Dodgers, Dave, you do surprise me. You must be a sentimentalist. But I can use this."

"You should know all about sentimentality," Dave said, "mooning after the daughter you lost years ago."

Michael smiled again but held the gun steady.

"You are trying, aren't you? But I don't make stupid mistakes, Dave, you should know that. Now give me your keys."

Reaching into his pocket for the keys, Dave said, "You don't have to do this. Whatever I know, the sheriff does, and you don't stand a snowball's chance in hell of getting near Allie."

Michael took the keys.

"But you're smarter than Briggs," Michael said. "And this is personal, between you and me. I saw the way Allie looks at you. And Kelly too. But you could have had that lying bitch if you had only let my daughter alone."

Dave saw a tiny opening.

"She is good, you know. Too bad you chose Grace."

Michael's face spasmed in anger, and Dave lunged at him, grabbing his gun hand. He spun until he had Michael's arm twisted and extended, and the gun dropped.

"That's right, just hold him for me," a voice said.

Dave turned toward the voice, and saw the glint of the sun off a rifle barrel. Leonard stepped out of the trees. Kyle was in front of him, with his hands up. Leonard tossed Kyle's revolver into the underbrush and with the indifference he might use to swat a fly, brought the butt of the rifle down on Kyle's head.

"I owe him at least that much, for setting me up at the hotel," Leonard said. He walked toward them. "Let him go, Abrams. I want him. The idea was I would be in the room when the police came. I was just supposed to talk some sense into Leaping Frog, tell him not to testify, give him traveling money." He lifted his rifle to his shoulder. "I have no beef with you, Abrams, especially since you've been helping my sister and my niece. But Mr. Gallagher here, he and I have business to settle."

"I should have hit you harder," Michael said, "so you would stay put. But I didn't want to kill you. That wouldn't have done me any good. It's all in the balance."

"I woke up and saw the bodies," Leonard said. "This porno movie was on full blast."

"Just to get somebody's attention," Michael replied.

"I didn't wait around to find out," Leonard replied.

"We can still work things out," Michael said.

"I don't think so," Leonard replied.

"Well..." Michael began, but then stepping down hard on Dave's foot, he broke free. Dave saw Leonard shoulder the rifle, and he dove out of the way.

A bullet crashed against a tree trunk above Michael's head. Dave looked at Leonard who was sighting at Michael. He started to pull the trigger, but then he brought the weapon down and frowned. He ambled over to Dave. The scar on his cheek seemed to be whiter and deeper against the taut, angry flesh of his face. He reached into his shirt pocket for a cigarette and lit it.

"That son of a bitch," he said. He pointed to Kyle. "When he comes to, you can ask him what happened at the hotel, who killed Leaping Frog and his woman. That's why I didn't kill him, so he could tell you, and I'm letting you live too, so you'll tell my family, my sister and her daughter, why I am doing this. Nobody else matters. Now turn around."

"He's getting away. We can go after him together."

"No."

"One question, then. Did Robin shoot Charlie?"

"No."

"Did you?"

"That's two questions," Leonard said, "Turn," he said, and Dave did.

After a few moments, hearing and sensing nobody behind him, Dave looked over his shoulder. Leonard was gone, and Kyle still lay where he fell.

Kelly sat at the dining room table nursing a cup of coffee, her eyes fixed on the cruiser and beyond the driveway. She felt herself smile when she saw Dave's blue baseball cap above the wheel of the Caddy as it pulled into the driveway. She got up to go into the kitchen to pour another cup of coffee.

She had just replaced the carafe on the warmer when she heard a voice shout "Mrs. Abrams," and then a thud, as though a heavy object had fallen. The sounds seemed to be coming from the front of the house. She hurried to the window and saw the face beneath the blue baseball cap. She glanced beyond it to where Deputy Ormond lay on the ground next to his cruiser. She grabbed the cordless telephone on the table and pressed 911, but realized, after a moment, that she had not heard a dial tone. There was a tapping at the window. Michael smiled and held up a piece of telephone wire. The next moment he was through the door and standing before her.

"The cordless still needs a cord," he said, and tossed the wire on the table. "I hope you don't mind, but I didn't want us to be interrupted while we finish our business."

"We finished our business years ago. What did you do to Dave?"

"Not what I intended to do. I left him out on the trails, but he's a clever fellow. He'll find a way home."

"Why don't you just leave? We have nothing to talk about."

"I suppose not," he said. "But you know what I want."

"She's not home," Kelly said, a little too quickly. "She's staying with John."

"Well, that's funny. I passed by John's place on the way over here, and he was out in one of his orchards. I even tipped my cap to him. I guess he didn't wave back because his arm is in a sling. But I didn't see a sign of Allie."

"She's there, nonetheless. She's not much interested in cherry trees."

A creaking of floorboards floated down from upstairs, and Michael turned his eyes in that direction.

"That's just the dog," Kelly said. "He probably figured out that an unwanted guest was in the house." She looked past Michael and through the window. The deputy lay still on the ground, but then she thought she saw his arm move.

Michael continued staring at the stairs.

"Well, you were half right," he said. "Here comes the dog, with Allie."

Kelly took a quick step forward while he was still looking up and threw her fist at his jaw as hard as she could. He responded a moment too late to avoid the impact but he managed to tilt his head so that her fist glanced off the side of his mouth. She started to swing again, but he grabbed her arm. Then he reached behind him with his other hand and pulled his pistol out from his waistband.

"I was hoping we could be more civilized about this." He turned his glance toward the stairs. "Come on down Allie."

"No," she shouted. "Mom, what should I do?"

"Stay right where you are," Kelly said. She could see Deputy Ormond on the driveway. He was not moving.

Michael followed her glance.

"He won't be getting up for a while," he said. "But we don't have much time. Either your husband or my disgruntled employee will be here." Blood trickled from the corner of his mouth. He swiped at it with the back of his hand and then stared at the red blotch on his skin. "You know," he said, "maybe if you had done this years ago..."

"Forget it, Michael," Kelly snapped. "Don't try to play me."

His expression changed from a false and fixed smile to hard determination.

"No, play time is over." He pointed the pistol at Kelly's head.

"Come on down here, Allie. I don't want to hurt your mother. But like she says, we have nothing to talk about, and I didn't come here for her."

"Don't," Kelly yelled, but then she heard Allie's slow tread on the stairs. A moment later and she was at her side, leaning over, holding Hooper's collar. The dog growled deep in his chest and strained toward Michael. He lowered the pistol at Hooper's head.

"Shut that dog up," he said.

"You wouldn't hurt him," Allie said.

"Yes," he said, his voice now gentle. "I've killed three people, just this week. A dog, more or less, won't make any difference."

Kelly again looked out of the window. A figure holding a rifle was standing over Deputy Ormond who was stirring on the ground. The figure nudged the deputy in the ribs with the rifle barrel, and Ormond lay still on his belly with his hands behind his back. Kelly turned to Michael, but this time he had not followed her eyes. He was staring fixedly his daughter.

"Come here," he said. "We're leaving."

Dave saw the nose of another car pulled off onto the side trail. He walked over to Kyle and knelt on the boy's chest and searched his pocket to find the car keys. Kyle groaned but did not try to get up. Dave found the revolver in the underbrush where Leonard had tossed it. He pointed it at Kyle.

"Get up," he said.

Kyle rubbed the back of his head and sat up.

"Over there," Dave said, pointing to a beech tree. "Sit over there."

Kyle nodded and sat with his back against the tree trunk.

"Take your belt off," Dave said, "and give it here and hug the tree."

He tied Kyle's hands to his feet around the trunk of the tree.

"Stay put," he said. "I'll need you later. For now, I'm going to borrow your car."

It was an old Nissan Sentra. Dave laid the revolver on the seat and tried the key. The Sentra coughed a couple of times, and then started. He gripped the wheel in frustration, visualizing Michael getting into his house somehow, with Leonard hot on his heels firing shot after shot. He ripped the wheel to the left and headed back in the direction he had come. He glanced at Kyle as he drove by. The young man lay in the dirt, his arms and legs strapped together embracing the tree. He lifted his head with an imploring look. Dave stepped on the accelerator.

Just as he reached the point where the trail joined pavement his way was blocked by a pickup truck. He leaned on the horn, but nobody responded. He got out and ran up to the truck. He could see that the cab was empty. As he reached the vehicle, the face of a young man peered at him over the tail gate. His eyes blinked in the sun, as though unaccustomed to the light.

"Would you move your truck?" Dave called. "I've got to get by."

The young man did not respond for a moment, and then he nodded his head. He disappeared behind the tail gate and whispered something to somebody in the bed of the truck. A female voice, just audible, responded. Dave waited. The whispers continued, growing in volume, until the female voice rang out clearly in the quiet air.

"Just tell him to wait a minute, goddamn it."

Dave, though, did not wait. He stepped closer to the truck, and as he did the young man stood up, his hands buckling his jeans. Behind him, a slim young woman was gathering her clothes. She held her shirt in front of her and glared at Dave for a moment, Then she brushed her hair away from her eyes and dropped the shirt.

"Have a look," she said.

Dave took the revolver from his pocket and showed it to the couple.

"I'm in a hurry," he said. "You don't have to bother getting dressed. Just move your truck, and I'll drive by. Then you can get back to what you were doing."

"Okay," the young man said, taking a step backward. "Just let me find my keys."

Dave cocked the hammer of the revolver, and the young man vaulted over the tail gate and scurried to the far side of the truck. He disappeared for a moment, and then opened the passenger side door. He slid behind the wheel, keeping his head shielded by the back of the seat. The engine started and the truck lurched down the path. Dave eased the hammer down, shoved the revolver into his pocket, and ran back to the Sentra. As he reached the paved road, he saw the young woman standing with her arms crossed over her naked breasts and resolutely shaking her head back and forth. He turned onto the road and gunned the engine. The little four cylinder sputtered, teetered on the edge of a stall, but then revved up.

"Just tell me one thing," Allie said, her eyes stealing a glance past Michael at Leonard, who was handcuffing Deputy Ormond.

"Nothing to tell, and no time to tell it," Michael replied. He turned toward the window, but only the deputy was visible. Leonard had disappeared.

"I want to know about Robin."

"Is she your little Indian friend?"

"Yes."

Hooper continued to strain against the leash and pulled Allie a step toward Michael. Kelly snatched the leash from Allie's hand and hauled the dog back.

Michael seemed to think for a moment. He turned his intense eyes on Allie. "Your friend's father had become a liability. I had to remove him. It was supposed to be a simple hit but your friend got involved. She tried to kill her father..." He stopped and rubbed his eyes as though losing the thread. "You know, that wasn't very nice, was it?" Allie shook her head obediently, and Michael smiled. "Well, I guess it depends how you look at it. Maybe you'd like to do the same to me."

"No," Allie replied. "I just want you to go."

"We'll be going. Shortly. Your friend botched the job, and I had to finish it while she stood there with her eyes closed. It's really better to leave those things to those who know what they are doing."

"You would let her take the blame, then, wouldn't you?" Allie demanded.

"I only conduct business," Michael said. "I don't deal in guilt." He stepped toward her, pointing the pistol at Kelly. "I'm going to take my daughter now."

Allie shrank away as Michael reached toward her. Hooper hurled himself at Michael, a deep growl resonating in his chest. Michael kicked the dog, catching him on the side of the jaw. Hooper tried again, and this time fastened his powerful jaws on Michael's gun hand. Michael switched his gun to his other hand and brought its butt down hard on Hooper's skull. The dog dropped but did not immediately loose its grip. Michael was pulled down to his knees but pried the jaws open and shoved Hooper away with his foot. Allie knelt over the dog and cradled his head.

"Daddy," she said, her voice caught between accusation and terror.

Michael clutched at the bleeding wound on his hand. He wrapped his good arm around Allie.

Kelly took a step toward them, and Michael aimed the pistol at her.

"I'll go with you, Michael," Kelly said.

"I'm sure you would. But you can't say 'daddy' the same way. No, that won't do."

The front door swung open, and Leonard stood with his rifle aimed at Michael's head.

"It's my play now," he said.

Dave had the Sentra at seventy-five on the rolling and twisting road. He climbed the hill approaching John's farm, and the little car dropped down to fifty, and then forty. He downshifted to third and accelerated again. As he hit the crest of the hill, he rammed the gear shift lever into fourth. By the time he hit the level road at the bottom of the hill, he was back up to eighty. His foot held the accelerator to the floor and the engine whined and clattered, and the steering wheel vibrated in his hands.

A quarter of a mile before his house he downshifted to hold his speed up one last, curving incline. As he caught sight of the gray mailbox that marked his driveway, two vehicles roared toward him under a cloud of dust. The first was the Caddy. His Caddy. He turned his head and saw the blue baseball cap. Behind the Caddy rattled a pickup truck. He could make out two figures hunched over in the cab as the truck swayed around the curve. They passed him and he screeched the Sentra to a stop at the foot of his driveway. He saw Kelly rushing toward him, her mouth shouting words that he could not hear. Behind her, Deputy Ormond stumbled, his hands behind his back and his balance unsteady.

Kelly reached the Sentra and yanked open the passenger side door.

"He's got Allie. And some crazy bastard with a rifle has got the both of them."

"I saw them go by me," Dave said. "The guy with the rifle is Leonard Asebou."

Deputy Ormond, his hands still cuffed behind him, staggered up to the car. Kelly pulled back the passenger seat and shoved him into the back of the car, where he landed in a heap on his side.

"We need your damn gun," she said as she threw herself into the car. She slammed her door behind him.

"My cruiser," Ormond said.

"No time," Kelly replied.

Dave wheeled the Sentra around on the road.

"Do you have any idea where they might be headed?" Kelly asked. "Leonard said something about taking this back to where it started."

The scene played itself out in his mind, as he recaptured the images of Michael alone in the Caddy, followed by Allie and Leonard in the truck. Michael wasn't running, not with his daughter in the cab of the truck. No, Leonard must have told him where to go, and Dave suddenly knew where that was, just as surely as he had known that Robin would be hiding in that stone silo. They couldn't get there too fast, not with Leonard pushing that battered old heap. Maybe he could catch them before they arrived.

He caught sight of them about a quarter of a mile ahead on the shore road heading toward the beach. The Sentra couldn't make much better speed on the hills than the truck, and so even though they gained a little on each straight away, he could see that they weren't going to be able to catch them. Then a loud metallic sound told him they would he would be lucky to make it at all.

"Sounds like you threw a rod," Deputy Ormond said from the back of the Sentra. "I told you that you should have let me take my cruiser."

"You'd have had a hell of time driving it," Dave said. The Sentra was still moving, though a good deal slower, and the temperature gauge climbed toward the danger zone. "We'll get there."

"I could have radioed for help," Ormond said.

"Yes," Kelly replied. "You've told us. But that's my daughter in that truck, and I couldn't wait."

The Caddy and truck were no longer visible ahead of them, but before too long they saw the turnoff for Peterson Beach. The Sentra struggled badly and as they reached the parking lot, it quit. Dave let it coast for a few feet, and then slammed on the brakes. He and Kelly were out of the car at the same moment.

"Folks," Deputy Ormond said. "The key to these things is in my pocket."

"Right," Kelly said. She leaned back into the car, and took his pistol from its holster. Then she dug out the key and dropped it on the seat next to him.

Dave waited for her to catch up to him, and then they both ran off toward the far end of the parking lot where the Caddy was stopped with the truck right behind it. When they got a little closer, they could see that the Caddy was sitting on the edge of the lot with its nose pointing through the break in the fence Charlie had fallen through. The Caddy's brake lights were on, and Michael clutched the steering wheel. The truck's wheels were spinning against the asphalt, filling the air with stench of burning rubber.

Leonard turned toward Dave and Kelly, his face dark with sweat and fury.

"My daughter, you bastard," Kelly screamed. She pointed the deputy's service pistol at Leonard. "Where is she?"

Leonard stared at her, then backed the truck up a few feet, shifted gears, and rammed it into the rear of the Caddy, which inched forward from the impact, but did not go over. It pivoted on a tree stump that jutted up from the side of the cliff. The front wheels were over the side. Michael pulled the steering wheel first to the left and then to the right, as though to steer the car away from the edge, but the front wheels only danced uselessly in the air. Leonard rammed the truck into the back of the Caddy again, and the car shuddered a little further over the side, but did not go over.

A figure appeared at the side of the Caddy and grabbed the passenger door handle.

"Allie," Kelly screamed.

"I've got to," Allie said. "I've got to try."

Kelly ran toward Allie, who now had the door open. Dave took out his gun and charged the truck. Leonard kept his eyes straight ahead, as he maneuvered the truck again and again against the rear of the Caddy. Kelly circled the truck to reach Allie. Dave saw the Caddy begin to tilt a little more downward over the edge, and he shot his revolver in the air. Leonard glanced at him for a second, but turned back to the Caddy, and spun the truck wheels until they smoked.

Kelly saw why Michael had been pulling at the steering wheel. Leather straps circled his wrists and were tied to the spokes of the steering wheel. His wrists were raw and bleeding, and Allie was working to unknot the strap on Michael's right wrist. The car seemed to tilt ever so slightly forward, and Kelly leaned into the car to pull Allie out. Michael freed his right hand and seized Allie's arm.

Allie looked first at her mother and then back to her father.

"We've got to get him out of here," she said.

Kelly lifted the heavy revolver, cocked its hammer, and pointed it at Michael.

"Let her go," Kelly said.

"No," Michael replied. "The only thing stopping this car from going over the side is my foot on the brake. Pull that trigger and you lose your daughter. Now, you just back off."

Kelly backed out of the car.

"Just keep your foot on the brake," she said.

"I'm going to let go of you," he said to Allie, "but you stay right where you are." He released Allie's arm, and began working on the strap on his left wrist. The car started to move again, and he jammed his foot down harder on the brake.

"Allie come to me. Now!" Kelly screamed, but the car slid over the edge, and as it did it turned to the left so that the passenger door swung into Kelly, knocking her down.

"Allie," she screamed.

The thrusting log caught the rear undercarriage, holding the car. The wood began to crack under the 5,000 pounds of car.

Dave was at the side of the truck pushing the gun through the window against Leonard's head, and he saw the Caddy tottering, with Kelly grabbing onto its rear bumper as though she could hold it there, and he brought the barrel of the revolver down hard on Leonard's head. Leonard slumped toward the passenger seat. Dave climbed in and turned the ignition off. He looked up just in time to see the Caddy go over the edge.

He jumped out of the cab and joined Kelly at the edge, watching as the huge car bounced down the cliff, then turned one almost graceful cartwheel before landing upside down on the stony beach. A second later it exploded into flame.

Kelly grabbed Dave's arm and turned him away from the wreck. Then he noticed that she was pointing to a place about ten feet from the edge. Her eyes blinking in the smoke that now rose from the fire stood Allie.

They clambered down to her. Blood seeped from a deep gash on her forehead, but otherwise she did not seem to be seriously hurt. She was rubbing her left arm with the palm of her right hand in circular motions of growing intensity, more akin to the movement one would use to wash a stain than ease a hurt.

"He pushed me out," she said, and then she turned her eyes toward the flaming wreck. She snapped her head back, as though the heat of the fire had singed her eyes. "He almost had his other hand free, and then he pushed me out."

"It'll be all right," Kelly said, and she pulled her daughter to her. Allie collapsed against her mother's side.

"Will it?" she asked.

Kelly ran her thumb gently over the cut on her daughter's forehead, and then she stroked her hair, and finally she forced Allie's fingers free of their convulsive grasp on her arm, but she could find no more words.

CHAPTER TWENTY ONE

ROBIN stood between Frankie and Dave in the harsh morning sun outside of the court house. A few feet away, a television camera was trained on Heilman. He held a document.

"This is the ballistics report that confirms what we had suspected, that a gun in the sole possession of Michael Gallagher shot Charlie Williams. Mr. Gallagher was connected with an organized crime operation based in New York. In addition, we have sworn testimony from Kyle LeBraun, an employee at the hotel, that implicates Mr. Gallagher in the Resort Hotel murders. We have worked out an arrangement with Charlie Williams' wife and daughter, who we now see were unfortunately drawn into his criminal ways, but who, nonetheless do bear some legal responsibility for taking the law into their own hands. The arrangement is fair and just. Perhaps Mr. Abrams would care to comment."

A television reporter thrust a microphone toward them, but Dave brushed it away.

"No comment, and no questions, please," he said. "You have the statement from Mr. Heilman's office, and we have nothing to add."

The television reporter, a young woman with short red hair and freckles, turned her back and faced the camera.

"As you can see, Frankie Asebou and her daughter have been released under an arrangement worked out by their attorney, Mr. Dave Abrams of New York, and District Attorney Heilman. Mr. Gallagher was killed in the bizarre incident at Peterson Park, but Mr. Leonard Asebou, Frankie's brother, still faces charges of obstructing a criminal investigation. Mr. Abrams has said he will represent Mr. Asebou, should he be charged. The police have closed the hotel murders case, ascribing guilt in that matter to Mr. Gallagher. Police now say that Mr. Asebou worked for Mr. Gallagher until they had a falling out over Mr. Gallagher's attempt to frame Mr. Asebou for the hotel murders."

Dave ushered Frankie and Robin toward his car. Allie leaped out to embrace Robin. For a moment, Frankie would not let her arm drop from her daughter's shoulders, but then she stepped back.

"I suppose I should thank you Mr. Abrams. But how can I when I won't be able to have my daughter for a year."

"I'm sorry about that," Dave replied. "But I couldn't do any better. Rehab for you and a year's probation was the best deal I could get. Briggs wanted to keep you in jail and to put Robin immediately into foster care with a good Christian family and strip you of your parental rights altogether. We got something better than that, at least."

She lowered her head. Her eyes, which he had been accustomed to see either hot with anger or cold with bitter resignation, now moistened.

"But a year," she repeated.

"She'll visit you, with Livonia, every weekend."

"I don't know if I can," she said.

"Yes you can, because you must. If not for yourself, then for her."

Robin pulled away from Allie and fixed her eyes on Dave.

"Mr. Abrams, what does it mean to say that I am a ward of the state? Aren't I my mother's daughter?"

"Yes," he said. "But for the next year, the state is taking responsibility for you."

"But who is the state? And what does it know about me?" She shook her head. "Do not try to answer," she said.

She walked to her mother and they embraced. Dave saw the television cameraman angling for a shot, and he interposed his body to block the camera's view.

Livonia's station wagon and John's old sedan were parked next to each other at Peterson Park Beach. John stood at the railing looking down at the beach. The Caddy was gone, but a slight indentation of blackened stones testified to its fiery landing. Livonia and Robin were below in the circle of scorched rock.

Allie brought her hand up to the beaded earrings she now wore and then started down the stairs to the beach.

"Let her go, alone," Kelly said. "Then we'll follow."

After a moment, Kelly and Dave made their way down the steps to the beach. Livonia looked up and held her hand, palm outward, to say they should stay. She turned to the two girls who were sitting cross-legged in front of her. She picked up a scorched stone.

"O-ko-me-se-maw, tell us about the Trickster," Robin said.

"Yes, grandmother, please," Allie said.

Livonia turned the stone over and over in her hand and then handed it to Allie.

"This is the story of Nanabush," she said, "and how the snails got their shells. Nanabush can take any form he likes. Sometimes he looks like the priest in the church, and sometimes he wears a fine suit and drives a big car, but this story is about long ago, before the priests and the men with fine suits and big cars, a time when Makinak, the Great Turtle, lay in his pride beneath the waters of the great lake. Just as he does now, though some people do not know this."

She spoke, and the girls listened. Above them, a heron drifted in lazy circles in the cloudless sky.